story of an extended New England family beleaguered by loss, misunderstandings, and terrible secrets from the past. It is also a story about the power of redemption and self-fulfillment. Ms. Britton understands everything there is to understand about the Maine coast, from the way fog 'both muffles and amplifies sound' to the fishing techniques of ospreys. Best of all, she understands how, through love, the human heart can overcome just ab   Mosher

Praise for

Her Sister's Shadow

"A touching, intricate account of painful memories that radically shape lives."   —*Publishers Weekly*

"Katharine Britton's debut novel, *Her Sister's Shadow*, about time, memory, family, love and death is a book for the ages. Because of the skill in the plot, the complex characterization, and the lyricism of the prose, the book is a deeply satisfying read. It's also very wise. Britton tells us that 'It's best to share secrets, but only if they're yours.' Words that ring true for all of us, but especially for the protagonist of *Her Sister's Shadow*."
                              —Ernest Hebert, award-winning author of
                              The Old American and *Never Back Down*

"Anyone with sisters, secrets, or a family house where memories are stored will be held captive by this haunting story of love, loss, loneliness and the healing light of truth. *Her Sister's Shadow* by Katharine Britton is the quintessential summer holiday book. It invites you to linger in the garden, breathe the salt air, listen to the hiss of the tide. And best of all, it is a story that will not let you go."

—Sally Ryder Brady, author of *A Box of Darkness*

"In prose both evocative and precise, Katharine Britton creates the fictional town of White Head, Massachusetts, and the house in which the Niles sisters grew up, with such assurance that readers will feel certain they should find both on a map. *Her Sister's Shadow* is a story of loss, grievance, and the permutations of time, rendered with disarming honesty."

—Catherine Tudish, author of
Tenney's Landing and *American Cream*

"Anyone who has lived with long-held family secrets will relate to this story of two aging sisters who can't escape their tragic past, or their abiding sense of, what—duty? nostalgia? love?—that reluctantly brings them together. Evocative, compelling, and exquisitely written, *Her Sister's Shadow* will make readers reconsider the resentments within their own family relationships, and how time is too short to let past events shadow the future." —Joni B. Cole, coeditor of *Water Cooler Diaries*

Titles by Katharine Britton

HER SISTER'S SHADOW

LITTLE ISLAND

Little Island

. . .

Katharine Britton

BERKLEY BOOKS, NEW YORK

THE BERKLEY PUBLISHING GROUP
Published by the Penguin Group
Penguin Group (USA)
375 Hudson Street, New York, New York 10014, USA

USA | Canada | UK | Ireland | Australia | New Zealand | India | South Africa | China

Penguin Books Ltd., Registered Offices: 80 Strand, London WC2R 0RL, England
For more information about the Penguin Group, visit penguin.com.

This book is an original publication of The Berkley Publishing Group.

BERKLEY® is a registered trademark of Penguin Group (USA)
The "B" design is a trademark of Penguin Group (USA)

Library of Congress Cataloging-in-Publication Data

Britton, Katharine (Katharine Fisher)
Little island / Katharine Britton. — Berkley trade paperback edition.
pages   cm
ISBN 978-0-425-26635-9
1. Family secrets—Fiction.   2. Maine—Fiction.   3. Psychological fiction.
4. Domestic fiction.   I. Title.
PS3602.R5345L58 2013
813'.6—dc23

2013010873

PUBLISHING HISTORY
Berkley trade paperback edition / September 2013

PRINTED IN THE UNITED STATES OF AMERICA

10 9 8 7 6 5 4 3 2 1

Cover photos: *Woman* © Lee Avison Photography/Arcangel Images;
Colored Light Circles #1 © Alexey Romanov/Thinkstock;
Colored Light Circles #2 © moggara12/Thinkstock;
Wood Planks © ideldesign/Shutterstock.
Cover design by Judith Lagerman.
Interior text design by Kristin del Rosario.

For Maggie
Friend, companion, and teacher—in life and beyond

Acknowledgments

My heartfelt thanks for their contributions large and small:

Amin, who helps keep my world right side up on a weekly basis; Mary C. Breen; Beverly Breen, for her gentle manner and acerbic wit; Doug Britton, for his love and support; the Fraser family, owners of Dan & Whit's where, if they don't have it, you don't need it; Chris Ivanyi; Linda Kennedy for her amusing anecdotes about island and inn life; Nowell King; Margot Lewin for her close reading and for listening to me over too many cups of coffee to count; Polly Medlicott, the kind of friend and editor every author wants; Lonnie and Kathy Morton, owners of the Harbor Gawker in Vinal Haven, Maine; Margo Nutt; Ron Schneider, for his help investigating the SOL of an OUI in 1991; Suzanne Simon, who really did go after an escaped dog with a bag of salmon treats in hand and a bear loose in the neighborhood; Jennifer Unter, Jackie Cantor, and the folks at Berkley Books for their stewardship and editorial wizardry.

Gathering

. . .

· Chapter One ·

JOY

I sat at our kitchen table amid the remains of a hasty breakfast, letting the silence slowly swallow me up the way the stealthy tide steals in and surrounds Spectacle Island, stranding unwary visitors. An hour earlier I'd watched my husband and son set off for Cornell, my son's trunk, suitcases, skis, computer components, tennis racket, desk lamp, and new bedding filling the back of our Highlander. Soon I would be on my way to Little Island.

I didn't think my mother would have chosen this weekend for my grandmother's memorial service had she remembered that Friday was the twentieth anniversary of the crash, and yet I couldn't imagine that she'd forgotten. No mother could forget such a thing. So, I'd begun to believe it was a sign: all of us together again, without the "outlaws," as Daddy humorously (if unoriginally) refers to my husband, Stuart, and to my sister's husband, Daniel. I took a large gulp of coffee but couldn't swallow. My throat felt constricted, something hard lodged there, as each passing moment carried my son farther away, and my journey to Little Island closer.

Earlier this summer, I spent the better part of a day roaming from Kohl's to Macy's to Beds 'n Things, searching for the perfect ensemble for Rex's room, finally settling on a red rug, blue-and-white-striped sheets, and a blue comforter with red piping. My selections were masculine yet soft, warm yet light. I found them at my very first stop but kept going, even though I hate shopping, wanting them to be perfect.

"S'great, Mom. Thanks," Rex said, and stuffed them into his duffel.

I don't know what kind of acknowledgment I'd hoped for—No, that's not true. I did. "These are awesome. You're the best, Mom. I don't know how I'll make it without you. In fact, you know what? I'm not going. I'm staying here with you."

Ridiculous, but true. I'm not proud of it, but there it is. I'd prayed half the summer that some event would delay his departure, and then spent the rest of the summer trying to recant my prayers—as futile as trying to cancel an e-mail sent in haste. I was worried, you see, that the prayers might bring on some catastrophe. Sitting here—his chair empty beside me, the memory of him so fresh I half expected to turn and see him standing at the sink—I simply didn't know what I would do without him, without his cross-country and track meets, dances at the high school, college applications and campus visits, his meals, laundry, and the comforting sound of his size-eleven footstep clomping up and down the stairs. The too-silent house now seemed like a taunt.

"I disinvited Daniel," Tamar had said on the phone the other night. "We had a fight," she told me. "A big one."

I was surprised to get my sister's call. It was unusual for her to open up to me. Usually she confides in her twin, Roger, and vice versa. "About what?" I asked.

"Oh, nothing. Stupid misunderstanding," she said. "You know how it goes."

I said I did, but I really didn't. Stuart and I rarely fight. I don't like fights; there were too many in my family. There was sure to be at least one big one this weekend.

The clock was ticking too loudly above the kitchen sink, and I thought again about my family, alone together on Little Island for three days, with no referees. Then I remembered that Tamar was bringing her twin daughters: not referees but, perhaps, buffers, someone to focus on other than the five of us. I hadn't known what to say when she shared this news, not recalling Tamar ever having traveled alone with her girls. And so I said nothing. Silence does not guarantee absolution with my sister.

"I'll be fine, Joy," she'd snapped. "And thanks for the vote of confidence."

"You don't need my vote, Tee. You've got more than enough already." As soon as the words were out of my mouth, I could hear my mother's voice in my head, chiding. The edict she delivered throughout my childhood: "Be nice to your sister. She's younger than you." And then, later, "Joy, be kind. Remember, we almost lost her."

I resent this immutable stance presented by my mother: Tamar will always be younger and we will always have "almost lost her" in the crash that altered our lives in so many unexpected ways. And, although I am the eldest of the Little children, I am not my mother's prized firstborn. That spot will always belong to Abigail, who died in infancy. What did that make me? I was not quite three years old when Roger and Tamar came along. *Came along*, as though my twin siblings were foundlings our parents discovered one morning on the broad granite step beneath the inn's kitchen door and decided, on a whim, to keep.

I tried another swallow of coffee and thought about the fun I could have with her twins, Hal and Nat: bake cookies, play dress-up from the trunks in the attic, and collect beach glass. (My mother lugs a box of bottles out to Sunset Point every Thanksgiving, to ensure a good crop on the beach below the inn the following summer.) And then I thought again of my own child, no longer a child, and of my husband not beside me this weekend. And this thought sent me spinning, like Alice, twirling down into that storybook earth. Dizzy, I lowered my head onto the kitchen table and stared at the crust of toast on Rex's plate. Beside that lay the little paring knife.

I picked up the crust and held it in front of me like some sort of treasured artifact. I knew I needed help, but Stuart was an hour into his trip, and it was too early to wake anyone else. Reaching for the knife, I told myself, *I'll just hold it.* It was an old castoff my mother gave me when I married Stuart; its handle was worn and its serrated blade dull. But I pressed the blade, ever so gently, into my thumb, liking the resulting puckering dents, liking the feeling, wanting to press harder, knowing I shouldn't.

Did Alice fear her fall, I wondered? Or did Alice, just a child, believe that she would land safely? Unlike Alice, who floated gently down her rabbit hole, a portal to a great adventure, I was plummeting, with no adventure awaiting me at the bottom. I pressed the knife just a little harder, because physical pain is so much easier to locate and manage than emotional.

On the fleshy mound at the base of my thumb, I could see the faint white scar where I'd pressed that other knife, over and over, always in the exact same spot, startling myself alive with the pain, the sudden flow of blood. I knew I should put the paring knife down and stand up.

"Do something, anything, related to the task," Tamar once told me is an antidote to procrastination. What was I procrastinating now? An endless succession of days and weeks that would become months, and then years, with no child giving them purpose. Also, three days alone at the inn with my mother, father, and twin siblings. At this, I pressed the knife against my thumb a little harder and drew a bit of blood. It surprised me. I hadn't thought the blade sharp enough, hadn't thought I was pressing that hard.

Stuart would walk in tomorrow night—I could picture it clearly—and find me here, knife to thumb, mustering all available strength and concentration to draw in each new breath to replace the last. Not acceptable. But the effort to raise my body from that kitchen chair seemed as unimaginable as hopping off the footbridge leading to Little Island and riding the current to the other side: a Little family tradition. I sucked away the bright thread of blood.

"Feelings mean we're alive," Dr. Kilsaro told me when I was first sent to see him two months after I began cutting. "Be grateful. Don't judge them as good or bad, but as indicators of how fully alive you are." I never told him the reason I cut myself. Never told him that sometimes, being alive felt more like a burden than a gift and demanded some accompanying pain.

Do anything related to the task. There was nothing I could do about the endless stretch of empty highway that was my life without my son, but I could pack for the weekend. I lifted my head from the table and ate Rex's crust. Pressing a paper napkin against the cut on my thumb, I stood, tossed dishes into the dishwasher, and climbed the two flights of stairs to the attic to get my suitcase.

When I flicked on the light, there, scattered beneath the eaves, stood a half dozen boxes that I had, years before, carefully labeled *Rex Toys*, *Rex Books*, *Rex Camp*, *Rex Soccer* . . . I breathed out and wondered if I would find sufficient reason, this time, to take in another breath. My thumb throbbed, and I could see a faint smear of blood on my robe. I needed to get out of this house.

I didn't see my overnight bag and guessed that Rex had taken it to college, which was why I grabbed the Pullman case and rolled it behind me as I fled to the second floor. I launched the big bag—ridiculously large for the few items I'd need for a weekend at my parents' inn—onto the bed, went over to the dresser, and yanked open the top drawer. Reflected in the mirror—in addition to my haggard face—was our king-sized bed flanked by our nightstands. A single book was the only item on mine, while Stuart's housed yesterday's coffee cup, his back scratcher, a flashlight, a water glass, and a tissue box. A trail of papers, books, and magazines spilled off the table and into the piles on the floor.

In front of me, on his side of our dresser, stood a pile of loose change, three pairs of cufflinks, several slips for the dry cleaner, a dish that Rex had made in third grade in which Stuart kept orphaned buttons, some shells from our family vacation in Florida last March, an oversized paper clip holding several crisp twenty-dollar bills, his comb, a roll of pennies, and two finger puppets from the play I had recently put on at the library. My side? My jewelry box and a single dried rose from the bouquet Rex gave me on Mother's Day. I knew then that I wasn't only concerned about the loss of my child and this weekend in Maine. Sometime in the past twenty years, I had gone missing.

SEPTEMBER 9, 1991

Daddy and I were playing gin rummy in the Games Room. Mom was chatting with Grammy in the entryway. It was just past ten o'clock when the phone rang. Daddy waited two rings to see if Mom would get it. She did the same, and so the phone rang four times before anyone answered.

"Hello?" I heard him say, as I rearranged the cards in my hand and considered the seven of clubs lying faceup on the discard pile. I listened to see if it was someone I knew calling, maybe even someone for me. Bonnie had gone to the party at the quarry with Roger and Tamar, and I knew she'd call as soon as she got home to tell me how it went. But since Roger and Tamar weren't home, I doubted that she was either.

I kept waiting, but Daddy didn't say anything for the longest time. I started to think it might be some sort of recorded message, or a telemarketer, running through her script. Daddy is too polite to interrupt.

Finally he said, "Where?" And something about the way he said it made me put down my cards and stand up. I had no idea what the call was about, but I knew I wanted to flee. Mom had stopped talking as well. It's funny, how we know when something isn't right. It's that sixth sense that animals trust and rely on, but that humans often discount in favor of reason. But I couldn't leave the room without going right past Daddy, and that would bring me even closer to the thing I wanted to run away from. He was talking again, but in a low voice so I couldn't hear his words. I kept staring at that seven of clubs, willing Daddy to hang up and come back in, pick up his hand, and say, *That? Oh, nothing. Town business*, or, *Just someone calling about room rates.*

Finally he did hang up, but he didn't come back in. Instead, he started talking to Mom. I heard her say, "Oh, no. No, no, no."

I sat down, picked up the seven of clubs, and discarded the ten of diamonds.

I was still sitting there, staring at that seven of clubs, now in my hand, when my parents came in a minute later. My mother was shaking. Daddy was talking softly to her, and she was nodding, but I had the sense that she didn't hear a word he said.

That the call had something to do with Roger and Tamar, I was certain. The year before, another recent high school graduate, drunk, had drowned in the quarry during this annual island party, celebrating the end of summer. "What happened?" I asked, not really wanting to know. Daddy looked at least ten years older than he had just ten minutes before. "Is it Roger?"

Mom held out her arms, and I moved into them, although my instincts still called me to run.

"There's been an accident," Daddy said. "Do you want to stay here with your mother?"

"No," Mom said. "We're coming."

And so we all went out to the car and drove the dark, winding road to the site where Roger's VW missed a curve and rolled twice before smashing into a tree. The hood was freakishly crumpled. Police and ambulance lights gave the whole scene a nightmarish glow, and shattered glass covered the road like ice.

Standing there in Stuart's and my bedroom, amid the tangible evidence of my nonexistence, I realized that when Stuart returned we would be alone for the first time since we married. Really alone, not waiting up for Rex, born not quite nine months after our wedding. Something about this awareness made me panic. What would we say to each other over dinner? How would we spend our evenings and weekends? Would he still want me? Would I still want him? I started to pull out sweaters and jeans for my weekend in Maine, and before I knew it, nearly every article of clothing I owned had gone into the suitcase, then into a canvas bag, and finally a cardboard box retrieved quickly from the attic. When I was done, my bureau and closet were empty—except for the ankle-length linen dress I hadn't worn in ten years and the white blouse with the tags still attached. Everyone needs a white blouse, I thought when I bought it. Apparently not. And still I felt myself spinning and twirling down that rabbit hole, as inconsequential as a dust bunny. But the spinning, I decided, was starting to slow.

And so I moved on to my desk and packed up my computer and a ream of paper; filled a box with my favorite books; added my stapler, calculator, and thesaurus. I took it all out to the car and returned to the house, wandering from room to room, filling another box with photos, my grandmother Little's Wedgwood teapot, the clay mold of Rex's hand, more photos, and my jackets from the back hall. I filled a tote bag with clogs and another with hats, then added an evening bag.

I did all this as if in a dream, still Alice, but now wandering about, desperate to find the exit from Wonderland. In truth, Alice's tale has always haunted me, reminding me of the summer after third grade when my parents sent me off-island to camp. Tamar and Roger remained at home, of course. I arrived late, and by then all the other girls had become fast friends, knew where the crafts tent was and where to eat lunch, had formed groups and chosen skits for the performances we were required to put on the last day. I spent the first few days alone and lost before being assigned to a group of girls who made it clear they didn't want me in their skit. Standing there in my silent house, I sensed that if I didn't leave, and quickly, I would again find myself, like Alice, an inadvertent vagabond in my own life, aimlessly roaming about asking passersby the way out, knowing they did not speak my language and wouldn't understand the reason for my question.

I filled one bowl with cat crunchies for Pinklepurr and another with fresh water, scratched the cat's head, walked out the door, climbed into my car, and drove north toward Maine, wondering how I would make it through this weekend, wondering, again, if it was some sort of omen, us all being alone together on this date, wondering how one went about locating a lost self.

· Chapter Two ·

Grace Little surveyed the front lawn of Little Island Inn and decided she'd made a terrible mistake. She should never have put in sod this late in the season. *What was she thinking?* She'd had to water it every day, and now the ground was soft and squinchy; people's shoes might get wet on Saturday. The big blue ceramic urns of ornamental kale (another mistake) stood like sturdy beacons at each corner of her garden—the garden of someone trying too hard to make an impression. Grace could feel her mother's silent concern.

She sighed, and her Glen of Imaal Terrier, Sophie, now sitting at her feet, turned a stoic, cataract-clouded gaze her way in a show of sympathetic solidarity, before limping off to her den beneath the potentilla, near the steps at the end of the inn's wide front porch. Even Sophie seemed to know that this departure from Grace's usual gardens of wildflowers, herbs, and blowsy, no-fuss perennials was misguided. Although Grace could not recall her mother ever growing anything more than the occasional basket of red-and-white-striped petunias—

which she would hang from a hook on whatever outdoor space was available in whatever apartment Grace and her mother had been currently living—her mother had requested flowers, and Grace wanted to honor that request. Joan had asked so little of Grace in life, given herself so little. Grace wished her mother were here to guide and comfort her, to sit beside her in the Adirondack chairs on the inn's now-emerald lawn, watch boats motor in and out of East Haven, and tell her everything looked lovely. But that was precisely the problem. Her mother could not be here to help plan her own memorial service.

The day her mother died, Grace found a manila folder in the drawer beside the bed. It contained what looked like a page torn from a diary and a photograph of her mother, quite young, standing on a beach with two other little girls. On the back of the photo, in faded pencil, someone, not her mother, had written: *Joanie, Callie, Cornie, July 1937.* Grace could make out little of their surroundings. On the scrap of paper, in her mother's familiar looping hand (although rounder than Grace was accustomed to) was written:

Grace
Flowers
By the water
Have fun!

Grace deduced that these were Joan's wishes for her service and had set about granting them. While she believed she'd fulfilled Joan's first two—however imperfectly, given the gaudy garden and sodden lawn—she'd fretted over her mother's final directive for the three months since her death. Just this week, she'd added it to her to-do list, hoping it might summon forth a few fun ideas. As yet, the two words now anchoring the list remained a distant and daunting finish line that Grace felt certain she would never reach. (A friend had asked her recently what she did for fun. Grace stared mutely back and finally blurted out, "Watch movies," although Grace hadn't seen one in years.) She loved her family; they were everything to her. But *fun* was not a word she associated with their gatherings.

Grace reviewed her mother's note one last time, before carefully folding and returning it to her pocket. There she felt the envelope, delivered just the week before, its slender profile belying its weighty contents. Grace sighed, wishing her mother had provided just a little more detail with her final written instruction.

"It's three days, Daniel. Three days. I can certainly take care of my own daughters alone for three days." Tamar stood at her kitchen sink, finishing the last of her coffee, as her husband poured brightly colored puffs of cereal into two plastic bowls. "I wish you wouldn't feed them that stuff. It's pure sugar. And where are they, by the way?" She dumped the last swallow of her coffee down the drain, put the cup in the sink, and strode out of the room. "We're going to be late." At the bottom of the stairs she called up, "Nat? Hal? Come on. We need to get going." Tamar wished Roger had agreed to meet her at the rest area—not so very far out of his way. *DVD.* "Hon, is . . . the movie in the Volvo?" she called. The girls liked one in particular, but Tamar couldn't remember which and didn't want to admit that to Daniel. "Natalie! Haley!" Two identical faces peered over the top of the railing, and the twins clomped down the stairs. "Don't you look nice! A little breakfast? Go see

Daddy. I'll be right down." *Mouthwash.* She could not abide the lingering, stale taste of coffee.

She dashed up the stairs and hurried down the hallway, past the twins' room, shut the door on their unmade beds and a floor littered with discarded outfits, and went into the master suite. She swigged some mouthwash, checked her hair and makeup, opened drawers and cupboards one last time to be sure she'd remembered everything, spit, and headed back down to the kitchen, where her daughters were wrapped in their father's arms. "Okay, junior woodchucks, everybody ready? Uncle Roger will be waiting for us at the ferry. Won't it be fun to see him?" She turned to Daniel. "Suitcases in the car?"

He nodded. "Drive carefully. Call me when you get there, so I know—"

"Yes. Of course, of course. We'll be fine. Won't we, girls?"

"Can we stop for fried clams and ice cream?" the twins asked.

Tamar looked accusingly at Daniel.

"I thought you might stop at that place in Wiscasset." He was spooning up the remains of his daughters' cereal.

She checked her watch. "I don't know, girls. I told Nan and Pop we'd be there for lunch."

Daniel frowned and checked his watch.

"But Daddy said—"

"Right, but Daddy didn't know. Maybe we can stop on the way back."

The girls tightened their grip.

Daniel pried them off. "Time to go, sweeties. I'll see you Sunday." He turned to Tamar. "What time will you be home? We really need to—"

"We'll see how the weekend goes. I'll have some work to do, so, not late."

He nodded. "Be good. I love you," he said, kissing each of the twins on the dark, shiny top of her head.

"Kiss, kiss," Tamar said to him, and headed out the door.

Daniel nodded. "Drive carefully."

Tamar made it through the tangle of roadways and round-abouts that snaked their way between White Head, Massachusetts, and I-93. She'd plugged in *Wallace & Gromit* as soon as they left the driveway, and the twins—who'd probably seen it a hundred times—were reciting the lines along with the characters. She checked her voice mail at work. Nothing. The office didn't open for another half hour. Once she got past the Tobin Bridge and onto I-95, she'd stop and make some calls. The girls would want a pee break by then, she figured, and maybe she could get them a snack so they'd forget about the fried clams and ice cream: too much fat, too much sugar. Empty calories. That was the trouble with people today: They'd forgotten what food was for. It's not entertainment. It's not a drug. It's nourishment, sustenance. You are what you eat. She truly believed that.

She glanced in the rearview mirror, dazzled, as always, by the sight of her two little girls. They were so . . . perfectly identical. Even Tamar sometimes had trouble telling them apart. She would have preferred dressing them differently, not just to avoid awkward confusions, but because clothes said so much about a person. But the twins' tastes were identical: the pinker and sparklier, the better. Tamar disliked pink. Everything she owned was black, white, gray, or blue, except for one red "power jacket." Pink was a power diffuser. *Don't ever give people a reason to discount you*, she'd been told in law school.

She wore nothing frilly, nothing plunging or seductively short, nothing fuzzy. Soft was okay. She had a drawer full of soft scarves. Lawyers don't always want to threaten either.

She could see the bridge up ahead. Good. No traffic yet. She accelerated and pulled into the left-hand lane, quickly getting up to seventy. Then traffic started to slow. "Come on, people, stay out of the passing lane if you're worried about gas consumption," she snapped at the blue mini-compact ahead of her. She glanced in the mirror. The twins stared back. "Finish your movie?" They nodded. She started it again. She reached over to check the glove box, flipped through manuals, spare napkins, granola bars, pens, plastic cutlery . . . no DVDs.

She glanced up to see a line of taillights glowing directly ahead. She hit her brakes, hard. The suitcases slammed forward; the DVD case flew off the front seat and clattered onto the floor. Tires squealed. Tamar gripped the wheel so hard she was sure she would rip it right off, shut her eyes, and, as she did, heard that other set of shrieking tires, on that other road, twenty years earlier. Her heart raced as she waited for the impact.

A horn blared. She took several deep, shaky breaths and opened her eyes. The cars ahead of her were moving. The girls were holding hands, mumbling something. "Okay back there? Sorry about that. I was seeing if Daddy had another movie."

Two heads disappeared from view. Tamar put on her blinker and moved into the center lane, dropped to fifty-five, and tried to slow her racing heart. The heads reappeared. Nat held up a small cardboard box. DVDs. A dozen at least. "Well, isn't that wonderful!"

The girls stared at her with an expression that, had it been coming from one of the partners at her firm, Tamar would have instantly recognized as dismissal. She was only thirty minutes from home and already out of control, already regretting her decision to leave Daniel behind.

Eight years earlier, in the delivery room, one pink, mewling baby in each arm, Daniel snapping photos, she'd sensed that she would fail as a mother. During the next few weeks she'd known it. The twins would keen, simultaneously, rousing her from the deep sleep into which she could fall any time, anywhere, summon her from even two floors away, and send her running to the nursery. She felt as though her nerve endings had been whittled to fine points and left, raw and exposed. No sooner had she changed one twin and dressed her than the other spit up, or began again to wail. The babies clung to and soothed one another, more than they ever let her soothe them. Dishes remained dirty, laundry piled up, the house lay as fallow as an unplowed field. She had no time to eat, never had uninterrupted sleep, rarely sat down. The truth of her failing stuck like a fishbone in her throat. She began to resent the twins, despise Daniel, berate herself. She'd been only too happy to abdicate the "mother" role to Daniel and return to the firm, where she was competent, respected, and, most important, in control.

Persistence is always rewarded, right? *Her boss had told her that.* "I was thinking of stopping in York. Stonewall Kitchens?" Tamar said to her daughters. "Remember that place? They have the wonderful bakery and all kinds of interesting gadgets? We can get muffins and pick up some blueberry jam for Nan and Pop. Would you like that?" Tamar had kept her gaze fixed on the road and cars ahead as she spoke. When she checked the rearview mirror, she could see that the girls were intent on their movie, once again reciting the dialogue. "Plus they have really nice restrooms," she muttered, and returned her focus to the road, easing back up to sixty-five.

· Chapter Three ·

JOY

It was quarter past eleven when I drove my car off the Charles Philbrick and onto East Haven. Main Street was congested, and I covered only half a block in ten minutes. That was fine. My mother didn't expect me until a little after one. I pressed my thumb into the steering wheel, felt the little wound open. Felt a little better.

I wondered what Rex and Stuart were doing just then. Unloading the car at Rex's dorm, meeting his roommate, getting ready to head out somewhere for lunch. I thought about pulling into the next empty parking space and going into the Harbor Gawker for a crab roll. Take a little time for myself. This was something I'd need to get used to doing with my son gone. Free as a bird, I was! An image flashed before me of oil-soaked pelicans huddled at the water's edge during the terrible BP oil leak in the Gulf of Mexico the previous summer: flightless, sightless, suffocating. I continued down Main Street, past several empty parking spaces, in the direction of Little Island.

I drove past George and Kit's General Store, where Bonnie Day and I used to stop every afternoon for candy when we were little and, later, to look through the fashion magazines. In their window, a handwritten sign, faded with time, declared: *If we don't have it, you don't need it.* I was happy to see that the bookstore, Second Hand Prose, where Bonnie and I traded in and bought books every week, was still open. The church, where we ascended from lowly shepherds to angels who got to wear glittery tinsel halos and stand in the upstairs windows in the annual Christmas pageant, looked freshly painted. Our senior year I was chosen as Mary, which was hard on Bonnie. But even she knew she was nobody's image of the Holy Mother. In eighth grade, she'd been selected to play Buttercup in the local production of *H.M.S. Pinafore* (she had a lovely voice) and so didn't begrudge me this honor.

I turned right on East Main toward Little Island, slowing as I passed Maisie Day's yellow cottage. Her hydrangea hedge looked in need of a trim. I was hoping to see her broad back bending over her award-winning dahlias, some the size of dinner plates. If I had seen her, I might have stopped in, maybe had the conversation that I'd wanted to have for twenty years. But the garden was empty—of humans, that is. One of Maisie's corgis was patrolling the grounds. I knew I would stop by to say hello sometime this weekend, although it was hard for me, all those photographs of Bonnie lined up on tabletops and mantel, looking at me, her expression so hard to read. All the Littles have tried, in small ways, to atone, to let Maisie know that we haven't forgotten her daughter, killed in that crash twenty years ago.

• • •

Grace would later say that it all began with that phone call. She had been standing at the registration counter, reviewing upcoming reservations but thinking of her mother, dead then just two days. She picked up the receiver and said hello, distracted by the sight of her garden: old plants, root balls exposed, scattered across the lawn. New plants in black plastic pots lined up like passengers waiting to board. Gardening was therapy for Grace, and she'd done quite a bit since her mother died.

"Is this Grace Little?"

The voice on the other end was her mother's. Grace felt her heart flutter like the wings of the moths that dance around the porch lights in the evening. She knew it couldn't be her mother, of course, but Grace had so fervently wished, in the past forty-eight hours, to hear her mother's voice just one more time that for one dizzying instant, she believed her wish had been granted.

She'd been with her mother at the end. Not at the precise moment of her death—her mother was much too private to permit herself to die in anyone's presence, even Grace's—but she had seen her mother just moments after she died. Joan waited to make her departure until Grace slipped into the kitchen for coffee. "Shows the depth of a mother's love," the hospice nurse said, when Grace tearfully summoned her. "Tell you the truth, most folks aren't all that helpful at the end. Try too hard to keep their loved ones here. Even when they think they've given them permission to go. See it all the time."

So Grace knew perfectly well that the woman calling was not her mother, but the tone, soft and sweet, was so familiar that she had to shut her eyes to hold back sudden tears.

"This is Callista Clark," said the owner of her mother's voice.

Grace tried to place the name but was distracted by images of her mother, calling from a pay phone in heaven. "Your mother's sister. Your . . . aunt."

This was impossible. Grace's mother was an only child.

"I do apologize for calling like this, but my sister and I decided it would be best to call before we wrote."

The voice, Grace could now hear, was clearly not her mother's; the syllables were more clipped, the timbre richer. "I'm sorry, there must be some mistake," Grace said. "Who did you say this was?"

Another voice came on the line. "This is Corintha Weatherby. Joan's older sister."

This second speaker's voice was more authoritative than the first, and far more so than her mother's. "We understand that Joanie didn't tell you about us, and we wanted to respect her wishes while she was alive. But now—" There was a moment's silence on the line, and when the woman continued, her voice had lost some of its hard edge. Corintha spoke for a few minutes, and then said, "We wondered if you're planning any sort of service. We'd love to meet you."

While Grace might have enjoyed sharing her mother while she was alive, she wasn't feeling quite so generous now that her mother was gone. On the other hand, she was curious. They were family. Joan's family. The calendar lay open in front of her, and she could see the entry for September 10, where, many months before, Gar had written, *Joan's visit*. Grace picked up a pencil, erased the word *visit*, and wrote *memorial service*. "Yes," she said. "A small gathering. Just family and a few friends. A . . ." She hesitated over the last part. "Fun celebration."

"That sounds perfect," said Corintha with enthusiasm.

Before she hung up, Corintha asked Grace to e-mail her any

questions she had about the Carlton family, Grace's mother, anything Grace wished to know, and promised to send her a letter, providing the answers. Grace said she would but never did. Corintha's letter, unsolicited, arrived two and a half months later.

JOY

At the causeway, I stopped and watched eddies pucker the surface of the water, like an invisible hand shirring fabric, and tried to imagine myself jumping. A moment's unease, brought on by thoughts of the structure (which is rather old) giving way and plunging me, and all my belongings, into the current made me inch my car forward so that I was most of the way across. I've always been more comfortable *by* the water than *in* it, or even on it, liked best to sit in an Adirondack chair on the inn's front lawn, with the tide high, holding the island in a tight embrace. There is a paucity to low tide that I find troubling: the craggy, barnacled underbelly of the harbor exposed; the seaweed, looking limp and exhausted, lying on the rocks. High tide is a time of abundance, when those fat, brown bladders dance beneath the water's surface, and the island looks cosseted and well fed, as though the harbor were pregnant and waiting, contentedly, for the big event: the moment when the tide turns and sends water surging down the creek, beneath the causeway and wooden footbridge, and out into Isle au Haut Bay. I could see the bay, sparkling in the distance.

I wondered, sitting there on that causeway, when Daddy would make us "ride the rip" this weekend. At sixty-seven, he was at some risk of a heart attack, given the water temperature—

just slightly fewer degrees than his age, according to the sign at the ferry dock—but that wouldn't stop him. Edgar Little is a man of action and a man who lives by tradition. A tradition that involves action, such as jogging around the island and jumping off the footbridge into the incoming tide, would never be sidestepped. This year, that was fine with me. Because this year, I had decided, was the year I would jump.

Chapter Four

Roger was beat. Williston to Rockland in just over five hours: a record. He'd blown through Littleton, Bethlehem, Gorham, Augusta . . . pushing the whole way. *Why?* He didn't know. It was just something to do.

He turned his attention to the cars being disgorged from the mouth of the ferry and decided they looked like Jonahs being spit out by the whale. He put down his window and inhaled. The air smelled like creosote and clam broth. If they could put that scent in an aerosol can, he'd buy a case of it. He smiled to himself. That wasn't a half-bad idea, actually. He ran through a list of names of people he might talk to when he got home. Not that he'd call any of them, but the exercise gave him a momentary lift, the passing notion that he might still make something of his life. He pictured himself shaking hands with influential people at parties. *Hi, Roger Little. Patents. I hold quite a few, actually.* Where there was one, others were sure to follow. He just needed to get the ball rolling, he mused, imagining the conference calls, luncheon meetings, business trips, the Porsche or Audi he'd buy once he sold the truck . . . What Roger really wanted to do, though, was to take over his parents' inn.

A gray gull paraded along the seawall in front of him, looking very stern, reminding him of his former headmaster, who strode around campus, arms folded behind his back, forehead furrowed, challenging "his boys" not to disappoint him. Roger supposed gulls had good reason for looking so pissed off, so ready to be disappointed, subsisting, as they did, on garbage and dead things. He couldn't say what had given the headmaster that look. Perhaps it was Roger himself, he conceded.

The sun felt great, and Roger slumped down in his seat, folded his arms across his chest, and tried to stretch his legs. His six-foot frame couldn't go far in the truck cab, and his shoulder was starting to complain. He should have taken more breaks on the drive over. He grabbed a bottle of Vicodin from the glove compartment and swallowed two with the tepid dregs of the beer he'd opened after lunch. Probably not a great idea, but he wouldn't be driving until he got across to East Haven, and then it was only a short ride to the inn.

He climbed out of the cab and hoisted himself gingerly onto the hood—grimacing as pain radiated down his left arm—and carefully laid his back against the windshield. He tilted his baseball cap down over his eyes to block the sun. The doughnut, eggs, sausage, home fries, and pie he'd hastily consumed at the Miss Downeast Diner on Route 1 were talking to him. He really couldn't eat stuff like that anymore. Shouldn't, anyway. His cholesterol was high last checkup. But there was no way he could drive by it without stopping. *Pie Fixes Every-*

thing, their sign said, and Roger had to agree that this was almost true.

Besides, the Littles had always stopped at the Miss Downeast on their trips to visit Grammy, and he wanted to honor her in some small way. He pictured them, Mom, Dad, Joy, Tamar, and himself squeezed into a booth, or sometimes their parents at one and the kids at another. Usually that didn't last long. Roger would misbehave and be called back. Tamar would want to come with him, and Joy, not wanting to sit alone, would come as well. He chuckled.

His father tipped generously to make up for the spilled drinks, dropped food, piles of soggy napkins, the pinches, shrieks, tears, and sword fights with the cocktail daggers that came in the BLTs—*who would give those to a family with three lively children?* Come to think of it, why did his mother let them order BLTs? None of the kids liked them. Only ordered them for the swords. Tamar would always sneak Roger into the ladies' room, ignoring Joy's insistence that it wasn't right. She would come in, too, in the end, and the three of them would listen to the *Bert and I* recordings played in a continuous loop, laughing as though they understood the jokes. Gar and Grace retrieved their offspring only when female customers complained to the manager about the long wait for the restroom.

Roger could feel his back seizing up and shifted position, exhaling slowly to relax the muscles. He'd pay for that drive. Was his halo pinching a bit, his mother would ask? No! *Yes*. He should have met Tamar and the girls at the Maine rest area like she'd asked. Resentment is a funny old thing. Like swallowing poison and expecting the other person to die, as the saying goes. On his best days he was free of it. Letting it go, keeping it simple. Anyway, he wanted his truck with him on the island, and Tamar wouldn't have wanted to stop at the diner. Its menu featured no forty-grain bread; no fat-free, unsweetened yogurt; no organic field greens, or free-range, hormone-and-steroid-free, humanely harvested animals. It was hard to believe, sometimes, that they were twins. Tamar would undoubtedly bring bags of groceries with her to the inn, which would also be short on foods she was willing to eat. Tamar had no idea how burdensome her "clean and sustainable" lifestyle was. Or maybe she did. It was hard to know with her.

He cracked his eye to check the time. When did she say she was arriving? He sensed she'd be here soon, sensed that she was close by. One twin always knew, somehow, where the other was, what the other was feeling. He was starting to relax, like a roll of tarpaper, unfurling and softening on a hot roof. He shut his eyes and pictured himself driving from the ferry terminal on East Haven to the inn. His inn someday, maybe. *(Would he have the courage to broach this with his dad this weekend?)* To his left was the sardine cannery (closed), and on his right, the Fisherman's Co-op and Walter Fifield's lobster pound. Roger reflected for a moment on Walter's sister, Loraine, his high school sweetheart—the one that got away—wondered where she was and what she was doing, whether she was happy . . . He paused for just a moment and allowed himself to wallow in a little *what if* before continuing his virtual tour.

After the gas dock was the Harbor Wharf with the Flying Bridge restaurant. His trip took him past the boatyard, where he looked to see what boats were for sale and mentally chose one to buy. He paused at Maisie's cottage, said hello, patted the corgis, admired the garden, and asked if she needed any help this weekend. She'd always been so nice to him, even after all that happened. From there he turned onto Island Lane and crossed the causeway to Little Island, stopping to check the tide and watch the current.

Roger felt himself rise now and hover above Little Island. He could look down on his parents' big shingled inn: the original part and the "new wing," added in 1958, when his grandmother, Isabelle Little, converted the old family house into an inn, as the Little family fortune began to decline. He drifted above Little Cove, Sunset Point, Peg's Point—*Who was Peg? Some cousin of his father's*—Seal Cove, Land's End, Sand Beach, and Spectacle Island. This ride was fantastic! Effortless! Vicodin was a really nice high. He was being blown along by a steady, light breeze. He could actually feel it on his face and neck . . .

He opened his eyes and turned his head to find his twin sister inches away, blowing gently into his ear. "Hey."

"Hi." Tamar climbed onto the hood and snuggled in next to him. "Cold."

"Impossible. Even you can't be cold today." He pulled her tight to him.

She buried herself in the crook of his shoulder. She fit there better than any other woman, except possibly Loraine Fifield. He'd always suspected that this was how he and Tamar had spent their nine months in utero, him sheltering her from tight waistbands, occasional bumps of oars, and the heavy books that their mother had rested on her swollen belly. Tamar had probably been cold even then.

"You looked like Sophie having one of her dreams. Were you chasing a rabbit?"

"Flying, actually. Over the island. Would be still if you hadn't woken me."

She smiled and shut her eyes. "Let's fly over together. Ready?"

"Where are the twins?" Roger asked, wondering if she'd decided, in the end, to leave them with Daniel.

She shifted onto one elbow and glanced in the direction of the ferry terminal. "Should I not have left them in there alone? Do you think they're okay? I mean . . ." She turned an uncertain gaze to Roger, paused, and then whispered, "I'm a lousy mother."

Roger felt uneasy. "Hey, let's all go get ice cream at that place on Water Street," he said. "They have gelato. I saw a sign."

But his sister's gaze had shifted out beyond the entrance to the harbor, where the low, hazy shapes of islands—including East Haven and Little Island—were just visible. "The ferry leaves in twenty minutes."

"Let's take the one o'clock," Roger said, tucking a stray hair behind his sister's ear.

"And give Joy some time with Mom and Dad to soften them up?" she said.

"Is Joy there already?" Roger asked, but knew the answer as soon as he said it.

"Of course she is," they said in unison, and laughed.

"Yeah, okay. Let's take the noon." Roger shut his eyes, hoping to reclaim the easy, gentle rocking of his high.

She began to massage his shoulder. "How's it feel?"

"Like somebody peeled it apart and stitched it back together. Badly."

"Ow." She pretended to plump his shoulder like a pillow, and then lay down, resting her head on it. "Feels good from out here." .

"I don't recommend it." They lay awhile in silence. "Also, *shoulder surgery* is really hard to say three times fast."

She tried. Failed. "You're right. Glad you got so much out of the experience." They giggled and relaxed into the truck's warm hood.

Tamar inhaled deeply. "Smells good. Like creosote and—"

"Clam broth."

She nodded. "Someone should stitch it into little pillows."

"Pillows. Good idea." Roger made a mental note. Pillows were better than aerosol cans. He cracked open an eye and studied the top of her head. "Are those gray hairs?"

"You are in a very vulnerable position for someone making comments about gray hairs." She wiggled her fingers in the direction of his armpit. "You, who are a full twenty minutes older than me."

"Witch!" He recoiled and rolled onto his side, where he encountered his two nieces, Hal and Nat, standing beside the truck, their faces now level with his and just inches away.

They looked like carbon copies of each other, he thought, with their pale faces and dark hair cut just below their ears, those almost-black eyes. *It was a little creepy, really.* Their heads looked too big to balance on those thin necks and narrow shoulders. Like Tamar's had at that age. Roger had clearly gotten the bulk of the nutrition in their mother's womb. The girls wore matching pink T-shirts with glittery decorations and pink pants that landed just below their knees. Even their sneakers were pink. Whatever happened to dressing identical twins in different colors so uncles could tell them apart? "Girls."

"We want—"

"Ice cream. There's a store—"

"Up the hill."

Roger stared at them, wondering which was which. "An excellent suggestion. What flavor do you like?" he asked the one on the right, hoping for some helpful, identifying clue.

"Cookie dough," they said together. "It can make you sick."

"Natalie," Tamar said, without raising her head. "Say hello to your Uncle Roger."

The twin on the right said, "Hello, Uncle Roger." The twin on the left (*Haley, then*) immediately repeated it.

Roger smiled.

"No ice cream. It will spoil your lunch." Tamar hugged her jacket around her. "Besides, it's too cold."

Roger stared for an instant longer into the twins' flat, black eyes. Their gazes were more probing than inviting, just like the looks he'd gotten from his father all his life: assessing, trying to understand, to find some sense of kinship after Gar had returned from talking with Roger's headmaster, or calling some irate parent or store owner, or bailing Roger out of jail and delivering him to the treatment center, or, later, visiting him in prison. Still, Roger had always felt his father's gaze to be tinged with hope, however tarnished, a certain . . . admiration for how Roger always bounced back.

Hal fished something out of her pocket: gum, already chewed (*please, God, let her not have picked that up off the sidewalk*), bit it in two, and offered half to her sister. They both chewed, and then, as though on a signal, turned their focus from Roger and began a small hand movement together. Perfectly orchestrated: index fingers touched, thumbs hooked, hands clasped. Second hands came up, and the intricate dance expanded—Roger watched, mesmerized—*snap, clap, curl, bump, clasp*, on and on it went, and then they started to chant as they continued to bump fists and walk fingers over palms. "Ah, ram, sam, sam!

Ah, ram, sam! GOOLIE, GOOLIE, GOOLIE, GOOLIE, ram, sam, sam! Ah, ram, sam! Ah, ram, sam! GOOLIE, GOOLIE, GOOLIE, GOOLIE, ram, sam, sam! AHHH DAHHH AHHH DAHHH! GOOLIE, GOOLIE, GOOLIE, GOOLIE, ram, sam, sam, sam . . ."

"Ice cream," Tamar blurted. "Go."

The twins stopped their chanting and stared at their mother. Even Roger was startled. He opened his mouth to say something, then simply handed her the keys, knowing that no one wants parenting advice from someone without children. "Stay warm." He slid gingerly off the hood.

"But hurry." Tamar took the keys. "I don't want to miss the noon ferry."

The twins resumed their chanting, and, Roger noted, did not glance back once as they trotted up the hill behind him.

The roof of the church had been sheared right off, and the metal pipe bent nearly in half. Gar looked for evidence to confirm his suspicions. Sure enough, there were the claw marks. *I'll be damned. Little Island has a bear.* He unscrewed the platform that had secured the bird feeder to the pipe and placed the now-roofless structure on the ground. With the season nearly over, he'd wait until next year to put up another. Maybe he'd make a boathouse this time, or a lighthouse. Or a miniature version of Little Island Inn. He turned to look at the shingled, three-story structure, its porch wrapping around the front, the matching towers at each end, flanking the gabled roof. Doable. He probably had some leftover shake shingles in the shed. But where would he find the time? Maybe this weekend, he and Roger— He stopped himself. Might want to wait to see what kind of shape Roger was in before signing him on for any projects, he reminded himself.

He'd need to paint the trim again next summer and do some work on the dock. He sighed. It was all getting to be just a little too much for him, although he hated to admit it. He made a mental note to call Jason Coombs to come haul out the float next week, acknowledging that he'd probably forget by the time he got back to the office. Grace had suggested he get one of those handheld devices that all the kids carry these days. Something he could tuck in his back pocket and pull out every time he needed to jot something down. "I have that," he'd said, "It's called a pad of paper." Problem was that neither was waterproof, and Gar was forever dropping things in the drink, forgetting that his glasses were on top of his head and bending down to secure a line on the *Kestrel*. Three pairs just this summer. Last year it was the master keys to the inn. The tide had been low, thankfully, and he was able to reach down and grab them off the bottom.

He hated that he was getting forgetful. Nothing serious. He'd been to the doctor and passed all the memory tests with colors flying. Had a CAT scan: mild cognitive impairment. This was a relief to Gar, but not as much as he'd hoped. A good, old-fashioned case of "the dwindles," Grace said when he reported the doctor's findings.

He'd sunk the pole for the feeder into a cement footing, the only way to secure anything with the granite ledge that lay just a few inches below the lawn, so he'd need a hacksaw to cut it off. He made another mental note to paint the end red, so people could see it. Maybe he could get Roger to help with that at least. Next summer he'd buy a smaller-diameter pole and insert it into the old one.

Grace was above him on the lawn, staring at her new sod. He'd told her it was too late for the grass to set roots in the topsoil that she'd had trucked in, and that it wouldn't grow, despite the water she lavished on it. It would look fine for Saturday's service but would probably die over the winter. Which was okay. They didn't aim for a perfect lawn at the inn. Coastal Maine was too rocky, the climate a little too harsh to sustain one. So theirs was thin and weedy with many brown patches. Clover kept it looking green. People didn't come here to look at grass, they came to look at the water, and Little Island Inn offered plenty of that. Grace and Gar had run out of water-related names for their guest rooms, after Ocean, Harbor, Sound, Bay, Cove, and Reach, and so named the other half Cliff, Osprey Nest, Cormorant, Garden, Puffin Roost, and Sunset. Guests assigned to those rooms always asked whether they'd have a water view. Grace and Gar always assured them they would. Gar picked up the damaged bird feeder and headed toward the tool shed for his saw. *Call Jason Coombs and, damn, what was the other thing?*

· Chapter Five ·

Joy arrived first, and early, as Grace knew she would. She could see her eldest daughter, stopped on the narrow causeway leading to Little Island. Grace shifted one of the Adirondack chairs, noting that its legs left dents in the damp sod. Poor old Joy. Forty-one next month—hardly old from Grace's vantage point of sixty-four—but Joy had seemed old since the day she was born: self-contained and seemingly self-reliant. Although Grace knew how fragile she really was, like a monarch butterfly, their wings strong enough to carry them three thousand miles from Maine to Angangueo, Mexico, and yet so delicate that the slightest touch by a human hand renders them useless. Grace wondered whether butterflies would describe themselves as fragile or powerful—and which Joy would choose.

When Joy was first placed in her arms, Grace had held her so tightly, afraid that she, too, would be taken away, as Abigail had been. But this daughter—how that responsibility-laden word had filled her with a sense of duty—was perfect. Grace saw the slight upward curve of her own mouth, her mother's lovely straight nose (Grace's own nose being, she'd always thought, rather too short and pugged), and Gar's brilliant blue eyes. Even so, Grace found herself face-to-face with a complete stranger. This realization—that Joy was entirely her own person—came as quite a shock.

The pause on the bridge, Grace guessed, was an attempt to shrink the time between now and when Joy was expected. Joy *couldn't* be late. Her need to please others and to ensure that everyone around her was happy was too strong to resist. Those are tough roles to assign oneself, especially in this family. It was a very different need than her sister Tamar's: to win, to be "in the loop" (her expression, not Grace's), to be in control—perhaps because Tamar's own life had spun, literally, so unexpectedly, so badly, out of control the night of the crash. Certainly Roger's life had spun even more wildly out of control that night. Then again, Roger was at his best in a crisis, which was perhaps, Grace acknowledged, why he'd become so adept at creating them.

Grace sat down on the arm of the chair. She knew this weekend was the twentieth anniversary of the crash and chose it anyway, because this was the weekend every year when her mother came to visit her at the inn. Right after Labor Day, when the crowds had lessened, because Joan, even after all those years, was afraid to be too much out in public. Grace wished with all her heart that she were waiting for her mother's arrival rather than planning her memorial service. Gar would have driven down to Handley to fetch her, while Grace made a nice lunch: lobster rolls, tossed salad, and a lemon-blueberry tart. She'd had the discomfiting feeling all week that Joan was waiting for her down there, sitting in the upholstered chair in her small living room, her overnight bag neatly packed and resting beside her, her coat folded carefully across her lap. What she wouldn't give to be able to spend one more day, even one more *hour*, with her mother. To hear her voice, see her sad, gray eyes, her beautiful nose, touch her soft skin. What would she do with that day, that hour? What would she say if she could?

Grace had known the end was coming and spent as much time with her mother as possible, trying to store up the details of her face, to breathe in her scent. It hadn't been enough. Her memory was fading as surely as the colors of a sunset. It seemed unfair—wrong—to Grace that a life could be so easily expunged after death. She'd cleared out her mother's room, given away some of her clothes and books, packed others in boxes and sheathed them in plastic and placed them in the attic. Other items she integrated into her own household: a couple of old kitchen gadgets now nested in drawers, several sweaters were stacked on the shelf in Grace's closet, a pair of old sneakers stood by the back door. Although they didn't fit Grace, the sight of them gave her the comforting sense that her mother was close at hand. She wanted her mother with her. So much so, that Grace sometimes felt herself floating, as if Joan's spirit were a balloon that Grace was holding, and the balloon was trying to rise, and Grace's weight not quite sufficient to keep them both earthbound. It was tiring work. Grace sat in the chair and closed her eyes.

Joy was watching the current, Grace knew. All the kids did this when they returned to the island for the first time after a long absence. In Joy's case, she was probably dreading the requisite run and riding of the rip. How Grace loved it! She could feel the three feet of free fall from the wooden footbridge, the jolt of the cold water, the hug of the current, wrapping itself—

like tentacles—around her and pulling her under the bridge. Once through, the current tossed riders into an eddy that swirled toward the flat rock below the Findleys' house. But there was always a moment when Grace would wonder, with a mixture of excitement and hope, whether the current would keep its icy grip on her and pull her all the way up the creek, beneath the causeway, into the harbor, and then what? Where would the current stop? How far would she be carried? Out into the reach, and then Hurricane Sound, and over to Rockland, or Camden? No, at best she would end up at the gas dock on East Haven, having collided with a few boats in the harbor along the way.

Her fantasy of being borne to faraway places was never more than just that. The eddy always caught swimmers and brought them safely to shore. Gar made certain of this, timing their jump with the last moments of the incoming tide.

Grace hadn't ridden the rip once that summer. Why was that? Age? She hoped not, but she and Gar were both slowing down. His dwindles were beginning to worry her: items and words misplaced with increasing frequency. She adjusted another chair so it faced more directly toward the harbor—noting that its legs had also made deep indents in the damp sod.

Grace glanced back at the creek. Why was Joy *still* stopped, unmoving, on the causeway? Something was wrong. Grace knew, even from that distance. Well, she thought, retrieving the slender envelope from her apron pocket, intending to read it one more time, *I'll burn that bridge when I come to it.*

Bottledarter's missing. The contents of Gar's tackle box lay scattered across the table: his El Squid Senior, some prowlers and plungers, bunker spoons and bullet heads. He was seated in one of the forty-some chairs in the inn's dining room, which looked undressed and homely without its usual sea of blue-checkered cloths, unifying the tables of mismatched wood, scarred with coffee cup rings, dings, and gouges. Grace probably took them off to wash, he thought. Later, she would put flowers on each table and on the sideboard and have a pot of coffee and perhaps some cookies or a loaf of zucchini bread for the kids to snack on. Funny how those little touches bring a room to life. His mother, when she ran the inn, had a whole staff of employees to help and never managed so many nice touches.

Times were different then, he supposed, as he gazed down at the green-and-blue super pogy that was giving him a startled glassy glare from the pile on the table. People didn't expect as much: a bed, a clock, somewhere to put their clothes. Private baths were unheard of. Now guests wanted a television in their room, a private bath with amenities, snacks available at all hours, Wi-Fi . . . Grace and Gar had converted a few former closets to private bathrooms by putting antique wardrobes in the larger rooms, and Grace had ordered plush terrycloth robes to hang in them. She'd stocked the baths with refillable dispensers of shampoo, soap, and lotion and had Gar build a fire pit, where they held weekly roasts with her homemade marshmallows. They'd drawn the line at television in the rooms but did install a big flat-screen in the Games Room. Wi-Fi and cell phone connections were still hit or miss out here, but Grace insisted they create a "business center," so they'd converted the former gun closet near the registration desk, where guests could check their e-mail and print out their boarding passes.

Grace had Tamar's husband, Daniel, design a website and

take photos of the grounds and harbor to post there and on Facebook. *Facebook!* Gar was highly skeptical of this site. He didn't understand it, and he distrusted things he didn't understand. If he had his way they wouldn't have a computer at all. He didn't like being so instantly connected to the outside world, or the feeling that people were peering in at them without their knowledge, passing judgment based on a few photographs and reviews from former guests. He and Grace always provided comment cards, but some guests felt the need to withhold their opinions from the innkeepers themselves and instead deliver them to the world at large under some anonymous pseudonym. Cowards. Gar did insist that they maintain the old paper registration system, where he could always find a guest's record.

Gar had to admit he'd ordered a few nice lures online at good prices. But then, feeling guilty, he'd bought a few he didn't want or need at George and Kit's. George would know that Gar needed new lures and wonder why he hadn't come in to buy any. Gar needed George and Kit's: hard to run an inn on an island without a general store. So, in the end, ordering the lures online had cost him more. The world was simply getting too complicated.

He stared down at the empty cubby in his tackle box. *Where the hell was his bottledarter?*

· Chapter Six ·

JOY

"Hello?" I called into the inn's empty entryway. I parked my huge suitcase near the registration desk, a captain's table that my parents had found years before in an antique barn on Route 1. Daddy restored it after my mother extensively researched its history and read up on the proper method and materials to bring it back to life. Daddy wanted it left as was, wormholes and all. A guest berth from the same ship—*Constellation*—served as a settee.

"Hi, honey." Daddy's voice was coming from the dining room.

I headed through the living room with its enormous field-stone fireplace, where we'd hung our stockings every Christmas. "Sorry I'm a bit early." I kissed the top of his head and sat down.

"Are you?" Daddy sounded surprised. He wasn't, but I appreciated the effort he made. He was studying my face. "Anything wrong, sweetie?"

"What? No!" I beamed and hoped the result was convincing.

"Just a little tired. The traffic was terrible." The effort of trying to be perky exhausted me. I wanted nothing more than to go upstairs, lie down, and sleep for, oh . . . forever, or at least for the next three days. Daddy had the contents of his tackle box spread across the table and looked like he was in the middle of something important. I didn't want to disturb him. Besides, I knew he would ask about Stuart and Rex, and the mere mention of Rex's name was likely to send me spinning back down that rabbit hole. "When are Tee and Roger coming? Tee is still bringing the twins alone, right?" I rolled my eyes. "That will be interesting. How will she get any work done?" My tone was facetious. I could hear it, and so could Daddy, judging by his raised eyebrows. I knew I should apologize but couldn't summon the words, my mind too occupied with the anticipation of negotiating the tides and currents in my family this weekend, not to mention missing my child. And then there was the fact that I'd just . . . what? Run away from home? I felt as helpless as the bits of flotsam I'd just watched being borne beneath the footbridge and out into the bay.

Daddy was looking at me, concern evident in the creases— so much deeper than I remembered—bracketing his mouth and running between his brows. Then he smiled. "Your mother's been gardening like a madwoman for three months. Why don't you go outside and say hello? See if she needs a hand. She's had some—" He started to say more, but stopped.

I looked out across the lawn, which seemed an unnatural shade of green, to the Adirondack chairs arranged in their usual semicircle facing the harbor. Beyond them, lichen-covered rocks led down to the dock, the float, and my parents' trawler, the *Kestrel*. "The lawn is as green I've ever seen it," I said. "Wet summer? Or did you fertilize?" It looked like sod, although I couldn't imagine my parents installing sod. I looked more closely. Yes. Unquestionably. Sod.

"Go on out and tell her how nice everything looks."

My mother's garden is usually a tangle of coneflower, bee balm, and butterfly bush—"magnets for winged pollinators," she likes to say—along with Queen Anne's lace and other assorted wildflowers, with morning glories vining throughout. She manages to make this look not only intentional but fabulous. When I tried it, my garden looked chaotic and weed-choked. But this year, my mother's garden, framing that kelly green lawn, looked like an overdecorated salon, and I hate to lie. I really hate to lie. So I didn't want to go out there and tell her how nice everything looked. Besides, my mother would sense something was wrong and start asking me questions and ferreting out answers I couldn't, or wouldn't, give, in an attempt to fix me.

Fortunately, I didn't see her and said as much to Daddy. "I'll just run my bag upstairs, and then go look for Mom."

"Let me give you a hand." He started to rise.

"No, no. Looks like you're busy." I pressed him firmly back down into his chair and hurried back through the entryway, took the key for Sound—my favorite room—from its little drawer in the antique apothecary cabinet, and, as quickly and furtively as possible, rolled my enormous suitcase toward the stairs. Breathing hard, I hauled it up two flights and rolled it down the hall, stopping in front of the door to Sound. I love the meanings contained in those five gold letters on their midnight blue background: *reliable, discreet, and trustworthy.* No matter that the room was named for Hurricane Sound, the body of water that presses itself against the west side of East Haven.

Once inside, I surveyed the double bed with its antique spread, crocheted by Daddy's great-grandmother. A faded, hooked rug covered most of the uneven wide-planked floor, waxed and polished to a high shine. A wardrobe stood against one wall, the closet having given way to a private toilet and sink. The shower was shared, down the hall. The windows in the bowed tower gave a magnificent view of the harbor, East Haven, and Penobscot Bay. On special occasions, when we were kids, and the inn had few or no guests, we were allowed to invite friends over for the night. I always invited Bonnie, and we always slept in this room. My parents have a book of Audubon prints, and we liked to page through it, selecting our favorite. Bonnie's was the indigo bunting. She never knew how brightly plumed she was.

I opened my suitcase. Tamar and Roger would take the adjoining rooms, Cliff and Cove, on the second floor and stay up late, one having slipped into the other's room, and whisper together, as they'd done throughout our childhood. Although, back then, all three of us slept in the new wing, where the summer help used to bunk when Daddy's mother ran the inn and hired college kids, including our mother, to wait tables and help in the kitchen. I would lie awake, listening to my siblings' whispers through the thin walls. I couldn't hear their words, just a sibilant sound, like distant surf, punctuated by their laughter. Some nights their murmurings would lull me to sleep. Other nights I would lie awake for hours. Nothing excludes a third person quite so successfully as two other people whispering.

Impulsivity often leads to regret, I have learned, and my hands shook as I dug through the layers of skirts, dresses, slippers, T-shirts, blouses, sweaters, shoes, and pants. It's best to think hard about consequences before one acts, something I had not done that morning. I bit down on my thumb and watched the small seam redden.

Tamar watched Roger drive his truck onto the ferry. He said he didn't want to walk from the dock to Little Island with his duffel, and gestured to his shoulder. Roger didn't like to be without wheels. Wheels meant independence, freedom, escape: the only way Roger could spend a weekend, she knew, back on the island with their parents.

She ushered the twins to the loading gate, one small hand clutched tightly in each of hers. They reminded her of the training wheels her father had attached to her bicycle when she was around the twins' age. She demanded that he take them off. They didn't train, they enabled, and thus postponed learning. Falling is what trains. She knew that even then, and fell until she got it. She clung now to her daughters' small hands, still sticky with ice cream, wondering how many times she would fall this weekend, whether she would have it down by Sunday and could return to White Head able to manage the ambiguities of motherhood: juggling job, parent-teacher conferences, school plays, volunteer obligations, a messy house, and her crumbling marriage. She exhaled slowly, suddenly grateful for the balance and support on either side.

Tamar and the twins were in the bow, standing along the starboard railing, staring silently out into the harbor when Roger sneaked up, grabbed Hal, and made as if to toss her overboard. She squealed and kicked, barely missing his groin.

"What the—" Tamar whirled around, saw her brother, and swatted him.

"Ouch. Bad shoulder."

"Bad idea."

"I was just goofing around."

The girls were hugging each other, and Tamar touched them both lightly on the head, uncertain whether her comfort was needed or desired. "Tell them that."

"What do you think about self-loading ferries?"

Tamar squinted at her brother. "Is this a riddle?"

"No. I just thought of it when I was parking. Some sort of lazy-Susan affair. You drive on and it slides your car one notch to the right, then the next car drives on, and when the whole thing is full, someone flicks a switch, and it lifts up, and there's another belt below it . . ."

Roger was getting excited about his idea. God, he was just a blown-up version of the freckle-faced ten-year-old he'd once been. "Genius."

He patted his pockets. "Maybe there's someone on board I could talk to. Maybe one of the guys parking cars."

"Roger, your design would put them out of a job." Tamar handed him a pen and a creased envelope, and he made some quick sketches. "Did you remember to move our stuff?" Tamar had put their suitcases in the back of Roger's truck, along with three bags of food she'd brought, and told him to lock them in the cab after he parked. Nothing and nowhere was safe these days. Laconic crime had become the new norm.

"Sure."

He hadn't. She knew this instantly. "Go move them."

He snapped to attention and saluted. "Want a beer?"

Tamar raised an eyebrow. "A beer? I thought you . . ." She glanced down at the twins, who were quietly reciting the words to *Wallace & Gromit*.

"Turns out it wasn't recovery so much as remission. It's no big deal. I brought a few for the road."

"For the—"

"Not literally."

She had to stop before things got ugly. "No thanks." She'd get him to take a run with her later, she decided—he needed the exercise anyway—and talk to him about his drinking.

Roger shrugged and headed back to his truck, and Tamar stared resolutely forward, impatient for the ferry to leave, and thought back to the fight she and Daniel had had the week before. He'd accused her of being a negligent mother, an "absentee wife." Said the girls "hardly knew her." To retaliate, she'd told him that she would take the girls up alone this weekend. She said it to hurt him. He loved the inn and her parents almost as much as she did. Maybe, in the case of the inn, more. She said it because he was right, and she needed to prove him wrong.

She'd called Joy, intending to ask if she'd help her look after the girls, but Joy had stayed oddly silent on the other end of the line. It was the same sort of silence Tamar got when she'd told her she was pregnant eight years earlier. In the end, she hadn't asked. Three days of total immersion was just the thing to kick-start the maternal instincts that Tamar was sure must lie dormant somewhere inside her.

She glanced down at her daughters' identical glossy heads and made a resolution: This weekend she would tease them, like Roger, and make them laugh, let them eat whatever, wherever, whenever they wanted, snuggle with them and read together, the way her mother did when she visited . . . The ferry gave three blasts of its horn as it reversed away from the dock.

The twins grabbed tight to the rail and peered over the side, bouncing slightly with excitement. Tamar touched their hair again lightly, feeling as though she were in a foreign country unsure of the customs, afraid of the food, wary of strangers.

"Let's have a cookout tonight. On Sunset Point," Grace, with her head and shoulders buried in the refrigerator, called to Gar from the kitchen, unsure whether he could hear her. She knew he loved cookouts.

"It should be right here," Gar called back from the dining room, gazing with deep concern at the empty cubby in his tackle box, bracketed by the bunker spoons and bullet heads. He'd taken out all the lures, sorted and replaced them. No bottledarter.

Grace reversed out of the refrigerator, bringing with her a large package of frozen ground beef wrapped in white paper. The bundle made a dull *thunk* as she set it on the counter. "What do you say?" she called.

"I said it should be right here," Gar called back. He selected a bright yellow zigzag and dangled it at arm's length. "What fish could resist you?" Hearing nothing from the kitchen, he called out again, "I bought it last year and never used it." He poked through the lures with one finger, hoping Grace would call back that she'd seen his bottledarter in the back hall or the boathouse. He selected the pogy and held it up, admiring the way its body shimmered in the sunlight. "Aren't you pretty?" he said, just as Grace appeared in the doorway.

"Why, thank you." She winked at Gar as he lifted a startled gaze to his wife and said, "Hm?"

"We'll put everything in the Garden Way cart and take turns pushing. Wouldn't that be fun?"

Gar stared. Sometimes no response was the best response when his wife had been talking to him and he had not been listening. Often she talked right through his silence, taking it as tacit agreement. He always worried a bit about what he might be agreeing to, but it had worked for well over forty years. She was holding a white butcher paper–wrapped package and saying, "I should have taken this out last night."

Seemed safe enough, so he nodded. "Do you remember my saying that I'd lost my bottledarter?" he asked. But Grace had disappeared back into the kitchen.

"Do we need a salad?" she called as she rummaged through the crisper. Hearing no reply, she answered herself. "It's so hard to eat with plastic forks. How about coleslaw? Good idea! I'll order a tub from the Harbor Gawker. Perfect." She backed out of the refrigerator.

Gar was standing in the doorway, looking quizzical. "Bottledarter?"

Grace simply smiled.

She hadn't heard a word he'd said. He could tell by the look on her face. Her dear face, so comforting and so familiar, although it bore little resemblance to the young woman he'd married. Her once-sculpted jaw was now buried beneath fleshy cheeks. He still loved Grace's body, despite its extra girth. More to love! Her once-brown hair had faded to the color of bleached driftwood. He thought about crossing the kitchen and wrapping his arms around her, kissing her neck and earlobes. He'd grab her capacious backside, and they'd knock out a quick one right here on the kitchen floor. He felt a stirring in his loins, and then remembered that the twins were coming soon; Joy was already here. Besides, "a quick one" was no longer a guarantee for Gar. A quick anything, for that matter, unless it might be forgetting someone's name. He was quick enough at that these days.

It seemed only a few years ago that they had sat in this very kitchen, so young, so full of plans for the inn, their whole lives ahead of them. Then the children arrived, grew up, and left. And how much longer would he and Grace be able to run this place, do all the maintenance? He'd always hoped that maybe one day Roger would take it over. But Roger hadn't developed the kind of responsibility one needs to run an inn. He had dreams rather than ambition, was undependable and irresponsible, and a substance abuser. Besides, he'd never expressed any real interest. Gar sighed. He supposed every father has high hopes for his son. For some fathers, he supposed, those hopes were realized. No, Roger was better off working at that store, selling bicycles and kayaks, better off on the mainland. An island, especially a small one, isn't right for everyone.

It required planning and time to get to and from Little Island. This was as it should be. But some people didn't like boundaries, felt hemmed in by them. Not Gar. He felt protected, secure. At night he liked to look over at the lights on the mainland and imagine all those people driving around, thinking they'd be happier at the mall, at the movies, at someone's party. People energized by the hustle and bustle of crowds, enlivened by neon and flashing lights, reliant on that external energy to galvanize their own dim lives. Gar loved that there were no traffic lights or streetlights on East Haven, and essentially no streets on Little Island, only a dirt lane or two. He loved that his home was his workplace. Gar had never found anywhere to match his little island home.

Grace was unwrapping the white butcher paper to reveal a mound of frozen ground beef. *Had she said something about a cookout?* He hoped not. Eating at the inn would be so much easier. No bugs, no building a fire, no grilling in the dark. "Anything wrong?"

"Joy," was all Grace said.

He nodded. He'd noticed something when Joy came into the dining room to see him, but he'd been preoccupied and didn't like to pry. He'd find her later and see if she wanted to talk. Joy would not open up to her mother. That much he knew. Ever since the crash, ever since Bonnie's death, Joy had become like the fiddleheads he'd find in the spring, coiled as tightly as a clenched fist.

He gestured to the block of frozen hamburger. "You'd best get that defrosted, Short, if we're going to have a cookout on Sunset Point."

Grace smiled. "Then we'll go find your bottledarter."

He returned to the dining room and fished a tangled ball of monofilament line from the bottom of the tackle box, a few silver jigs caught inside. After adjusting his glasses, he held the mess up to the light, then walked over to the bay window, where the sun shone in, highlighting the dust on the bare tabletops. He began to tease the strands apart, careful to avoid the hooks on the shiny jigs. One was always tempted to tug, but he knew to push gently. It took patience, but eventually, almost miraculously, space began to open up, and the knot released.

JOY

It took me quite a while to find my underwear, which I'd stuffed into an outer pocket of my suitcase. I hung a dress that I could wear to the service on Saturday in the wardrobe, placed a pair of shoes below it, and tucked one pair of jeans, two T-shirts, and a sweater into a drawer. My book went beside the bed, toilet case on the shelf in the bathroom, minus the shampoo. This went down the hall to the shower, where it looked so lonely that I carried it back and put it on the bureau. The big, bulging suitcase barely fit beneath the bed.

It was too nice a day to stay inside. So I decided to get it over with: go find my mother, come up with something nice to say about the garden, and head off any attempts on her part to fix my broken soul. After that I would sit in an Adirondack chair and take stock.

My mother was still not in the garden, which, on closer examination, looked even worse than before. It seemed too . . . careful. Too engineered. The heads of ornamental kale in their oversized blue urns looked like guests who'd mistakenly arrived in costume at a come-as-you-are party. There was no sign of the meadowsweet, Joe Pye Weed, spiderwort, and wild raspberries that usually grew happily beside her perennials, tomatoes, basil, squash, and thyme. And where was the milkweed? My mother used to say that you could always tell the Unitarians in town by the milkweed growing in their gardens. "After all, wildflowers are not weeds in God's eyes."

Settling into one of the Adirondack chairs, I decided my first task was to devise some sort of strategy to get myself out of bed each of the next 18,250 mornings of my life with no Rex to get off to school. To find some way to make it through the hours of each day, which, like the dotted lines on a highway, seemed endless and indistinguishable.

At the top of the page, I wrote *Possible Career Paths*. Below that I wrote: *Teacher, librarian, accountant, writer*. I waited. Nothing stirred inside me. And then I thought about my siblings, arriving soon, about my parents inside, waiting so eagerly for us all to be together again and I wrote: *Hired assassin*. I loved the Bourne movies, Matt Damon, so sure of his every move. I added: *confident, precise, impeccable timing*. On a new line, I wrote: *Navy SEAL*. These men and women—*did they let in women? I could be the first!*—belonged to an elite team that made daring rescues, giving no thought to their own safety. I wanted to be part of an elite team and wrote down *elite team*, then realized that any team or group—or family—would do, and crossed out *elite*. I'd need to overcome my life-long fear of the water, of course, to pursue that one. Perhaps, I realized, I would have accomplished both this weekend after I jumped from the footbridge. I was warming to my task, and so below that I wrote: *Explosives expert*. How thrilling to arrive on the scene with my suitcase of tools, knowing precisely where to set the charges to topple bridges and skyscrapers, without so much as cracking a window in neighboring structures, forever altering the landscape. On the next line I wrote: *Umpire*. Umpires call the shots. They're in charge of a baseball game as much as anybody. I would always be fair, not let my attention wander for even a moment. And, if a pitcher took too long on the mound, wasting everybody's time and making the game run long, he'd pay. The outfits, however . . . dowdy. I wrote: *Jackets more tailored and less funereal*.

Maybe it was a silly list, but I felt better, lighter. Tamar was right: Doing anything related to the task *did* help. I closed the

book and leaned my head back against the chair. The next
sound I heard was the horn from the noon ferry.

The ferry issued its single blast as it entered the harbor.
Roger squatted down beside the twins, waiting for the moment
when he would first catch sight of the inn. And there it was!
God, he loved this place. Staying hadn't been an option twenty
years earlier, but he believed now was the time to make his
move. "When we were kids we used to run along the shore and
wave to people on the ferry."

The girls turned dark, serious eyes to him. "Why?"

"For fun." He pointed out the trawler docked below the
inn. "How about I take you guys around the island in the *Kestrel*?" The twins' expressions remained unchanged. He glanced
at Tamar. She shrugged and shook her head. He wasn't a great
student of body language and nuance, but she looked the way
Roger felt when he needed a drink: uncomfortable and slightly
lost. That beer he'd offered would have helped her a lot. God
knows, Roger felt better. Wouldn't want to face his old man's
assessing, disappointed gaze cold sober.

He pointed out the lighthouse at the height of the land, its
beacon barely visible in the bright sunshine. "A lighthouse
keeper, now there's a job. Not many left. Most lights are auto-
mated now." Roger deeply regretted that he had been born too
late for that occupation. The twins stared, unblinking, at the
light. He pointed to the inn and named all the bedrooms.
"Which do you want?" The twins studied him, looked back
toward the inn, and said, in unison, "Puffin Toast." Roger
laughed. "Roost. Puffin Roost." Four dark eyes flashed up

briefly, then back at the inn, and the murmuring recommenced. "Ah, ram, sam. Ah, ram, sam. Goolie, goolie . . ."

He could see the Adirondack chairs set in their usual semi-circle on a bright green lawn, brighter and greener than he remembered. *Home.* He shaded his eyes, trying to make out the lone figure sitting in one of the chairs—probably Joy—as the ferry made its turn toward the dock, and passengers began stirring around them, making their move toward the exits.

"Shouldn't you be back at your truck?" Tamar asked him.

Roger snapped his fingers. "The self-loading is done with conveyor belts, so your car is waiting for you on the dock. Want to come with?"

Tamar shook her head. "We'll walk." The twins started to whine. Tamar shushed them. "Just bring our stuff in for us, will you?" she said to Roger.

He thought uneasily about the suitcases and groceries still in the back of his truck. He'd forgotten to lock them in the cab when he went back for his beer, as she'd requested. But, really, who'd steal someone's food? Especially *that* food? Besides, he reasoned, the twins had bright pink suitcases with orange flowers. Hard to wheel those discreetly off the ferry.

Tamar was frowning at Roger. "You left them in the back, didn't you? You jerk. If they're gone . . ." She looked down at the twins, who were peering up at her with matching, worried expressions. "Then Uncle Roger will buy us all new things!" she said brightly. From where Roger was standing, the girls didn't look pleased.

"See you at the inn." Roger gave her a peck on the cheek. "Suitcases and all." He strode off toward his truck, wondering just how drunk or sober he needed to be to approach his dad about taking over Little Island Inn.

When he arrived at the truck, he found an irate parking attendant and a line of cars.

"C'mon, fella," barked the guy, and a few drivers sounded their horns. Roger waved apologetically, motioned to his midsection, and mimed seasickness. The man in charge nodded toward Roger's truck to indicate that he needed to get a move on, but seemed less angry. Roger had that effect on people. Blessing and a curse, he had to admit. He waved as he pulled his truck forward. The attendant waved back. Roger would definitely talk to him about his self-loading ferry idea on the way home. He was pretty sure the guy would remember him. Who better to partner with on this than someone who made his living loading cars? *Park-o-matic. Load-rite. Ferry Fast. Get-on-board.* Roger tried out a few names as he rumbled across the metal ramp and onto East Haven.

He pulled into an empty parking spot near the Flying Bridge, having decided that one more quick beer would get him sufficiently loose to face his father. The restaurant was crowded. Waitresses, shouldering trays layered with plastic baskets of fried seafood and paper cups of coleslaw, weaved their way between tables topped with tumblers of iced tea and lemonade. Roger didn't recognize any of them, although he spotted a few he wouldn't mind getting to know. He smiled at a young brunette who looked . . . vaguely familiar. Was a time he was on a first-name basis with half the waitresses. Hell, was a time in high school he was dating half of them.

The smell of fried food reminded Roger that he was hungry. He checked his watch: one fifteen. His mother would have made lunch, and he didn't want to disappoint her. He grabbed a seat at the bar and ordered a beer. From his seat he could see Little Cove and the creek, with its causeway and footbridge. He thought of Tamar and the twins, making their way through town, and remembered their groceries and suitcases, still under the tarp in the back of his truck. They had survived the ferry crossing; be ironic if they got lifted here on East Haven. Hard to imagine it, although he'd done his share of petty crimes here: breaking into empty rental properties and leaving the water running and the lights on; shoplifting candy, small toys, cigarettes, and once a baseball mitt from George and Kit's, which his father had discovered and made him return. The waitress delivered his beer. He drained half of it.

One time he got Walter Fifield and a few of their buddies to undo the screws on the *Welcome to East Haven* sign and rotate it 180 degrees. They attached a small plaque that they made in shop class that read: *At some point in time, the entire world flipped upside down, except for this one sign, on this small island, in Maine. No one knows why.* What kid didn't do stuff like that, he reasoned? Neither of his sisters, he had to confess, as he pulled five dollars from his wallet and tossed it on the counter.

He moved to the window so he could see the inn, nestled in the tall firs above the cove. So serene. So settled. He pictured himself hosting big pancake breakfasts on Sundays, clambakes on Friday nights, taking guests out in the *Kestrel* for fishing trips and tours around the islands . . . If only he had someone to share that life with him. Below, cars slowly nosed their way across the metal ramp into the belly of the ferry. He watched until they were all loaded, then made his way back downstairs and out the door to his truck. Time to face the music.

Gathered

. . .

· Chapter Seven ·

JOY

"What would you girls like for lunch?" Tamar was guiding her twins along the buffet line. "You like turkey, don't you?"

"No," they said.

"Why not?" Tamar asked, sounding truly puzzled.

That is not a question you ask an eight-year-old, I wanted to tell my sister, *unless you are prepared for the answer.*

"What would they like?" My mother had studied the cheese, ham, turkey, roast beef, bread, lettuce, tomatoes, mustard, mayonnaise, chips, pickles, olives, potato salad, forks, knives, napkins, plates, and pitchers of both iced tea and lemonade. She wore an expression of deep concern. "Sorry about the tablecloths. I haven't had a chance to iron them yet."

Who but my mother still irons tablecloths?

"It looks funny," the twins now said in response to their mother's question.

"How about roast beef?" Tamar's voice held a desperate edge.

Identical faces scrunched into identical frowns.

This was going to be a very long weekend for someone. I tried telepathy. *Ask them whether they want turkey or roast beef. Give them a simple choice.* I certainly wasn't going to say it aloud. Tamar's temper was the minefield through which my family tiptoed. This made me wonder whether Jason Bourne had a sibling who held his family hostage—as Tamar often did ours—intimidating them into silence. Was this what compelled Jason to kill people for a living? A hired assassin, I realized, probably couldn't have my overdeveloped conscience or sense of familial duty.

"How about peanut butter and— Damn!" Tamar said.

The twins giggled, and our mother frowned, probably deciding whether to correct Tamar for swearing in front of her children. She decided on humor (a time-honored Little tactic) and said, "I don't believe we have any of that."

"Nope. Used the last of it this morning." Daddy was layering ham and turkey onto a slice of rye bread. I couldn't blame them for taking the easy road. It was early in the weekend. No sense setting Tamar off yet.

"Roger has my stuff in his truck," Tamar moaned. "Including my peanut butter and jelly."

"I have peanut butter and jelly, for heaven's sake." My mother started toward the kitchen.

"Mine's organic."

My mother looked so flummoxed by this statement that I stalked over to the buffet and began to make myself a sandwich. To hell with Tamar's temper. I could get her girls to eat a sandwich. I layered on turkey, a slice of cheese, pickles, lettuce, and then slid in a few potato chips and topped it all with a second slice of bread. The twins studied my every move. Taking my place at the table, I took a big, crunchy bite, never letting on that I knew the twins' eyes were trained on me and that chip-lined sandwich.

"Mmmm." I took another bite, and only then let my gaze drift toward the girls. "What?" I asked in mock innocence. "Don't tell me you've never tried this!" I winked at Tamar. She scowled back. *Dangerous waters: Tamar does not like to be bested.* But I didn't care, this was fun. When I stood and headed back to the buffet table, the twins paddled after me like ducklings.

Just then the kitchen door slammed, and Roger's voice called out. "Hi, all!"

"In here," Tamar immediately called back.

Roger strode into the dining room and surveyed the scene. As always, when my brother entered a room, the energy level went up. "The garden looks great, Mom. And, Dad, that lawn!" He moved over to the buffet. "Wow, what a spread. You're amazing. And I'm starved." He wrapped our mother in his arms and rocked gently to and fro. "Dad." He crossed the room and grabbed our father's outstretched hand. They clapped one another on the back, smiling, but I could already feel the tension between the two, like the discordant tuning of an orchestra before a concert. The tension would build until something set one of them off. What would it be this time? How long did we have?

"Hi, Jo-jo." He gave me a hug, and I felt flushed and slightly creased when he finally released me. Roger didn't stint on hugs. Roger didn't stint on much.

Mom checked her watch. "Oh, heavens, I should get going. I have a hair appointment at two thirty and some errands to run after that." As she started to leave, she said over her shoulder, "Any message for Loraine?"

A long silence ensued.

"Loraine Fifield?" I finally asked, glancing at Roger. "She's back on the island?"

"Owns a hair salon. Divorced," Mom added, also now glancing toward Roger, who was busy piling ham and turkey on a bulky roll.

He said only, "Really?" But it sounded too casual to me: a studied indifference.

"Been back since—" my mother started.

"Put chips in," the twins chirped to Roger, holding up their half-eaten sandwiches to reveal the layer of chips.

"Really? *In* the sandwich?"

I smiled: Roger had been the one to originate the concept of potato chip as condiment.

They nodded, eyes bright with pride. I detected dark clouds gathering above Tamar.

He added chips to his sandwich. "Like this?" Their heads bobbed, and he took a big bite. "Oh. Oh, wow! Now, *that* is a good sandwich. How did you ever come up with it?" He smacked his lips. "Someone should invent a flat, sandwich-sized potato chip just for this. *Chipwiches*. No! *Chipsters*. Whadya say? Are you in?"

The twins giggled.

"Did you, by any chance, bring in our stuff?" Tamar sounded sarcastic and was gazing with an expression of deep suspicion at the fans of lettuce on the tray.

"Sorry. Forgot."

"Don't get up," she said, although Roger had remained firmly seated and was now spooning potato salad into his sandwich—to the delight of his nieces. "I'll get it."

Tamar followed my gaze to the nearly untouched tray of lettuce and tomato slices and said, "You wouldn't believe the pesticides they spray on vegetables these days."

I wanted to snap that I wished she wouldn't polish her righteousness to quite such a high sheen; its radiance was positively blinding. But I could see my mother's expression across the room; it held a look of . . . befuddlement that I couldn't remember ever seeing on her before and could in no way account for.

"I'll give you a hand." Daddy stood and gave my mother a light pat on her bottom as he passed. Perhaps he'd seen her expression as well. I suddenly missed Stuart terribly. *Who would give my bottom a reassuring pat when I was sixty-four?*

"Back since when . . . ?" Roger took a big bite of his sandwich, and a large dollop of potato salad plopped onto his lap. "Quality control." He looked at the twins. "Take a memo."

The twins dissolved into a fit of laughter.

"What?" my mother asked, turning to Roger.

"Loraine," Roger replied, trying again to sound casual, even uninterested. "Been back since when?"

"Last spring. Her son was killed in Afghanistan. Jason, I think. Terrible." My mother shook her head, and she and Daddy headed out of the room. Only Tamar and I saw Roger lower the disintegrating sandwich back onto his plate and gaze out the window across the lawn.

After lunch I sat with Roger and Tamar in the Adirondack chairs. The sun felt good on my face, and I could hear the nearby hum of bees working the garden. From the harbor came the flutter of someone's outboard motor, and the wash of waves against the rocks. Above it all were Roger's soft snores. I felt, at that moment, for the first time since Rex left—or maybe all summer—at perfect peace.

"These quizzes are so stupid," Tamar said, looking up from the magazine she was reading. "My ideal mate will be either a lawyer or doctor; divorced, not widowed; like travel; be independent." She paused. "Which would you choose, uncertainty or doubt?"

"Really? It asks that?"

"No, I'm making up my own questions."

I shrugged. "Neither." My serenity was ebbing like the tide.

"You have to pick," Tamar insisted.

"Doubt?" Roger ventured, sitting up and rubbing his eyes.

"You sound uncertain." Tamar laughed. He laughed, too, although I was pretty sure he didn't get the joke. "Challenge or opportunity?" Tamar asked.

"Challenge," Roger responded. "No question."

"Opportunity," I said.

"Some people view challenges *as* opportunities," Tamar added, and Roger and I both groaned.

"Which seminar did that kernel come from?" I tilted my face back to the sun.

"What? Change Management, but it's true." She sounded testy. "Okay, endings or conclusions?"

"Conclusions. Definitely," I said.

"Me, too," Roger agreed, and we smiled at one another and bumped fists. I loved these moments of being one of two in our group of three. I was nearly always the third wheel.

"Obviously," Tamar said, louder than seemed necessary to carry the short distance between us. "Stupid question. Regret or remorse?"

"Can I have a different one?" Roger asked after a brief pause.

"No. Choose."

Roger was not a deep thinker, preferring to dwell in the realm of the practical, the tangible, the real, than in the theoretical. Anyway, the choice between regret and remorse was like the choice between tofu and seitan, two ghastly foods that Tamar once recommended I try. I wondered why she was asking this. But she was staring intently down at the magazine, and I couldn't see her expression.

"Remorse," I said, suddenly not feeling like being careful. "Remorse suggests having taken action and feeling guilty about it. It assumes a conscience. With regret you feel *bad* about what you've done, but not necessarily guilty." I cracked an eye to look at Roger. He was repeatedly pressing his toe into the damp sod, making little squelching sounds. "You can also regret *not* taking an action, but you can't feel remorseful. I'd rather do something, feel remorse, and make good on it, than do something and just feel bad."

"Well, that's easy for you, Joy," Tamar said. "You've never done anything bad enough to feel regret or remorse." She laughed and looked at Roger for confirmation, but he continued to press his toe into the damp sod, watching the water bubble up around his foot. "I choose regret, because remorse is something you can only feel about your *own* actions," Tamar said. "Whereas it is possible to regret someone else's."

Roger stamped his foot into the sod and was rewarded with a small geyser of water. "Next question."

The ferry blew its horn then as it steamed into the harbor, and we turned to watch. I could see my two little nieces, far out on the rocks, scampering along, waving. A few passengers on-board waved back. I glanced at Tamar, but she seemed intent on the magazine, so I turned back to watch the girls. Neither one was wearing a life jacket, and I wondered whether they knew how to swim.

SEPTEMBER 9, 1991
JOY

Bonnie and I were spending a last afternoon at Sand Beach before our return to college: me to Dartmouth, her to Northwestern. The tide was high and so Spectacle Island looked a long way from shore. We were discussing our plans for the evening.

"Highlights," Bonnie said. "Just a few streaks. Like yours."

"That would look nice," I said, examining my sun-bleached hair for split ends. "You can give me a trim."

"Want layers?" she asked.

"Do you know how?"

"How hard can it be? Just cut some hair a little shorter."

I didn't think that was all there was to it, but agreed to let her try. Whatever. It would grow out.

"You sure you don't want to go to the quarry?" she asked, for the second time.

"I'm sensing that you do," I said, rolling over on my stomach. "Untie my strap, will you?"

She undid the strings on my bikini top. The sun felt hot for September.

"Want sunscreen?" she asked. "You don't want to burn."

Bonnie was fair and had to be careful in the sun. I shrugged, doubting I'd burn much this time of year, but let her rub some on.

"No, not really," she said. "I mean, the quarry parties are fun, but . . ."

I knew what she was thinking: *Who wants to go without a date?*

"Besides, I think it might rain." She stared out to Spectacle. "I'm going to swim out."

"Okay. Be careful," I said, although Bonnie had captained the high school swim team and there was no reason for me to worry.

Bonnie stood and headed down the beach. I sat up to watch her. We were alone, so I left my bikini top where it lay on my towel. She walked the length of Sand Beach and, without breaking stride, continued right into the water until it was up to her knees, thighs, waist, and then she dived under. I watched her strong, sure strokes cut through the water as she made her way to Spectacle.

· Chapter Eight ·

At two forty, Grace blew into A Cut Above, Loraine Fifield's hair salon, two rooms above George and Kit's general store. "Loraine?" Grace called into the empty space. "Sorry I'm late."

Loraine stepped out from the back room and gestured to one of the stools facing the big mirror. "Hi, Grace. How are you?"

"Tired," Grace said, surprising herself. My God, it was only Thursday. The kids had just arrived. She couldn't be tired yet; she had to make this weekend fun. "Roger said to say hello," she added. Not quite the truth, but Grace couldn't see the harm. "Hopes you'll stop by on Saturday." Loraine's face in the mirror looked solemn. "I told him you were back."

Grace had always liked Loraine, had hoped that she and Roger might make a go of it. And they might well have, if not for the events of that last summer. They'd been young but seemed to have a real connection, Loraine providing the ballast that Roger lacked.

Loraine didn't seem as pleased with Roger's invitation as Grace had hoped. She looked, in fact, troubled.

"What are we doing today?" Loraine swirled a plastic cape around Grace's shoulders and snapped it secure. "Want to try something different?"

Grace stared at herself in the mirror. She looked old. And frumpy. When she was a little girl, she'd had very long hair, and her mother used to wash it for her in the kitchen sink. Grace would stretch out on the counter, and Joan would wet her hair, lace it with Breck shampoo, and lather it into a foamy white mound. They would pretend Grace was going to a ball, and Joan would style the froth into a towering beehive.

Grace remembered her mother washing and setting her own hair on those bristly, brown rollers, and then drying it under a puffy white bonnet attached to a fat hose that snaked its way into a plastic traveling case. She'd used a rinse, Frivolous Fawn, for years, partly trying to lose herself in case Grace's father came looking for them and partly trying to look young so as not to lose her job. Her mother enjoyed going to the hairdresser but wouldn't spend the money. So Grace always treated her when she came for her annual visit. They looked at magazines and discussed recipes, knitting patterns, house designs, gardens . . .

Grace had never colored her hair or put any curl into it. She'd been wearing essentially the same style her entire life, just shortening it as she grew older. "I don't know . . ." Grace ventured, meeting Loraine's eye in the mirror. *Would it be fun to try a new hairstyle? Would Joan think so?*

Loraine's eyes twinkled. "C'mon," she said, as if she'd read Grace's mind. "It'll be fun."

JOY

I watched Tamar from the third step. "Thanks," she said over her twins' heads. She had changed into running shorts and shoes and was stretching her right thigh as she held on to the banister, her heel tight against her rump. "Mind Aunt Joy, girls."

"Will you be gone long? I was actually thinking of—" I stopped, noting the twins looking at me, their gazes guarded, as though prepared for disappointment. "Making cookies. I don't suppose you'd want to do that, would you?" After a brief hesitation, the girls nodded, smiling shyly.

Tamar shifted and stretched her other thigh. "Cookies. Great idea. The girls love doing that. Don't you?"

They nodded uncertainly.

I suddenly understood the reason for Tamar's recent telephone call. It hadn't been to share the news about her fight with Daniel to forge a more sisterly bond. She'd wanted to book me as a babysitter. I had no doubt that Tamar was going on this run with Roger—

As if on cue, Roger limped down the stairs in shorts and hiking boots. "Ready."

"Ready for what?" Tamar looked at his heavy footwear. "I said *run*. We've got to get you in shape for tomorrow morning. Dad says the tide will be right at oh-nine-hundred hours."

I never checked ahead to see when the tide might be right for the requisite run and leap: at its almost-highest point, right before it turns. I shivered, thinking about the cool air and cold, dark water swirling below the bridge. But I was resolved: This year I would jump, come what may.

"I want a real run, not a Roger run." Tamar was pressing her heel into the floor behind her now, stretching a calf.

"What's that mean?" Roger didn't sound offended, merely curious. I admired that about him: He always assumed good intent. Didn't let people get to him.

Tamar changed feet. "You are wearing hiking boots."

"I'll bet you have trouble keeping up." Roger swiveled half-heartedly at the waist a few times.

"Bet not."

"Let's race."

"Up to the Dietrichs'?"

"Go!" Roger took off, letting the door slam behind him.

"Hey. That is not fair," Tamar called. She pressed a button on her watch and scampered after him, calling back, "Thanks, Joyous."

"You're welcome," I said, as the screen door again slammed shut.

JULY 1983
JOY

"We'll meet you at the school playground in twenty minutes," Tamar said. "Roger just needs to pee."

They were both wearing bathing suits. "I'll wait," I said.

"No, Joy. Roger doesn't want you listening."

"You are," I pointed out.

"That's different."

I didn't press. Instead, I went outside, but dawdled behind the inn, where I could see both doors, as well as the front lawn. It wasn't that I wanted to go to the beach. It was that I didn't want Tamar and Roger to laugh at me as I waited for them in town, while they went off to Sand Beach, or wherever they were headed. Too many times Tamar had caught me in her mean little deceit.

Before long, I saw them slip out the front door. "Wait up, guys," I called, trotting after them.

Tamar immediately started to run and pulled Roger with her. He allowed himself to be tugged along for a few steps but then stopped. "Why are we running?" He sounded truly puzzled.

"I thought you said school playground," I said when I caught up to them.

Tamar's gaze was cold. "We changed our minds. We figured you'd left, like I told you to. But you were probably listening to Roger, weren't you? We know you listen to us at night."

"I do not."

"Do so."

"Then don't talk so loud."

"Cut it out, guys," Roger said. "Let's get going."

"Where?" I now wished—laughter or not—that I had gone to the school playground, or better yet to Bonnie's. Her piano lesson would be over soon, and I could have heard the end of it. Roger's adventures usually involved water, or fire, or both.

"Silver Beach," he said. "I found a boat." He was really excited.

"*We* found a boat," Tamar corrected. "I saw it first."

Roger shrugged. "We're going to row it around to Seal Cove."

"Why?" I asked. Our parents had a perfectly good rowboat, the *Miss Katie*, tied to the dock below the inn. *Why not go out in that?* "Whose is it?"

"Nobody's! It just washed up." He sounded amazed at this unexpected blessing.

"I think I'll go over to Bonnie's—"

"No way, Jose. You wanted to come." Tamar now had me by the arm. "You're coming." She marched me off toward the trail through the woods to Silver Beach. Roger fell in behind.

The boat looked as though it had been adrift for weeks, possibly months: bare wood exposed, slimy seaweed growing from the barnacle-covered hull. One oarlock, green with tarnish, dangled from a corroded chain.

"I don't think—"

"What, Joy? Don't think you want to go out in this? Should have thought of that sooner," Tamar said. "C'mon, Roger. Let's launch her."

"Hold on. We have to find paddles first." He began to search the surrounding beach.

I went up to the high tide line and fished a splintery board from the line of dried seaweed, lengths of rope, lost lobster buoys, and broken traps. "Here's something."

Roger's face lit up. "Perfect. Now we just need two more." He joined me in the search, and together we found a piece of driftwood and a foam cooler top. Tamar was bailing the boat with a twelve-ounce plastic cup.

It took the three of us quite a while to drag the boat across the stones to where the water had receded with the tide. Tamar and I climbed in, and Roger pushed off.

We'd gone only about fifteen feet from shore when the water inside the boat made it too heavy to paddle; it was going down much faster than forward. My heart felt like it was caught in my throat as I looked down at the water all around me.

"Let's paddle back," I said, the water now halfway up my calves. "We won't make it to Seal Cove."

"Scaredy-cat," Tamar said, but she began to bail the foundering boat, while Roger and I vainly attempted to turn it and head back to shore. Within minutes, Roger gave the command to abandon ship.

I'd chosen the cooler lid intentionally, predicting something like this, and now used it as a kickboard to paddle, terrified, the short distance back to shore.

"That was awesome!" Roger said, when we were all safely on the beach.

"Totally," Tamar agreed through chattering teeth. I tried to pretend that my shaking and chattering teeth were simply from the cold as well.

"But let's not tell Mom and Dad," he said.

"For sure," Tamar agreed. "Joy?" She managed to make that single syllable sound like a threat.

I nodded as I watched the tide slowly pull the half-submerged skiff back out to sea.

Chapter Nine

Roger was standing at the bend in the lane just above the inn, hands on his knees, trying not to lose his lunch, when Tamar caught up with him.

"You are the most pathetic thing I've ever seen." She punched a button on her watch.

"Then you need to broaden your social circle."

She jogged in place. "Maybe you shouldn't have stopped at the Flying Bridge for a beer." She lifted her right knee and hugged it to her chest. "I know you did."

"Makes a nice high with Vicodin."

"Jesus, Roger. I really thought you were done with all that."

Tamar was the moral conscience for the world. He wondered if she knew how tedious it was, and how she'd take it if he told her. There was no way he wanted to endure one of her lectures, not this weekend, not here on the island. He watched a red squirrel scamper across the lane, an acorn filling its cheek.

To head Tamar off, he said, "Do you think squirrels know that their bellies are white and furry and soft? And, if they did, that they'd be pleased?"

She took the bait and studied the squirrel. "No and yes." She punched another button on her watch and set off up the lane. "C'mon, let's at least walk fast."

Roger loped along beside her.

"I'm pissed at Joy," Tamar said. "Always with the I'm-the-best-mother-of-the-year and you-don't-have-a-clue attitude. My kids trotting after her to the buffet like she's the god-damned Pied Piper. Well, it didn't turn out so well for the kids of Hamelin, did it?" She stopped and jogged in place, letting Roger catch his breath. "I can't believe she would do that in front of the twins. Show me up."

Roger had no idea what Tamar was talking about. Her tirade didn't seem fair, though. After all, Joy was watching the twins for her now, and he supposed she'd had other plans—Joy always did.

"My God, look at you! Do you get any exercise?" Tamar was marching in place, bringing her knees nearly to her chin.

"Not intentionally. Last thing I want to do when I have some time off is move around."

They stopped in front of the driveways to the island's two summer cottages, just west of the inn. "Well, it's time we got you in shape. We're not getting any younger," Tamar said. "Let's jog down to Sunset Point."

"Seriously, Tee. My shoulder is killing me, and I feel like crap."

He watched her frown. She needed exercise, he knew, needed to feel her heart pumping. It was the only way she could be sure she had one, he once joked—the only time he'd ever made her cry. "You go for your run. I'm going to head back. We'll meet in your old room when you get done."

Her face brightened. "I'll probably beat you there." She glanced at her watch. "Damn, I forgot to stop it." Roger watched her raise her hand in salute as she raced off for Sunset Point.

It wasn't only that Roger didn't feel like running. He wanted time alone, time to think about Loraine, about whether he'd go see her. He knew he would. The only question was when and how and what he'd say when he got there.

JOY

I placed the dog beside the pumpkin. The tree, the four-leaf clover, the witch's hat, and the mitten were already laid out on the table. I took out a stick of butter from the refrigerator, set it in a glass bowl, and put it in the microwave to soften. Then I gathered colored sprinkles, vanilla, flour, sugar, and a mixer from various cupboards and assembled them on the counter. "Nat, you cream the sugar and butter."

Nat stared, unmoving.

"You have made cookies before, right?"

"Yes, but they didn't look like this."

"Ours come in a package," Hal added.

"We break off the squares, and Daddy bakes them."

"While we watch."

"Ah," I said. "Well, this will be much more fun."

I put the softened butter in a bowl, turned on the mixer, and added the sugar. "Nice and slow. Keep pushing the dough down with the spoon, like this, Nat, but don't get it tangled in the beater.

"Hal, you mix the dry ingredients." I handed her the sifter and a measuring cup filled with flour. "We need three of these, sifted."

Hal dumped the cupful into the sifter, resulting in a small explosion. A cloud of flour drifted across the counter and onto the floor.

"Okay, okay," I said, sliding a bowl under the sifter. "Let's try that again. We need salt and baking powder mixed in with the flour." These I measured myself.

Nat was peering intently at the batter, occasionally giving it a tentative poke with her long-handled spoon. "Good. I've got two eggs in here." I handed my niece a bowl. "Dump those into the butter and sugar."

"Look," Nat said in wonder as she watched the batter turn pale yellow. It was the same tone of awe I remembered using when my mother and I used to bake cookies together in this kitchen. That memory, dormant for so many years, stirred something inside me.

Hal was cranking the handle on the sifter for all she was worth, spewing flour up over the top onto the counter and floor. "A little slower, honey. Now let's add a teaspoon of vanilla." I handed the small brown bottle to Nat and guided her hand as she tipped it over the measuring spoon. Hal and I added the sifted flour to the batter in the mixer.

As we watched the paddle cut into the dough, I remembered kneeling on the vinyl-topped stool with its squeaky fold-down step that Nat now occupied, helping my mother mix up batter, and then waiting impatiently for it to set in the refrigerator.

How gently she put her hand over mine as together we pressed the cookie cutters into dough so grainy with sugar it made my mouth water and my teeth hurt to think of it. Releasing the tree, or camel, or star from its web was the tricky part. If my mother rolled the dough too thin, the cookie would stretch when I lifted it, and I'd end up with an elongated figure that browned too quickly. Not thin enough, and the cookies would swell into unidentifiable blobs. But my mother always rolled it just right. Just as I had done with Rex. . . .

My eyes stung. It amazed me to realize how close to the surface my sadness was lodged. So close that the slightest nudge sent tears spilling. *When had Rex and I last baked cookies together?* Ten years? Twelve? I thought of all the opportunities missed and now gone forever. Why hadn't I taken him to more Red Sox games, on monthly mother-son camping trips, out for weekly nights at the movies? Now it was too late. *Maybe, if I had done these things, he wouldn't have gone off to college. Would be here with me now.* I took a few deep breaths. Bargaining, I knew from my sessions with Dr. Kilsaro, was part of the grief process. Of course Rex would have gone to college. I knew perfectly well why we hadn't done those things: My son had gotten busy, no longer needed his mother, had grown up. Which, I acknowledged, was at least part of the reason my mother and I had stopped baking cookies together.

When I was little, once I had cut the first round of cookies, my mother peeled away the bits left over, formed them into a ball, and rolled it out, and I searched for a cutter that just fit the resulting tile of dough. It astonished me how many times we could repeat this. Finally, there was only enough left for me to either roll into a candy cane or press into a sand dollar. Bonnie's death had left a hole in my life, and Rex's departure had just made another one. What had I made from the days and months that remained after Bonnie died? What, I wondered, could I make of the ones surrounding me now?

"It has to set in the refrigerator for an hour," I said to the girls, realizing that they were staring at me. "Nan bought a new puzzle for the Games Room. Why don't you go work on that, and you and your mom can finish these up when she gets back. I think she might like that." The twins scampered off. "Don't leave the house without telling someone."

I went upstairs. My parents slept on the first floor of what we still called "the new wing." Above it, a half dozen bedrooms lined a long hallway, which is where we kids slept, growing up. Beadboard wainscoting ran the length of the hall, windows on one side, doors leading to the bedrooms on the other. Each room had a metal bedstead and a small dresser painted in a pastel shade. Mine was pale yellow. I walked down the hall to the shared bathroom, with its claw-foot tub, its thin stainless steel towel racks, and the peeling radiator that clanged and wheezed when you turned on the heat. The linoleum was worn through in front of the sink from the generations of us who'd stood there, brushing our teeth, washing our faces, dreaming. *Does anyone get the future they dream of?* I studied my reflection in the mirror. My summer-blond hair had already begun to fade along with my tan, and I could see faint lines at the corners of my eyes and mouth. A sliver of Ivory soap in its porcelain altar beside the toothbrush holder smelled sweet and faintly metallic: the smell of summer and of my childhood. I went into my old room and stretched out on the thin mattress, shut my eyes, and drifted off.

Twenty minutes later I woke to the sound of voices. I got up, tiptoed across the room, and pressed my ear to the wall. Roger was saying, "I didn't realize you went to church."

"It's kind of expected," Tamar replied.

"By Daniel?"

"No, the community. Part of the deal. I spend the time choosing hymns for my funeral."

"You might want to see someone about that," Roger said, and Tamar giggled.

I wanted to go in and talk with them but knew their conversation would abruptly stop as soon as I walked in. They would make room for me, on the bed or in the ladder-back chair, but not in their lives. They'd never made room for me in their lives. I drifted off again, listening to their soft murmurs, always on the other side of the wall.

Grace stared in the rearview mirror at the stranger with the curly brown hair. What is it about a visit to the hairdresser's that emboldens a person? Why, when Loraine said, "Want to try something different?" did Grace immediately assume that *different* meant better? She couldn't take in her whole head at once in that little mirror—*just as well*—so she tipped her chin down and peered upward to examine the unfamiliar nimbus of curls, where, just hours before, there'd been a close-fitting cap of gray. When she wagged her head side-to-side, the curls danced in what looked to Grace like a frivolous manner. She felt half-naked with her ears exposed. She had never considered ears particularly attractive, and hers were no exception. When Loraine held a mirror up so she could see the back, Grace had made appropriate, appreciative noises as she struggled to keep her face composed, all the while feeling her mother's aston-ished gaze peering down.

Since her mother's death—and the arrival of her aunts' letter—Grace had felt incapable of making even the most ele-mentary decisions. She felt adrift, a boat whose anchor was dragging with the rising tide. She missed having an adult in her life. A parent. Many times a day she would find herself in the grip of indecision, wanting to call Joan to ask her opinion. It was as if her mother had taken with her when she died the key to the room where the answers to everything were stored—answers to even simple questions like, *Want to try something different?*

With a heavy heart and a new hat purchased at George and Kit's, Grace made her round of errands: to CVS for bug spray, to the grocery store for supplies for Saturday's service, to the Gawker to pick up coleslaw for that evening's cookout. Then she headed home.

Grace heard the shrieks as soon as she stepped out of her car. She raced toward the kitchen door, trying to picture the crisis so it would be less shocking when she saw it: someone cut badly and bleeding; a fall, resulting in a cracked skull; Gar lying on the floor, having succumbed to a heart attack, her daughters hovering over him . . .

She burst in to find her granddaughters racing around the butcher-block table, each wearing nothing but underpants and a thin layer of pink paste; globs of it clung to their hair. The floor was also covered in paste, half an inch thick in places. Counters, cupboards, and chairs were dusted with flour, flecked with red sprinkles. The food from lunch, which someone had left out on the kitchen table—as well as the mixing bowls, beaters, and utensils that filled the kitchen sink—also bore this residue of red-freckled flour. Grace watched, openmouthed, as one of her granddaughters stopped to sprinkle water onto the floor, while the other madly sifted more flour.

When they finally spotted their grandmother, they fell silent.

"What's going on?" Grace asked, trying to keep her voice level. *Where was Tamar?*

"It wasn't slippery enough," Hal said, as if this explained everything.

"So we're adding water. To make it slipperier," Nat said.

Ask a stupid question . . . "Where's your mother?" Grace surveyed her kitchen, vainly seeking a paste-free zone in which she might stand.

"Upstairs. With Uncle Roger," they said.

Grace forced a smile and nodded. "Well," she said, unsure what to do next. She caught a glimpse of herself in the door of the microwave, curls escaping from beneath the broad brim of her new hat. The mind, she knew, eventually adjusts to what is, no matter how bad. *This is how prisoners survive in captivity*, she told herself. The new eventually becomes the new normal. Whether that was good in her case, she wasn't sure.

The two little girls gazed at their grandmother, their dark eyes now filled with foreboding, their eyelashes tipped with pink paste. They were making the best of the situation, Grace knew, thinking back to her own childhood. She remembered years and years ago laughing and laughing as she jumped on the trampoline in the rain at the Shore View Cabins, her mother looking on with a smile. Grace could guess, now, what that smile must have cost her mother. She took a breath, counted silently to five, and smiled. Tamar had whisked her girls off for a weekend to prove something to her husband, or possibly, Grace had to acknowledge, to her and the rest of the family, and then left them to go off with Roger. Was there any limit to her youngest daughter's selfishness? "So," she asked the girls now, "was it fun?"

The closest bathtub was upstairs in the new wing. Grace marched the girls up the narrow stairs and down the long hallway. The door to Joy's old room was open, and when Grace peeked in, she saw the familiar mounds of her daughter's hips and shoulders beneath the cotton blanket. She stood a moment, watching them rise and fall with the steady rhythm of sleep. So many mornings she had stood here, calling to Joy that it was time to get up. So many nights she had stood here just to reassure herself that her daughter was fine.

The twins were beside her, quietly flicking pink scablike clods of dried paste to the floor. "Girls, go on into the bathroom, please. I'll be right in."

They scampered down the hall, and Joy stirred, shifted, and glanced toward the door. "Hi." She lay a moment longer before adding, "Why are you wearing a hat?"

"Know where Tamar is?"

Joy tilted her head, listening. "Next door, with Roger."

Grace walked down the hall, where she could hear soft murmurs coming from inside what used to be Tamar's bedroom. She rapped twice. "Tamar?"

The silence that followed whisked Grace again back to her nightly visits when the kids were young. After leaving Joy's doorway, she would stop in at Tamar's and order Roger back to his room. If she'd let them, her twins would have stayed up all night, lying side by side, talking and giggling. Joy used to complain that she couldn't get any sleep with the two of them chattering on. Grace strongly suspected that jealousy more than insomnia fueled her complaints, but Joy denied it.

"Yes?" came Tamar's voice after a brief pause.

"Your girls need a bath." Grace heard rustling, and then footsteps crossing the floor. The door opened and Tamar appeared, wearing running gear, minus the sneakers. "What?" She stared at her mother. "Why are you wearing a hat?"

Joy had come out of her room and was standing next to Grace, who now pointed down the hall. "Bath. Your daughters."

The three headed down the hall and found the twins, naked, crying, and mottled with pink paste. "Oh, my God!" Tamar cried. "Joy . . ." The word shimmered with accusation.

"What do you mean, 'Joy . . .'?" Joy mimicked her sister. "You've been up here with Roger for"—she glanced at her watch—"thirty minutes. Didn't you check on them when you got back from your run?"

"Yes. Of course. They were in the kitchen, 'making cookies,' they said."

"Tamar, they're eight." Joy made no effort to disguise her disbelief at, or disdain for, her sister's ineptitude. "Do you think they can make cookies by themselves?"

"Joy," Grace said, wanting to head off a full-scale blowout, and Joy fell silent, pressing her lips together, obviously annoyed. Grace didn't want to upset Joy; she'd seen the cut on her thumb. If her daughter would only open up to her, like she used to, she was sure she could help. Grace felt the familiar pressure building inside her little family, but, just as when she heard a storm warning, she could only gather candles and kerosene lanterns, fill jugs and bathtubs with water, secure windows and lawn furniture. She could do nothing to prevent the coming storm.

First, Gar took everything off the shelf. Then he opened, one by one, all the drawers in his toolbox, lifted the lids on coffee cans filled with nails, shook out rags, crouched down and peered under the workbench. No bottledarter. He was staring glumly out the window, trying to think of other places to look for his missing lure, when Roger walked in.

"What brings you out here?" Gar was both pleased and surprised to see his son in the tool shed. Gar used to dream of the two of them undertaking a construction project together one day: building a boat, perhaps. But the years had driven them apart, rather than closer. After he'd turned fifteen, Roger hadn't set foot in the tool shed. At least, not when his father had been in it. Roger's work (for a time) as a contractor felt like a personal insult to Gar. Where had he learned the skills? When had he developed the interest? Why had he never wanted to spend time with his father doing any of the dozens of projects continually needed to keep an old inn up and running?

"Escape," Roger said. "Bit of a row at the house."

"Oh?" Grace had been struggling since her mother's death and the arrival of her aunts' letter. One never knows how a parent's death is going to hit them. Gar's father had been killed in World War II, so Gar had never known him, and his mother had slipped slowly into senility and drifted off into her own world seven years before she died. When the end came, it truly was a blessing. The woman he'd called Mother, who had been warm and loving in life, had left years earlier, replaced by a stranger whom, sadly, he didn't much miss when she physically left.

But Grace and Joan were close—although Gar suspected that their bond sometimes felt like a hug that goes on too long. It had been just the two of them, and while Grace didn't speak often or at length about her childhood, Gar gathered that it had been difficult. And lonely.

"A row over what?" Gar opened a drawer in the workbench for the fifteenth time, just for something to do. There would have been no reason for him to put the lure there. Nope, still just screwdrivers.

Roger was quiet a moment. "I believe I will plead the Fifth. Although I don't think I had anything to do with it. This time." They both laughed, but Gar could hear its hollow ring. Too often it had been Roger's fault. He and his father had spent much of his adolescence fighting. Gar used to shout recriminations at Roger over misdeeds that he couldn't even fathom. Never once had Gar broken into a house or stolen anything. He had hardly ever lied and never about anything important, had never gone for a joy ride drunk. Certainly never caused anyone's death. All of which Roger had done. Their relationship had deepened in the years since, both of them maturing, Gar acknowledged, but not enough for real comfort to take root. The soil beneath them, like that on the island, was simply not deep enough. Although he hated to admit it, Gar didn't trust his son. Especially since the crash. Roger knew this, he was sure.

Why they'd started to grow apart remained a mystery to Gar. They used to fish together from the dock, and Gar taught him to run the *Kestrel*, avoiding lobster pots and watching for channel markers. He remembered one afternoon, when Roger was about twelve, telling him he'd give him twenty-five cents if he could hit a baseball over the roof of the tool shed. Roger broke a window, of course, on his first try, but then sent one ball after another soaring over. Grace and the girls assembled to cheer him on. He put Gar out a good five bucks before he broke his streak. Roger then asked if he could try hitting one over the inn's roof for a dollar, although Grace quickly quashed that idea. *Was that the last good day?* Because, not long after, or so it seemed, Gar became, if not the enemy, then a spy for the enemy.

"Cleaning the place out?" Roger asked, picking up a hammer and testing its balance in his hand. They were strong hands, capable hands, callused and tough, and Gar felt a pang of longing, an ache, for the little boy who sent the baseball over the roof.

"No, looking for . . . a lure." Gar realized how ridiculous this must sound: the shelves bare, the hooks empty, the workbench clear. He laughed and shook his head. "Got a little ahead of myself, I guess."

Roger nodded affably. "It can happen."

They stood together silently, almost companionably—difficult with the space around them so littered with unspoken sentiments, some as old and rusty as the nails nesting in the nearby row of coffee cans.

"How are things going with the inn?" Roger asked. "Are you and Mom . . . ?" Gar watched Roger begin to arrange the screwdrivers by size in the drawer. "I mean, do you guys ever think about . . . retiring?"

Gar's eyebrows shot up. "Retiring? No. Why, did she say something?"

"No, no. I just . . . wondered if you'd thought about

what you might do with the inn if you ever . . . got tired of running it."

Got tired of running it? Gar knew Roger was up to something. "I can't quite imagine what anybody does without an inn to run; why everybody isn't running one!" And, all at once, Gar knew precisely what Roger was up to. "Are you thinking . . . *you* might want to take it over?" He hadn't meant to sound so incredulous.

"Maybe. Is that so crazy?"

Gar could hear the challenge in his son's voice, the defensiveness. He had to take care that Roger not goad him into saying something he'd regret. "No, not at all." Gar turned and began rifling through a stack of yellowed newspapers in an old cardboard box, just to avoid meeting Roger's eye. The lure would clearly not be in there.

Roger seemed preoccupied with the screwdrivers, and the two men remained in silence for a long, uncomfortable moment.

"Are you going to see Maisie this weekend?" As soon as the words were out of his mouth, Gar regretted them. It was a very bad follow-up. But he was unused to having Roger in his territory and was just trying to make conversation. No, he had to admit to himself, that wasn't quite true.

Roger's attention swiveled instantly from the screwdrivers. He looked directly at his father. "Probably." The word landed in the space between them and dropped like a lead sinker. His meaning was as clear to Gar as the big red *PRIVATE* that Roger had painted onto his clubhouse, Fort Danger, when he was ten. (The fort was simply a discarded cardboard box from their new refrigerator, over which Roger had thrown a plastic tarp.)

"No. Right. Sorry." Gar said, attempting to back away from Roger's implied *keep out* command. "I was just asking. This is . . ." *For God's sake, Gar, get off the subject!* His son did not need to be reminded that this weekend was the anniversary of Bonnie Day's death. After all, he'd caused it. And paid with three years of his life. "We should do some fishing this weekend. Would you like that?" Gar felt vulnerable, extending such an invitation. Times past, Roger would have laughed in his face and stomped out.

"Yeah, sure." Roger aligned the last screwdriver and shut the drawer. "That would be nice." He left then, but only after giving his father a half smile, and he turned back after a few yards. "I hope you find your lure."

Gar watched his son slowly cross the lawn back to the house, then lowered his chin into his hand and sighed deeply.

· Chapter Ten ·

JOY

At five thirty I watched my mother roll the Garden Way cart up to the kitchen door and start shuttling out a cooler of drinks, a picnic basket, coleslaw, a plastic container of hamburger patties, and several packages of rolls. She was tossing in pieces of firewood when Tamar strolled across the lawn. "What's all this? Are you running away?" She stared at the mountain of supplies. "With a lot of other people?"

"Cookout at Sunset Point. We'll build a fire, cook burgers . . ." Our mother opened the lid on the picnic basket. "Homemade marshmallows, graham crackers, and chocolate bars. You know what that means."

"Diabetes," Tamar said promptly. "Obesity. Tooth decay—"

"S'mores!" our mother said, seemingly undaunted, and then added, with a forced enthusiasm that didn't suit her, "Won't that be fun?"

Tamar wrinkled her nose. "I think we're all well past the s'mores phase, Mom."

Apparently not all of us, I thought, as I watched the twins slip silently up to the cart, hands extended toward the picnic basket.

Tamar spotted them. "NO chocolate before dinner." She snapped closed the basket's lid, and Hal and Nat rocked back on their heels. "After dinner. Maybe." The twins sidled off. I suspected they'd be back.

Roger emerged from the house, bearing an armload of blankets. "Dad told me to bring these out." He eyed the Garden Way cart. "Tell me we're not dragging this thing . . ."

"To Sunset Point. Yes, we are," Mom said, but her conviction was waning, and I knew she would soon back down and amend her plan in the face of her twins' resistance.

"We? You know who's going to end up doing most of the dragging. Correction: all the dragging."

"We'll pull," offered the twins, appearing again beside the cart.

"If I recall correctly, last time we did this," Roger said to the twins, "your father and I had to pull not only the cart, but the cart with you guys in it. And you were very much smaller then." Roger tried to tickle Nat, but she dodged his hand and ran out onto the lawn. He chased after her, but she moved farther off, giggling. Tamar and my mother turned to watch their game, while I watched Hal deftly lift the lid on the picnic basket and extract a chocolate bar. As I joined my mother beside the cart, I gave Hal a conspiratorial wink. "A cookout? Great idea, Mom!" My enthusiasm didn't sound any more genuine than my mother's had, but she looked inordinately pleased.

Tamar, however, was still annoyed. "Then we're going to take Roger's truck. Come on, Roger. Give me a hand. We can switch all this over in no time."

Roger ambled over, carrying Nat fireman-style, and dropped her into the bed of the truck before joining Tamar at the cart. They each grabbed an armload and walked it over.

"I'm sorry, I thought this would be . . ." Mom trailed off as the Garden Way cart quickly emptied.

Nat had scrambled out of the truck and now joined her twin beside their grandmother. Each took hold of one of her hands and stared solemnly up. Grace smiled down at them. ". . . fun." The apology of a waning moon as the earth's shadow makes it appear, each night, a little less than it was the night before.

"Anything else to bring out?" I asked.

Mom shook her head, staring at the now-empty cart. "Just your father."

Tamar climbed behind the wheel of Roger's truck, Daddy slid in beside her, and they bumped out the drive. Roger headed after them, pulling the cart with Sophie and the twins on board. Mom and I followed on foot. The twins shared the chocolate bar on the way down to Sunset Point.

When we arrived, Roger let go of the cart handle, dropped to the ground, and rolled onto his back, holding his shoulder. Tamar was lighting candles nearby. "Citronella? Really?" Roger asked. "Try something with Deet. It actually works."

Nat and Hal climbed out and scampered along the rocky point. Tamar lit another candle. "Do you know what that stuff is?" she asked, moving to sit beside her brother.

"Do you?"

"No, but if it kills bugs, it's not something I want to slather on my skin."

"You'd prefer a nice case of equine encephalitis?"

"Children, please," Grace said. They were like boxers, she thought, dancing around the ring, taking swings, dodging, tantalizing the crowd. Eventually someone would land a blow. Grace wanted peace tonight, harmony, fun!

Gar got a fire going in the makeshift hearth he'd built years before: large stones stacked in a semicircle, supporting a rusty grill. Flames lifted and dissolved into the sky. Gar, Grace, and her mother had come down here every year at sunset the first night of Joan's visit to have a full cookout, or a picnic, or drinks, and watch the sun slowly turn in for the day.

Life without her mother was like a song with the bass line removed, Grace thought. Notes, floating about with nothing to ground them. She wondered if her kids would feel that way about her when she was gone.

She sent around containers of carrots and celery sticks, grape tomatoes, and sliced cucumbers, followed by crackers and little rectangles of cheese. The twins grabbed handfuls of each item and experimented with various combinations: stacking cucumbers on crackers, pairing carrots with cheese, trying to re-create the magic of discovering sandwiches garnished with potato chips.

Roger stretched out on the rocks above the fire. Ever since lunchtime he'd seemed quiet—too quiet. Grace hoped he wasn't drinking or using again. Gar had told her how Roger had stopped by the tool shed, and what he'd said. She tried to picture him running the inn. Someday, maybe he would be ready. Someday, maybe, Gar would be ready to let him.

"I'm bored," Nat said.

"Me, too," said Hal. "We miss Daddy."

Tamar was sitting with her daughters at the far end of Sunset Point. "My heavens, it's only been a few hours!" She checked her phone for a message or e-mail from Daniel. Nothing.

Her daughters inched down the slippery rocks to crouch by the water's edge.

"Don't get your new sneakers wet," Tamar warned. *They looked too close. What if one of them slipped? Should she move down there with them? Would they like that?* She remained seated and uncertain.

"We're seeing how close we can get," Hal said, and Tamar could hear the unspoken *duh* at the end of the sentence. The waves were mostly small, but every now and then a sizable one came along, and the girls would retract their legs with shrieks and giggles.

"These are left over from big boats way out at sea," Hal said with such authority that Nat didn't question her.

Tamar glanced back at her brother, who was stretched out beside the fire, feet crossed at the ankle, his work boots worn down at the heel, the laces undone. She thought about Loraine Fifield, divorced and back on the island. Tamar knew Roger wanted to go see her, and she needed to stop him.

The girls were discussing the fort they were going to build in Aunt Joy's old room.

"Can we sleep there tonight?" Hal asked, turning to her mother.

Why Joy's old room and not hers? Tamar hesitated. She wanted them to sleep in the main part of the inn, so she could listen for small feet tiptoeing down the stairs, late—she remembered all the nights she and Roger had sneaked out and gone down to sit on the rocks—although she doubted her girls were that adventuresome. She wouldn't have been without Roger's strong, steady presence. She always felt safe with him. Safer than with anyone else. "We'll have to ask Nan." *Let her be the bad guy.* The girls looked at one another, and, from their expression, Tamar knew they'd seen through her good cop/bad cop routine. Duh. "Can I come see your fort?" she asked them.

The girls conferred. "When it's finished." Hal said.

"Tomorrow," added Nat.

Tamar shivered. *September days can fool you into believing they're part of summer,* she thought, *but not September nights.* She glanced back at her phone, wondering why Daniel hadn't responded to her message.

When dinner was ready, Gar topped toasted buns with hamburgers and hot dogs, and Grace spooned big dollops of coleslaw onto plates and added ears of roasted corn on the cob. The corn spurred a debate about the best method of eating it. Grace said she liked to eat around rather than down the rows. Gar insisted that eating fat end to thin was more efficient and left the best for last. Roger declared that he liked to eat it in a spiral, which made the twins giggle and boast that they liked to start in the middle. Tamar declared these last two methods controversial, possibly illegal, which made the twins laugh even harder and mime taking random bites of corn from their cobs. "Watch me!" "Look how I'm eating it." "This is what I do."

Later, Grace looked around at the little islands of her family. Her twin granddaughters were in a deep, sugar-induced stupor, mouths sticky with chocolate, marshmallow, and crumbs, lying in the crooks of their aunt's arms before the dying fire. Joy was pretending she didn't mind being excluded by Tamar and Roger, who sat huddled down by the water, their heads together, whispering, just like the old days.

Grace, wrapped in a scratchy wool blanket that smelled of cedar from the chest in the upstairs hallway, turned and stared out across the harbor. Whenever she'd been sick, her mother had muffled her in layers of such blankets. Grace knew it was her way of trying to protect her daughter. And Grace had never complained, even as she sweated beneath the strata of heavy wool. She had done the same with her three children, although by then wool had been replaced by fleece, which didn't offer the same heaviness, the same sense of being too well anchored for a child to be carried off by a high fever, or something worse.

She was surprised by another memory, of herself as a child, hiding in a stairwell, listening to her father and his buddies play poker, hearing snatches of conversation, the clink of ice cubes against glass, the shuffling of cards, coarse laughter. Her mother found her there and gently, but firmly, escorted her back to her room, climbing into bed beside her, holding her. It wasn't too many days later that she and Joan left the little house in Bangor and began their journey, moving every few years.

JOY

"It's just like it was when we were little," I said, more to myself than anyone else. "Nothing has changed." I was propped up against a rock, my nieces, like sticky parentheses, on either side of me, letting the fire warm our fronts as the damp night air worked its way inside our collars and cuffs. The sky had slipped from gray to pink to vermilion and finally settled on pale apricot, before dissolving back into gray. Across the harbor, halyards clanged against hollow aluminum masts. An immature gull patiently patrolled the perimeter, waiting for a snack.

"Actually, lots has changed," Tamar stated. "We're married, have kids, careers, homes . . ." She trailed off and glanced at her brother. "Okay, I guess Roger's still the same."

"Hey, watch it. I have a job."

"Yes, but the landscape hasn't changed," I insisted, although that wasn't what I'd meant. "It looks just like it did twenty years ago." I glanced over at my mother. She was stroking Sophie, whose head was in her lap, her eyes at half-mast. They both looked like they were somewhere very far away.

"Sunset Point looks just the way it did sixty years ago," Daddy said. "My mother and I used to come here for picnics at sunset. Back in the day," he said to the girls, "my grandparents kept horses at the inn and drove us down here in the wagon."

"I thought we could have a picnic at Sand Beach tomorrow," Mom said, coming out of her reverie and offering Sophie a bit of hamburger.

"You're forgetting about climate change," Tamar said. "It might look the same superficially, but the seas are getting warmer and rising because of it. Vegetation is changing, too; whole species of trees are dying out, not to mention animals and birds. I'm just glad I won't be here to see the awful end."

We sat in a stunned silence until Roger finally said, "You'd leave a party before the fight starts and the police arrive? That's just when the fun begins."

His comment reminded me of the night half the kids on East Haven ended up at a party at the inn. Our parents had gone over to the mainland for the weekend to attend the wedding of a daughter of one of Daddy's college roommates. Roger invited Walter and a few other guys over. Loraine was there. So was Tamar. Cars started pulling up the road, and kids piling out. More arrived on foot. They broke into the bar and drank their way through much of it, threw up in the sinks and in the potted plants in the hall, put cigarettes out on the rug. Their glasses left rings on the side tables. They broke a window, several plates, and a water pitcher. The item my mother seemed most concerned about was a funny old ashtray with pinecones glued to it. Something I assume she'd made as a girl in camp. Daddy was livid with Roger, who apologized and truly did seem contrite. "I didn't invite them. Hell, I didn't even know half of them," he kept saying. "I only invited Wally and a few of the guys." Daddy didn't believe him. Poor Roger, trouble seemed to follow him.

My mother pulled Sophie all the way onto her lap and kissed the top of her head.

"I'm beginning to believe that humans were an evolutionary mistake," Tamar said. "I just hope we leave something behind so the planet can regenerate."

"Tamar?" I nodded down at the twins, who were listening, eyes wide, their expressions somber. I wished someone would, just once, tell her to shut up. *She's younger. We almost lost her.*

"Have a little faith, Tee. It's better than not." Roger said.

Tamar looked as surprised as I felt. Roger never went against his twin. I sent him a smile of thanks, and he smiled back, which also surprised me. Roger and Tamar had swapped such looks many times throughout their lives. I'd learned to ignore their obvious bond, or at least pretend I didn't care.

Tamar saw our exchange and didn't look any too pleased. "Cockroaches," Tamar said. "They'll survive. Crows. Hyenas, maybe. Species that aren't fussy about where they live or what they eat."

The immature gull had kept one beady eye focused on the remains of my s'more, the other alert for predators. I tossed it a piece of marshmallow. Seemingly out of nowhere, a second gull swooped in, pecked at the first one, driving it off, and gobbled up the snack. "Oh, mean thing!" I said.

"What are you doing?" Tamar said. "We'll have the whole flock here."

"Seagulls," Daddy said. "They'll survive."

"All so selfish," my mother said. "No regard for anyone else."

No one else heard her say it, or noticed that when she did, she was not looking at the gulls.

"All aboard," Daddy called.

My mother stood and stretched. "How about it? Picnic lunch out on Spectacle Island tomorrow?" An outing to Spectacle had been a favorite Little activity. But tonight, whether because of the sugar we'd consumed after dinner, the dark, or the late hour, no one responded.

"Wonderful," she said, with sarcastic enthusiasm. "What fun."

SEPTEMBER 9, 1991

"I thought Bonnie was staying for supper," Mom said to me as we stood at the counter, shearing kernels off their cobs. My grandmother was the only guest that weekend, and Mom was serving lobster stew, corn bread, and a salad of tomato and fresh mozzarella, topped with roasted corn and bits of bacon.

I readied the knife for another cut. "I guess she wanted some time to fiddle with her hair."

"Yours looks very nice, Joy." Grammy was frying strips of bacon.

"You think?" To me, the layers that Bonnie had cut that afternoon looked rather ragged.

"It does. Very nice," Mom added.

She hated the thought that all us kids would be gone soon and I suspected was trying to imprint herself on each of us in some indelible way, to ensure we knew how much she loved us, to ensure that we would miss her, and would, after college, settle close to home. "What are you and Grammy watching tonight?" I asked my mother.

"*Thelma and Louise.*" She cracked a lobster claw. "Want to watch it with us?"

I shrugged, still upset that Bonnie was going to the quarry party and not spending the evening with me. Would I feel worse about staying home if I watched a movie I'd seen with Bonnie? Probably. Although, at that point, I didn't see how anything could make me feel worse.

Roger breezed into the kitchen. "Man, that smells good." He spun Grammy around and gave her a hug, snagging a strip of bacon from the oil-soaked paper towel.

"Oh!" Grammy said, as he grabbed her, and then, "Oh, you," when she realized what he'd done.

"Rookie mistake," I said, and Roger grinned.

"So what's this I hear about you not coming to the quarry tonight?"

"Scratchy throat," I told him. A lie.

"You do?" Mom sounded worried. Here was one of those moments she lived for, when she could avow her motherly love by fixing something. "Have you taken anything?"

"No, Mom. It's nothing." I sliced off another row of kernels.

"Careful with that knife, Jo-jo. I just sharpened it," Mom said.

"Did you know it's easier to cut yourself with a dull knife than a sharp one?" Roger was now eating his way through the tomato ends lying on the counter.

"We were going to chop those up and put them in the salad, Roger," I said.

"Oh, sorry." He ate another. "You can short me at dinner."

Daddy came in. "The new bird feeder's up."

"Thank you, dear. Now, would you mind taking a look at the shower on the third floor? It's dripping."

Daddy glanced toward Roger but said nothing. *As if.* Roger averted his eyes and ate another tomato end.

"Roger!" I waved the knife jokingly in his direction. "Next time you might lose a finger."

Daddy headed out of the room, passing Tamar on her way in. "Anyone seen my blue sweater?"

"I haven't ironed it yet," Mom said. "I can do it now if you need it."

"Ironed it? It's a sweater." Tamar stared at Mom with those impenetrable eyes of hers. She'd done this to all of us since she was a baby: taken our measure, as though unsure what to make of us. We still weren't sure what she'd decided. Looking into Tamar's eyes was like looking into the deepest part of Isle au Haut Bay on a sunless day. Try as you might, you can make out little of what lies beneath the surface.

Mom clearly didn't know how to respond to Tamar's rebuke. She'd thought she was doing her a favor. Grammy must have noticed Mom's hesitation, too, because she offered Tamar a piece of bacon.

"No, thanks. And don't put any in my salad. Do you know how hideous hog farming is? The conditions are abysmal, and hogs are highly intelligent, sentient creatures." She swept out of the room.

"Something you might aspire to someday, Tee," I said, and Roger laughed.

As she followed Tamar out, Mom gave me a disapproving glance. I was shearing off another row of kernels. The knife slipped, nicking my finger.

Later that night, Mom, Grammy, Daddy, and I sat together in the hospital until Tamar was out of surgery. I didn't know what to say, what to do, or even what to feel when I understood that Roger and Tamar had both survived but that Bonnie had not. The horror of it, my guilt, threatened to swallow me whole.

· Chapter Eleven ·

JOY

When we returned from our cookout on Sunset Point, Daddy claimed a bogus plumbing job to avoid dish detail. The twins, having recovered from their sugar collapse, disappeared into the Games Room with Roger and began a voluble game of Wii tennis, Nat issuing a loud grunt whenever she hit the ball, and Hal something between a screech and a wheeze. Sophie climbed onto her bed and began spinning in a clockwise direction, furiously clawing at the edges, impelled by some primitive den-building urge. Finally satisfied, she circled three times, flopped down, curled into a tight ball, and sighed heavily. Tamar, my mother, and I had a good laugh.

Tee turned the faucet on full and squirted detergent into the sink. "I always thought it was ridiculous to name a dishwashing liquid *Joy*." She submerged the big potato salad bowl, which wouldn't fit into the dishwasher. "Do they honestly believe someone's going to see it and think, 'Oh, I will be so much happier washing dishes if I buy this brand'?"

"Almost as bad as naming your child that," I said softly,

as Tamar clattered the long-handled grilling utensils into the sink.

"Joy doesn't seem like such a bad name." Tamar handed me the bowl to dry.

"That's because it's not yours." I handed the bowl back. "Still has potato salad goo on the edge. It's a burden. Raises expectations."

"*Prosperity* would have been a better name," Tamar said, shutting off the water. In the silence we could hear muffled grunts and wheezes from the next room.

When we finished the dishes, she pulled the plug in the sink. "C'mon, Joy. Let's check on the Williams sisters. Maybe they'll let us play a game of doubles."

After her daughters left, Grace rolled a piece of dog kibble across the floor to Sophie, who now lay with her head hanging off the side of her bed. Every few minutes Grace had shot one over, and Sophie would watch it wobble its way toward her. Without exerting any unnecessary effort, she'd project her tongue and lap it up. But Sophie eyed this last piece and left it untouched on the floor. Grace knew she should retrieve it before someone—herself, most likely—stepped on it, but she lacked the energy to stand. "This has been an exhausting day," she said aloud, envying Sophie's near catatonia.

Stand she must, however, because she needed to make the breakfast strata and let it refrigerate overnight. In the morning she'd bake it, when they got back from riding the rip, and they'd all eat in the dining room—*Tablecloths!* Grace pictured them laundered, folded, and neatly stacked, unironed, on top of the dryer. She did not have the energy to iron them now. The perfect, fun weekend Grace wanted to create in honor of her mother was disappearing like stars in a morning sky. Her mood brightened at the thought of the family's annual trek the next morning around the island to the footbridge. Grace knew that Tamar would set an unsustainable pace, which Gar would attempt to match, but he would fall farther and farther behind and eventually give up and wait for Grace, Roger, Joy, and the twins. For many years Gar was the one to set the pace. Grace sighed, regretting the inevitable passage of time that erodes family landscapes as surely as a swiftly moving stream erodes its banks. She sent another piece of kibble over to Sophie. It, too, remained untouched.

Poor Joy. Grace wondered how long she would stand on the bridge this year, trying to convince herself to hop into the cold, dark, churning water. It didn't matter to any of them whether she jumped, but Grace knew it meant a lot to Joy. It set her apart from them, or so she'd always thought. Nothing Grace said ever made any difference. She recalled Joy's recent comment about her name: "It's a burden. It raises expectations." *Was that true? Whose expectations, Joy's or other people's?* Grace was sure Joy hadn't known she'd overheard. She glanced over at Sophie, now resting her head on one of her stuffies and gazing dolefully up at Grace.

After reading Corintha's letter, Grace realized that although she had an idea of what her mother wanted after her death (*Flowers, By the water, Have fun!*) she had no idea what her mother had wanted in life. She knew her mother had not dreamed of constant flight and a meager existence in Framingham, then Manchester, then Lowell, then Worcester. Knew she had not dreamed of rising each morning to head off to whichever shop, plant, or office currently employed her, to sit at one of a dozen desks, filing, recording, answering telephones and questions; of taking fifteen-minute breaks and half-hour lunches each day, when instructed to do so; of packing a small lunch to save money and only occasionally splurging on a bag of pretzels or chips for her afternoon snack.

At night Joan used to watch the evening news during dinner, and then an episode of *Murder She Wrote* or *Marcus Welby*, or else knitted, read, or did a jigsaw puzzle. After her mother retired at seventy-five, she moved to a "bungalow" in Handley, Maine. That was how the real estate agent had listed the prefab. It was on a pond. That was all that mattered to Joan. *Was this her dream finally realized?*

When Grace was nine, her mother took her to "a resort," or so she sold it to Grace, the very word conjuring up images of wealth and opulence. There was little of either at that humble assemblage of one-room cabins. Shore View it was called, although the "shore" was just a patch of dirt, raked into a beach at one end of a small pond, heavily shaded and coated with pine pollen. It rained the entire weekend.

Grace's father did not come with them. At the time, Grace didn't know why. She and her mother played countless games of gin rummy and old maid and parcheesi, and assembled an entire thousand-piece puzzle of the state flowers. (Grace recently found one at George and Kit's and bought it for this weekend in her mother's honor.) She could still remember most of the flowers: Arkansas and Michigan both chose apple blossom; Minnesota picked the elegant lady's slipper; California, the golden poppy. Idaho chose syringa, as did New Hampshire, but they had the good sense simply to call it lilac. Maine's, of course, Grace had already known from growing up in Bangor: white pinecone and tassel. An embarrassment as much as a disappointment. Why not the lovely lupine?

When they finished the puzzle, Grace stood on her narrow bed and peered out the tiny window, high on the wall. A trampoline, rain drenched and abandoned, stood behind the row of little cabins. When the rain slowed slightly, she and her mother donned rain jackets and ventured out for a walk into air heavy with the smell of balsam. Grace edged closer and closer to the trampoline, which stood, altarlike, in a clearing in the trees. Finally, her mother said, "Go on, then. Give it a try."

Grace took off her shoes and socks and climbed aboard. Tentative at first, soon she was jumping, higher and higher, her hair, slick and dripping, landing with a *fwap* on her back each time she bounced. The details of the rest of their stay were still blurry, just like the landscape was when Grace was on the trampoline, soaring up and down and up again, raindrops clinging to her eyelashes, and mist softening the edges of the cabins and the tall pines—as if it had changed their very molecular makeup.

It seemed to Grace now that she could organize all the events in her life into those before the trampoline and those after. They did not return to Bangor after their "vacation" at the "resort," and Grace finally figured out why her father hadn't joined them for that trip, or ever again: Joan took great pains to be certain he couldn't, moving Grace every two years to a new town. Running.

Grace was pleased that she'd been able to give her own children a stable home. But sometimes she still felt an urge to run. At first, she'd been delighted to settle here, charmed by the knowledge that she could know, intimately, every nook and cranny of this little, bounded world. As the years passed, however, she'd found herself longing for greater range, less restraint. Though Grace loved Little Island, at times she resented the rocky border that so rigidly defined the less than one square mile of her world. At low tide, that world and the possibilities within it expanded, but only slightly. It wasn't really the perimeter of the island that kept her here, she knew. It was Gar, the inn, the guests, her children, the endless chores, her life. "Think how hard it would be," she said to Sophie, as she bent down and retrieved the errant kibbles, "to hold the name Grace."

JOY

"There's Grammy," Tamar said to me. She was paging through an old photo album that the twins had pulled from the cupboard and placed on top of a half-assembled puzzle of state flowers. Plastic-sealed pages, their edges yellowed, held faded photos, marking most, but not all, of the major events in my family's lives. Tamar bent in for a closer look. "Wow, look how young she was."

Roger and Daddy had joined us in the Games Room, and we four now gathered around the album to examine the snapshot of my mother and grandmother on the bluff above Sand Beach. Our mother looked so fresh-faced and thin as to be almost unrecognizable.

"Grammy was about fifty-five when that was taken." My mother had come in, wiping her hands on a dish towel. She turned the page. "Here she was the same day with you two." She pointed to a familiar picture of me and Tamar, standing with our grandmother. The two of us wore striped stocking caps that Grammy had knitted. Tamar looked annoyed, being made to appear pleased about such a gift, clearly beneath her.

"I was right around your age, girls," Tamar said, and her twins wriggled in for a closer look. I stepped aside to make room, then reached for a padded white album, buried in the pile, and took it to where the light was better.

My parents had worried about my choice of husband. It wasn't just his thirty years to my twenty-one, although that was part of it. (As the decades advanced I seemed to catch up with him. Now, his fifty to my nearly forty-one? Well, who can tell anyone's age in that range?) Tears welled as I stared down at my unlined face, framed by my wedding veil—Stuart, beside me in his tux, so handsome, so confident, and looking so much like Rex.

"Oh, here's Grammy in The Dress and The Hat," I heard Tamar say from across the room. "Here you go. Right here. Same dress, same hat."

"And she wore it to Grandma Little's funeral," Roger added.

"And the twins' christening," Daddy said.

"And Cousin Margot's thirtieth birthday party," I added, joining the others.

Every time we Littles get together, we dredge up stories to retell, like Grammy's recurring hat and dress. But only certain stories. It was like selecting only certain pieces of silver from the set on the breakfront to keep shined. No one in the family ever spoke about the crash.

"Homicide by vehicle while driving under the influence," was the judge's monotone verdict at Roger's trial. It was just one more sentence to him, just one more case resolved. I wondered whether the judge had any notion of what such words can do to a family. Roger and Tamar had not been the only ones to career off the road that night. They took the rest of us with them. I postponed my return to college until Tamar was out of the hospital and Roger's trial and sentencing were over. My parents closed the inn, canceling reservations made many months in advance, although they needed the income. For a time they were unsure whether they would reopen at all. We endured newspaper articles, looks from neighbors, Maisie's grief and crumbling marriage.

I kept one newspaper clipping about the crash. Just that morning I'd found it yellowing in a desk drawer and had tucked it into one of my boxes. "Roger Little Arrested for Vehicular Homicide," declared the headline. The article described the inn, Daddy's long family history on the island, and some details of Bonnie's brief life and sudden death. She gazed out from her senior class picture, eyes bright with hope and promise.

When I finally returned to college, I couldn't concentrate, missed classes, failed exams, lost weight. I had a little X-Acto knife that I used for cutting mat board. I was into photography then. The first cut was accidental, or nearly so. The knife slipped and nicked my palm. It startled me at first, and then fascinated me, as I watched the small crimson bead well up and run down onto the clean white mat. There had been so much blood at the crash site: all over Tamar's face, the seats, the dashboard. Bonnie's carotid artery had been sliced open when her head went through the windshield.

The next day, the little nick on my palm had started to scab over, and I found I could open it with just the least bit of pressure of the knife. So I did, and then, with very little effort or forethought, I made the nick a little longer. Eventually it extended nearly two inches across the base of my thumb. Not deep. Every night I would press the X-Acto blade in the exact same spot. My undergraduate advisor must have finally seen it, or maybe my roommate told. I never did learn who was responsible, but I was sent to Dr. Kilsaro for counseling.

It seemed especially mean to Grace that her family should bring up her mother's sartorial quirk on what was practically the eve of her memorial service. Tamar and Joy had begun rifling through handfuls of loose photos, looking for more evidence of their grandmother's singular devotion to that hat and dress. It was not what Grace wanted to remember about her mother, nor what she wanted her children to memorialize. Joan scrimped and saved her entire life, spending almost nothing on herself, and managed to leave Grace seventy-five thousand dollars—a huge sum for Joan. She must have been so proud. Grace hadn't known about the money until her mother's solicitor sent her the will and so she never thanked her, never told her how much it meant to her. She wished her mother had spent the money on herself: taken a true vacation, bought lunch out once a week, made an occasional visit to the hairdresser. Perhaps bought a new dress. She thought again of her mother's last requests: *Flowers, By the water, Have fun! Fun.* Grace had begun to resent, deeply, that last, freighted little word, shaped, ironically, like a rollercoaster—one ride she'd always loathed.

"That hat is . . ." Joy began, but left her sentence dangling, perhaps noticing Grace's silence.

"Ridiculous," Tamar supplied, digging through the stack. "Oh. My. God. Here's Roger with Beau. Speaking of ridiculous hats." A holstered Roger wore a cowboy hat tipped low over one eye. Their German shorthaired pointer, Beau, also wearing a hat, gazed patiently at the camera.

"My deputy," Roger said. The twins giggled.

"God, remember the time Beau . . ." Tamar launched into one of the many Beau stories. There were dozens, all centered on his acts of heroism, devotion, and obedience. The stories inevitably resulted in someone making a crack about Sophie, who was more . . . *self-preserving*, was how Grace liked to think of it. "Sophie-loafer," as her children often called her, had a bed in nearly every room, each attended by an overflowing basket of stuffed animals, and she had to be carried up and down stairs now due to her arthritis. This was something of a blessing, because when Sophie could still climb the stairs herself, she'd had a habit of going into guests' rooms, whenever she happened upon an unlatched door, and leaving a dog biscuit beneath a pillow or in an unguarded shoe. Grace found it endearing, a sentiment not necessarily shared by the guest.

Grace felt out of sorts as she listened to her children reminisce, so she excused herself and went back into the kitchen. No one looked up when she left.

JOY

I watched Roger and Tamar drift away from the photos on the table. Nat and Hal had long since lost interest in the albums and now stood, murmuring and playing their finger game: *bump, curl, snap, clap* . . . on and on it went. Their mumbling was mesmerizing. Daddy said he was going to the boathouse in search of something—I didn't catch what—and left. My focus shifted back to my siblings. Tamar was clearly trying to convince Roger of something . . . As soon as she glanced my way, I knew. *They wanted to go out somewhere together, and she was going to ask me to babysit.*

That was fine. There was no need for them to whisper. I'd have been happy to head upstairs with the girls. First I'd make them cups of warm milk with cardamom and honey, and then we'd select a few books from the library—

"Joy told you earlier that she wanted to what?" Tamar said loudly to Roger, but looking at me.

Roger was staring at me, too, now. Beseechingly.

I stared stupidly back. Roger and I hadn't spoken earlier.

"Tamar wanted to ask you to put the girls to bed and stay here to watch them," Roger enunciated each word carefully, as though sending me a coded message. "But I was just going to tell her what you said to me earlier. How you wanted to . . ." He trailed off, clearly hoping I would complete his sentence.

Good God, Roger, I thought. *For someone who's lied as much as you, you are unbelievably bad at it.* I searched in vain for a suitable verb phrase. Wanted to . . . wash my hair, read a book, take a walk? None of these would work. "Talk to Daddy?" I shouldn't have posed it as a question; I sounded uncertain, and I could tell from Tamar's expression that she wasn't buying it. "Yeah. I didn't realize I'd told you. Why?" I flexed all my acting muscles and believe that I managed to pull off a pretty convincing "innocent curiosity."

"Roger's going out. I want to go with him." Tamar could have bored holes in my skull with the intensity of her gaze. "Could you maybe put the girls to bed and talk with Daddy after?"

What the hell was going on here?

"Oh, I would love to, girls." I turned to the twins to avoid looking at either of my siblings. Roger's look was pleading; Tamar's murderous. "But Daddy's waiting for me . . ." *Where did he say he was going?* "In the boathouse."

"We'll wait. Go tell him you'll talk tomorrow on the run around the island. Before we jump off the footbridge." I could hear the taunt in this last line.

"I'm afraid it can't wait." It was now my turn to stare at Roger.

He took the bait. "Leave her alone, Tee. I'm just going to see some of the guys. You wouldn't enjoy it. We'll probably smoke cigars." He moved toward the door, and Tamar followed.

The twins, seeing their mother leave, fell in line behind her, pleading. "Please stay. Can we cook popcorn?"

Roger took advantage of the momentary delay and beelined for the kitchen door. "Don't wait up," he called back.

"I'm going to"—I pointed in the direction of the boathouse— "go talk with Daddy."

"About what?" Tamar's question sounded like a challenge. "Why don't you come upstairs and talk to us?"

"Nothing. I mean, just some stuff . . . I have some things I need to tell him." With that I turned and hurried from the room, calling back. "I'm just going upstairs to get a sweater first."

"Joy?" I could hear Tamar call, but I made straight for the stairs and mounted them, two at a time, pausing on the second-floor landing, listening. I probably would make a good hired assassin or secret agent: someone whose life depends upon her ability to lie. I climbed the second flight of stairs, went into my room, and shut the door. I didn't like lying, but Roger had given me little choice.

· Chapter Twelve ·

Roger wasn't ready to tell anyone. Not even Tamar. He'd figured he'd have a tough time getting away from the inn without her. Tee had pleaded. Given him her hurt look. Normally he couldn't resist. But not this time. Luckily Joy played along. She was a good old egg; always there when you needed her most. A rock. Mom had been so busy in the kitchen she'd hardly looked up when he left, which was good. He had a tough time lying to his mother. She always knew. Almost always. His father, thankfully, was down in the boathouse, and hadn't seen him leave at all.

He met Walter Fifield at the Flying Bridge, where they had a few beers with three high school buddies, and then went over to Walter's and drank forties until after midnight. Walter ran a lobster boat and had to get up early but told the others to feel free to stay. One by one, the guys made their excuses and left. But Roger stayed on. He didn't want to go back to the inn hammered, and so he made coffee and drank four glasses of water while he waited for it to brew, worried that Tamar, or his parents, might be up waiting. Didn't want them to see him like this. Didn't want to drive like this either.

He hadn't meant to drink so much, had planned to stay reasonably sober this weekend, maybe just a nip here and there to take the edge off, but he'd convinced himself that he needed a few tonight to "build rapport," something Tamar had learned in a sales seminar she'd attended—although he was pretty sure she wouldn't want to claim credit for its application here. It seemed to work, as Walter was pretty free with information about Loraine, giving Roger half the answer he wanted: Loraine was happily divorced and not seeing anyone—but Walter thought she was pretty happy about that last part, too. Then he clapped Roger hard on his bad shoulder and told him, "Go for it. Worth a shot. Always wished the two of you . . ." He left the sentence unfinished.

Roger had spent his childhood with these guys—up until he went off-island to boarding school his junior year—and it was easy for him to slip back into the old patterns, like they were all sixteen again. Even so, he wasn't one of them, and they all knew it. None of the others had ever lived anywhere but East Haven and never would; their whole worlds were bounded by Isle au Haut and West Penobscot Bays.

But although Roger had left the island, his heart had stayed behind. His dream, to someday own the inn, was made more perfect at the thought of Loraine by his side. He drove by her house after he left Walter's. Her lights were off. Whose wouldn't be at two A.M.? He wanted to hop out and bang on her front door, wake her up, take her in his arms, tell her how he felt. She still had to have feelings for him, right, given what they'd shared? But even hammered, Roger knew that such a confession would sound better if he were sober. He was a drunk, not a dummy.

He'd stayed mostly sober for ten years after he got out of prison. How could he not, with all that experience, strength, and hope being channeled his way? He remembered the exact day he decided to hop off the wagon. He was putting a roof on some guy's house, and it was about ninety degrees. The guy and his wife were floating around their pool on rubber rafts, shouting up instructions to Roger, who was clinging to their eight-over-twelve-inch roof, nailing on shingles. He took a good, hard look at his world and decided it really would look better through the bottom of a bottle, which pretty much ended his contracting career. He'd been drunk, off and on, but mostly on, for the last decade, always promising himself he'd get and stay sober if he ever had a good enough reason.

Now he did.

He looked up at Loraine's window and got a hard-on just thinking about her sleeping up there, how she'd turn her sleep-creased face up to him in startled surprise, then open her arms, and he'd roll in beside her and hold her. God, he could still remember that solid but soft body. Twelve hours. He could do anything for twelve hours, right? That's what they said. To-morrow he'd stop by her shop, clean and sobered by sleep, time, and a bracing jog around Little Island followed by a freezing-cold dip. They'd talk, she'd take off that little smock thing that hairdressers wore, close the shop, and they'd spend the day driving around to all their old favorite places, have lunch, make love, make plans . . . He sat in his truck, looking at her house, thinking about what might have been.

· · ·

By the time Grace had sliced the French bread and the tomatoes, chopped the basil, whipped the eggs with the cream
and spices for the breakfast strata, unloaded the dishwasher,
set up the coffeemaker in case someone wanted an early cup,
and scraped one last bit of the twins' pink paste from beneath
the stove, the others had gone to bed, and the inn was quiet.
Gar had wandered through earlier and mentioned that he
was going to look for his bottledarter down in the boathouse
one last time, and then wandered back through later, empty-
handed, and told her not to stay up too late, they had an early
reveille. She responded with a tired but, she thought, good-
natured groan.

Sophie was snoring softly. Grace curled up beside her on her
bed and squeaked one of her toys to wake her. Sophie rolled
over, offering up a belly freckled with age. Grace thought of
her arrival at nine weeks old, all spiky hair, skunk breath, and
needle-sharp teeth with just two speeds: flop-dog and psycho-
dog. She never walked anywhere, nor simply lay down. When
she wasn't tearing around, she was sleeping with enviable
abandon, often flat on her back as she was now, with her head
hanging off the edge of the bed. The two of them used to go for
long walks up to the lighthouse and through the fern brake and
the woods to the south side, where they would skip stones from
Silver Beach, and Sophie would bark ferociously at the eider
ducks paddling a safe remove from shore. But it had been years
since they did that.

When Sophie was about eight, Grace noticed a stiffening in
her gait. It didn't slow her down much; she simply put one rear
paw on top of the other and pogoed along. No self-pity; that

was what Grace liked about dogs. Sophie was now twelve, and Grace could see the signs: most of her day spent in the sound sleep of the very young and the very old—even, as she was mostly deaf, through thunderstorms, which used to send her scrabbling behind the couch, panting. It broke Grace's heart to see her old friend slowing down. Sophie's heart was strong, the vet said. No reason to worry, yet.

"Belly rubbin's? For me?" Grace loved rubbing Sophie's belly, and Sophie seemed to know this. Grace also loved Sophie's uncomplicated and generous nature, her unself-conscious acceptance of her looks, her clarity in asking for what she wanted. Maybe, Grace thought, selfishness is not always such a bad thing.

"Want to go for walkers?" Grace asked, "That would be some fun." Sophie gave Grace a disbelieving, accusing stare but then staggered to her feet and trotted gamely after her. Roger's truck, Grace noticed, was still not in the driveway. She checked her watch: midnight. *Uh-oh. Where would he have gone? Where would he still be at this hour?* She sighed, thinking of the many sleepless nights she had endured.

Sophie conducted her business quickly, but Grace wasn't quite ready to go in, so she took Sophie on a tour of the yard, exclaiming over the almost-full moon, the harbor with masts in silhouette against the bright water, the flowers bleached like old bones. When they completed their circuit, Sophie looked up at Grace and lifted first one paw, and then the other, from the dew-laden grass. "Okay, Sophie-bean. Time for beddie-boopers."

But even after Grace had turned out all but one light, trudged upstairs to check on the kids, and fallen exhausted into bed, she lay awake. Gar snored quietly beside her, more soothing than annoying, but not quite soothing enough to send her to sleep. Moonlight seeped around the edges of the shades, and she counted the slow rotation of the shadows cast by the ceiling fan and thought again about her mother—of all the nights that she'd lain, alone, in her bed after leaving Grace's father. Could Grace have done more to make her mother's life happy? A large tear formed and rolled slowly down her cheek.

A little after two, the moonlight faded, Roger's headlights swept across the shades. Only then did Grace finally allow herself to drift off to sleep.

JULY 1984

JOY

"I don't want to go ashore to some stupid old B&B," Tamar whined. "Can't we stay on board? Please?" This morning she'd begged to come along on this trip to North Haven, where my parents planned to look at, and possibly make an offer for, a small walk-in cooler at a B&B that was closing there.

I was thirteen—old enough, my parents believed—to watch my eleven-year-old siblings. That hadn't worked out so well the previous week, when Roger and Tamar had given me the slip, gone down to the dock, and set off a firecracker, splitting one of the pilings nearly in two. And yet they were to be left in my care again. Had we stayed home, I'd planned to take them to see *Romancing the Stone* with Bonnie. A movie theater, went my thinking, was a relatively safe place to harbor them. But then Tamar whined that she wanted to go with Daddy and Mom and, as always, she got her way. I was then dragged along to watch them while my parents negotiated the purchase of the walk-in.

After arriving in North Haven, Daddy dropped the anchor and pulled the *Miss Katie* alongside to row us over to the gas dock. I was already seated in the dinghy, my hands gripping the sides—although it was still securely tied and rocking only gently in the wake of a passing boat—when Tamar started making a fuss about staying on board. Tamar must have seen Mom's imploring look, directed my way, because she immediately said, "Roger and I will be fine here by ourselves."

Mom shook her head, still looking at me.

"Why should I have to stay just because she wants to? I didn't want to come in the first place."

"Because you're older and the twins can't stay by themselves." My mother's tone was firm.

"Why don't you stay?" I said to her. It seemed only fair. After all, she brought them into the world.

"No. You stay. Please, Joy?" Tamar's plea startled everyone, me most of all.

Daddy winked as he helped me out of the dinghy and gave my hand a little squeeze.

After our parents rowed ashore, Tamar said, "Let's play baseball."

"Baseball?" Roger was hunting around for a spare key to the boat.

"If you wanted to do that, we should have gone ashore, dummy," I said.

"No. You're the dummy. On the boat. It's fun. Roger and I played last night."

From Roger's puzzled expression, I knew she was lying. "We don't have any equipment," I pointed out.

"It's pretend. This is home base." Tamar indicated an area

at the stern. "That's first, second, and third." She pointed to logical spots on both sides and the bow.

"You be the referee," Tamar said to Roger.

"Umpire," I said. "They're called umpires."

"No, wait, Roger, you be the pitcher. I'll be the batter, and Joy, you be the guy who waves me around the bases."

"Base coach," I said. "This sounds kind of—"

Tamar cut me off. "Joy, go up in the bow and make the call when I hit the ball and start to round the bases."

"What if you strike out?"

Tamar glared. This whole thing sounded infantile and totally subjective, but still I was pleased to have been included, and so made my way forward. I couldn't see them from up there, but apparently Roger wound up, delivered a pitch, and Tamar connected, because I soon heard her make a loud popping noise with her tongue, and she came into view, trotting toward first base. "Well? What is it?" she demanded. "A single? Double? Home run?"

I shrugged. *Who cares?* "Home run, I guess."

"Yes!" Tamar pumped her arm, ran past me, and headed back to the stern, avoiding the cleats, coiled ropes, and boat hook lying on the deck.

"Okay, Joy, your turn to bat. I'll be the base coach, and Roger will pitch again."

I made my way to the stern and watched Roger take a few practice throws and pound his fist into his palm. I glanced toward the dock, wondering how long our parents would be gone. Roger mimed climbing the mound, then looked toward first and threw me the pitch. I didn't budge. "Why didn't you swing?" he asked.

"High and away," I said. "Ball one."

"What's going on back there?" Tamar called from the far side of the cabin.

"Ball one," I shouted.

Roger wound up again and delivered a second pitch. Still I didn't swing. "What was wrong with that one?"

"Nothing. Strike one. I was just seeing what you had."

Roger grinned. "I think you'll like this one."

"Hurry up!" Tamar called. "Don't be stupid, Joy. You always ruin everything."

I probably should have guessed then that she was up to something, but Roger delivered the pitch, I swung, putting my whole body into it, and watched an invisible ball arc up over the *Kestrel*'s bridge. I flung the bat aside and walked toward first base. When I reached it, Tamar was cranking her arm, hurrying me forward. "That was not a home run. If you hustle, I think you can make it to third."

"What? That was too a home run. If yours was, mine was."

"Was not. I'm the whatchamacallit. Now get a move on."

As I trotted to the bow, Roger appeared on the port side. "What's going on? That looked like an infield double to me."

"I'm going to throw it in. We'll get her out at home," she called.

Tamar mimed a catch, cocked her arm back, and released the imaginary ball. "Run!"

"What?" I looked at her as I rounded second and headed for third. "Roger said—"

"Hurry, Joy. I think you can just make it home, but you've got to hustle."

"But Roger said—" At this, my foot caught on a fender, and I pitched over the side.

"Joy!" I heard Roger shout.

Somehow I managed to grab the boat's gunwale as I fell, and I hung there, stunned, as Roger ran up and grabbed my arm. (There was no way I was letting go and trusting him to pull me back on board.) Tamar joined him and stood there, staring down at me. "What happened?" Her tone oozed with counterfeit astonishment. She probably put the fender there herself.

"Grab her other arm. Can you swing your leg up, Jo-jo?"

"Let's use the boat hook," Tamar suggested, grabbing it.

My fingers ached. The water was just inches below my feet. It was deep and cold, and I was not wearing a life jacket. If I fell, there would be no way to get me back on the boat.

"Shut up, Tamar," Roger said, "And help me get her back on board."

Tamar now reached down and grabbed my other arm, and I managed to fling one foot up over the side. Roger grabbed it with his other hand, and I relaxed my grip.

"Oops!" Tamar said, loosening hers. I felt myself start to tumble toward the water.

"Cut it out, Tamar," Roger barked, clamping down on my leg.

My jaw was clenched so tight I'm surprised I didn't break any teeth. I didn't say a word as Roger wrestled me, single-handedly, onto the deck, where the two of us lay a moment, panting.

"Okay, Roger. You're up," Tamar said.

I glared at my sister and, without another word, went below and shut myself in the forward cabin, not caring how much trouble the two of them got in before my parents returned, just so long as they didn't sink the boat. I wouldn't tell—even though I suspected she had planned it, probably hoping I'd fall in, just to see what would happen. *Be nice, Joy*; my mother's words rang in my ears. *She's younger. Someday*, I thought. *Someday.*

I never made it to the boathouse after leaving the Games Room. Instead I sat in my window seat, just like Bonnie and I used to do, letting the damp night air curl my hair. I liked Mom's curls and thought idly that I might call Loraine the next day and see if she could fit me in. Maybe I would get some highlights, or a few layers.

From downstairs I heard the twins' muted giggles and muffled running, and then the inn slowly shut down: Pipes complained as Tamar ran the water; a door closed, opened, and closed again. Then, slowly, night noises crept in; feet scampered on the roof, an owl called. There was a final creak as the inn settled. Later, I heard my mother's tired tread on the stairs. Even with our children grown, we mothers need to do our nightly rounds.

I waited a few minutes before slipping from my spot in the window seat and tiptoeing downstairs. I went out through the kitchen, which was spotless, the drainer piled high with bowls and mixing spoons, and I wondered what my mother had been cooking.

The moon was so bright I didn't need my flashlight as I walked down the lane, past the causeway to the footbridge, where I stood, staring into the dark, rushing water. *It wasn't so very far down. What was I afraid of?* I stepped over the railing and leaned out, imitating the position I would take the next morning, tried to visualize the sense of falling, of landing in the water, of the current grabbing me and shuttling me beneath the bridge. This was how Stuart had tried to coach me out of my water phobia. But even though I held tight to the rail, my heart raced and my hands shook. I retreated to the center of the footbridge, and then, still queasy, to the flat rock to which the bridge was anchored. Fifteen minutes passed before I was able to stand and make my way back to the inn.

Later, I heard Roger and knew from his failed attempt to climb the stairs silently that he'd been drinking.

· Chapter Thirteen ·

Something was not right. Grace rolled onto her side and looked at the clock: eight thirty-three. *A.M. or P.M.?* Grace hadn't slept past seven o'clock for forty years. As consciousness dawned, she remembered going to bed and lying awake, waiting for Roger, until the green numbers on the clock said two twenty-two. So, morning, then. But the inn seemed so silent. *Where was everyone?* They were planning to leave at seven thirty to ride the rip. She sat up. "Gar?" *Impossible! They wouldn't leave her behind.*

In the kitchen, she found Sophie curled up on her bed in the corner and the coffeepot half empty. Beside it lay a note. *Sophie's been out. Didn't want to wake you. You looked so peaceful. Love, Gar.*

Reeling with disappointment, Grace dropped into a chair. Sophie raised her head and fixed her with a solicitous gaze— *They left me, too*, she seemed to say. *Betrayed by our own people.* Then she curled back into an even tighter ball.

Grace had to concede that there was no way Sophie could

have made the long trek around the island. But Grace certainly could. She'd been looking forward to it. It would have been fun! She felt helpless, the way she did when a strong May wind began to strip the blossoms from their crabapple trees. Could she join them at the footbridge? If the group left at seven thirty as planned, and Tamar set the pace, they would already have run the rip and be clambering out onto the rocks on the other side, shivering their way into clothes, eager to head home to hot coffee and breakfast. She didn't want to hold them up. When the adrenaline wore off, it would be cold.

Grace rode the incoming tide alone once. It was nighttime, the year Abigail died. The moon was full, and she walked to the bridge, stripped, and plunged, scaring herself a little. But the ride was worth it. Back at the inn she told Gar—it would have been hard to hide her dripping hair.

He'd checked his watch as Grace stood, shaking—partially from the cold, partially from the excitement of her solo voyage—in the inn's kitchen. "The tide turns in twenty minutes. Think if you'd timed it wrong. Think if you'd jumped when the tide was going out!" He was shouting. "You could have—"

"What? Do you even know?" She shouted back. She'd been warned of the hazards ever since her first jump.

"Been swept out to sea, mostly likely. I don't know. But is it a risk you're willing to take?"

Grace was, in fact, but didn't say so. She needed something . . . big and bold and explosive to jolt her from the stupor she'd been in since her baby's death.

"Did you know the tide was right?" His voice was softer, but only slightly.

She tilted her head, neither acknowledging nor denying. She

had known, somehow, but not in a way she could explain, not in a way he would understand. A creeping numbness began to replace her excited shivering.

"You scared me. That's all. I need you, Short."

She'd nodded, thinking back to her recent ride beneath the bridge, alone and free—although *alone*, she knew from her mother's years of flight from Grace's father, did not necessarily mean *free*, any more than being with someone means you're connected.

Resigned, Grace poured herself a cup of coffee from the half-empty pot. While she hated to admit it, she didn't have the energy to find a suit and rush down to the footbridge. She turned on the oven, gave the egg batter another whisk, poured it over the layers of French bread, tomatoes, basil, and cheese, slid the strata into the oven, set the timer, and decided to iron the table-cloths while she waited for her family to return.

"You got in late."

"Early, actually. I'd call it early."

"Where were you?"

"Sis, really?" Roger cradled his cup of coffee as he ambled along beside Tamar, who was straining to break into a trot. A light morning fog still lingered over the island. They stopped at the end of Little Lane, where it turned into two ruts and disappeared into the woods. Gar, Joy, and the twins were somewhere behind them.

"I'm going to run a little," Tamar said. "I'll wait for you at Land's End." Roger nodded and watched his sister set her watch and sprint off down the trail through the trees. She was built for speed, like one of the racing bikes they sold at the store, with their carbon framesets and Shimano components.

He could hear Joy and the others singing: "I said boom, chicka, boom. I said boom, chicka, boom . . ." He hid behind a tree as they approached.

"I said boom, chicka-wocka, chicka-wocka, chicka—

"Boom," shouted Roger, jumping out in front of them.

The twins shrieked. So did Joy. Even Gar gave a startled "Oh!"

"Where's Tee?" Joy asked.

Roger pointed. "See that cloud of dust?"

"Where?" said the twins, gazing down the trail.

"She's waiting for us at Land's End. My guess is she will have circled the island three times by then. So stay to one side, girls. She doesn't slow down for anyone. Ever watch Road Runner?"

They looked up at him, their faces serious.

"Kidding. You know any other songs? That one's . . . great and all, but . . . Do you?"

"The cow kicked Nelly in the belly in the barn," sang the twins. "The cow kicked Nelly in the belly in the barn. The cow kicked Nelly in the belly in the ba-a-a-a-rn, and the farmer said it would do no harm."

"Nice," Roger retrieved his coffee cup.

"SECOND verse same as the FIRST," Nat sang.

"A little bit LOUDER and a little bit WORSE," Hal added.

As they started in together, Joy gave Roger a pained look.

"THIRD verse same as the FIRST. A little bit LOUDER and a little bit WORSE," the girls shouted.

"Girls!" Joy said. "Let's look for fairy circles." The twins looked skeptical, but intrigued. "Fairies plant mushrooms around the spots where they have their dances and sing-alongs. You have to look very carefully, along the trail, both sides, and in the woods. And be very quiet so you can hear them singing. If you spot a mushroom, keep looking in a big circle to see if there are others. Also look for discarded acorn caps, which, as everyone knows, fairies use as hats when it rains, and for tiny animal tracks, because fairies often ride mice and voles and chipmunks—if they're very wealthy—through the forest. When they're not flying, that is."

"I thought fairies were gay people," the twins said.

"Yes, Mrs. Kilsaro, I've heard that, too," Roger added in his best whiny schoolboy voice, his expression all innocence.

"First of all, that is not a nice term to apply to gay people. We don't use it. Second of all, don't tell me you've never read a fairy tale, because I know you have. Remember *The Counterpane Fairy?*"

The twins nodded. "And your uncle knows perfectly well that there are fairy circles in these woods, and just how hard they are to spot, because he once spent an entire afternoon looking for one after I told him that I'd heard singing in the woods. Remember, Uncle Roger?"

"My, God, I remember that." Gar gave a delighted laugh. "I thought we were going to have to pitch a tent for you out here that night."

"Thank you very much, both of you, for bringing that up. Perhaps my finest moment."

"You were always so gullible," Joy said. "I made a whole little fairy village, stacked up balsam cones and told you the fairies burned them for fuel, built a miniature stone fireplace, made little beds of twigs and moss, told you that maple seeds were discarded fairy wings . . ." Joy trailed off as she realized that the girls were listening intently.

"Are there fairies or not?" Nat asked.

"No one really knows, because no one's actually ever seen one. But there are fairy circles, so, probably yes."

The girls stared into one another's eyes, then set off down the trail singing, "The cow kicked Nelly in the belly in the barn. The cow kicked Nelly in the belly in the barn . . ."

"Damn, I almost had them." Joy and the others started slowly down the trail after them.

At Seal Cove, the water had covered the rocks just offshore—where, at midtide, the seals liked to lounge and belch out their seal songs. The group scrambled down the path to the stony beach, and Roger gave the twins lessons on skipping rocks. Fog danced above the surface of the water, trying to gain altitude. The sun peered weakly through the dense gray.

"Going to be a hot one," Gar predicted, and checked his watch. "We better pick up the pace, or we're going to miss our ride." He called the girls and led the group up the trail at the far end of the cove, through the hay-scented ferns, beach plums, and rugosa roses, to the lichen-stained boulders of Peg's Point. The fog settled again, hiding the sun, slicking the rocks, and dampening the undergrowth and their clothes, so that they were all soaked by the time they reached the broad rocky expanse of Silver Beach, where the fallen trunks of several long-dead trees served as trellises for beach peas and vetch.

"Look, girls. A pirate ship!" Joy pointed to the hull of an old sardiner that had been run aground and abandoned back when sardine fishing in the area began to collapse.

"That's a fishing boat," they said. "Not a pirate ship. Mom said."

"That's what it was," Joy countered, "It can be anything you want now."

A figure appeared in the mist. "Where have you guys been? I've been running in place for ages. Do you know what time it is? C'mon."

The twins sprinted toward their mother, and the others followed. Up the hill the group went at a jog, to Land's End: a sheer cliff dropping fifty feet to the water. They stopped to catch their breath and watch the fog march out to sea. Waves hurled themselves onto the rocks below with such force that spray rose thirty feet in the air. "Don't get too close to the edge, girls," Joy warned, as Tamar led the pack at a jog around the point. Just visible was the roof of the long-abandoned cottage they called the Rookery, set on a ledge in the rock below the path.

As they skittered down the steep hill to Sand Beach, Joy stopped to point out to the twins Spectacle Island, now surrounded by water. Gar was standing beside the bathhouses at the far end, calling, "Did everybody wear suits, or do we have to stop?"

"I'm all set," Tamar shouted. "So are the girls."

"Me, too," Joy said.

"I'm going *au naturel*," Roger said.

"You are not!" Tamar called back.

"Okay, then in my skivvies."

"You're changing. But hurry, I'm getting cold." Tamar ordered Joy to fetch some towels as she trotted off, followed by her daughters. Gar headed off as well, shouting, "Six minutes till the tide turns."

JOY

I had resolved to walk right out onto the footbridge and be the first one in. But when Roger and I arrived, Tamar was already standing out there. Daddy had always made a big deal about the precise timing of the jump, something about the strength of the current, the height of the water . . . I'd never paid much attention, always too concerned about the act itself. I now had five minutes.

The girls jumped last year, but last year Daniel had buckled them into yellow life vests and dangled them over the side of the bridge, holding tight to their wrists—first Nat, because she was seventeen minutes older, then Hal—their legs kicking furiously in anticipation of the water. Then he let go, and first one, and then the other, bobbed brightly beneath the bridge, their shrieks echoing in the dark. Daddy was waiting, knee deep, on the other side with Tamar. My mother was standing on the flat rock, holding a big towel and wearing an even bigger smile. "Oooooh," they all cooed, like pigeons, to the twins. "You did it!"

"It was scary," both girls admitted when the trip ended, "but not as scary or dark as nighttime and not nearly so long." Everyone laughed.

"You don't need life vests this year," Tamar was now saying to the girls. "You're much too big." Nat and Hal inched toward the footbridge, gazing at the water.

"Why's it so black?" Hal asked. "When you put it in a glass it doesn't look like that."

I often wondered the same thing.

Tamar was starting to look angry, waving harder now, calling the twins onto the bridge, saying something. But her words were lost to the roaring in my ears. Then Tamar jumped and was swallowed by the rushing, black water. The girls ran onto the bridge and peered over, clearly anxious. Up came Tamar's head on the other side. She was laughing and shrieking as the eddy carried her toward shore. "Oh! Ha, ha, ha. It's wonderful. Come on, girls. Just jump! I'll catch you. But hurry!"

Nat and Hal clung to each other. "We want Daddy," they said in unison.

"Daddy isn't here." Their mother's words sounded clipped. She pressed her lips tight.

Four minutes. All I had to do was walk out there, climb over the railing, lean forward—just like last night—but this time, let go. I tried to visualize it. Tried to hear Stuart's calm voice in my head. But my legs felt wobbly and my breathing was so shallow that I started to feel light-headed. What if I blacked out just after I jumped? "You don't have to jump from the bridge," I said, as much to myself as the twins. "You can go underneath and just push off. Want to try that?" I pointed under the bridge, thinking perhaps if the three of us went through together . . .

"There are crabs under there," Hal said.

"And trolls. You told us so last summer," Nat added.

I gave them a weak smile. "I made that up. About the trolls. And the crabs are much farther out." The twins inched away. They didn't like crabs. Even farther out.

Daddy and Roger, in a three-sizes-too-big suit, were on the bridge now. Daddy jumped, grabbed his knees, and did a perfect cannonball into the water, the spray rising and ricocheting off the twins, who shrieked and backed away. I watched him, too, disappear, and sure enough, he popped up on the other side like a rubber tub toy held under. He floated for a while with his skinny white legs out straight, and his long toes sticking up in the air, spinning slightly in the current. "Very refreshing. Nothing to it." He was talking to me, I knew, not the twins, although he was directing his gaze their way.

The twins inched onto the bridge, wanting to be brave for their mother, to show her that they weren't sissies. So did I. Roger climbed over the rail and stood, one hand holding up his suit, the other plugging his nose. He made a funny face, and then just fell backward and landed with a whack and a sploosh. We watched him disappear, and then reappear like magic, on the other side.

It looked so easy! I stood with my hand on the railing. *Hike first one leg over, and then the other*, I told myself, *lean forward, and let go*. Then I thought about the seaweed that might wrap around my leg and hold me down, and so I held the rail a little tighter, and worked a splinter into the cut on my thumb. *And what about jellyfish?* Who knew what was down there. I was being irrational, but that is the nature of phobias. Sweat had broken out on my upper lip and neck. My scalp tingled. My heart pounded. I backed away from the edge. Two minutes.

"Come on, girls. Be brave. Jump with Auntie Joy." Tamar was taunting me.

I turned, intending to climb right over that railing and hop in without giving myself time to back out. But just then I heard Tamar say, "They're not going to jump," as she climbed out of the water and wrapped herself in a towel.

Wait, who isn't going to jump? I was almost ready!

"Okay, so my suit? Now floating toward the gas docks," Roger said. "Toss me a towel, would you?" Tamar tossed him one, and the girls giggled as he, too, climbed out onto the flat rock and wiggled his bare bum in their direction.

Now there was no one in the water to grab me as I hurtled

by. I was certain that the eddy would not transport me safely to the rock, but would send me straight across the harbor, right into the path of the inbound ferry. . . .

One minute.

"Last chance, girls," Tamar said. "Don't be sissies. You'll be sorry."

I felt the sting of that comment, directed, I was sure, more to me than to them. It made me furious. Furious at Tamar for humiliating her daughters, for humiliating me. Furious at Daddy for upholding this detestable and dangerous tradition and inflicting it on us every year. Furious at my mother for tending more to the tasks on her list than the dynamics in her family. Furious at Roger for continuing to numb himself against life with drugs and alcohol, so he couldn't feel the consequences of the bad decision he'd once made. Furious even at Stuart for . . . being Stuart: kind, patient, providing for me as he allowed me to raise our son, but not protecting me from the void that would follow that son's departure, and for not being here with me now to talk me through this jump. *Why couldn't I just jump?* I fought back tears of rage and frustration. The twins had run back to the flat rock and were climbing, shivering, into their shirts and shorts, leaving me all alone on the bridge.

It had taken Grace several days after Aunt Corintha's letter arrived to work up the courage to open it. If her mother had wanted her to know about her past, she reasoned, she would have told her. She'd stood at the window in the dining room, watching the installation of the new sod, and felt a twinge of guilt as she slit open the thin envelope. Siblings, Grace knew, did not always get along.

Dearest Grace,

I kept waiting for your e-mail, and then realized what an impossible assignment I'd given you. You want to know it all, of course, and probably feel that is too much to ask. It isn't. There is more we can share with you when we see you. But let me begin by telling you a bit about us . . .

I am two years older than Joanie. Callista is one year younger. Daddy worked for U.S. Rubber Company, eventually becoming its president. Our mother headed up the auxiliary at the Yale–New Haven Hospital and volunteered at the New Haven Museum. We grew up in Guilford and spent summers at Prout's Neck in Maine. Joanie, as you know, always loved the water.

Grace recalled the caption on the back of the photo of the three girls on a beach: *Joanie, Callie, Cornie, July 1937.* The three sisters at Prout's Neck?

Joanie met your father at a bridge party after the war. (Did you know that Sam was in the Army Air Corps?) She brought him to the house for our annual Christmas party, and we all liked him very much. Daddy liked him so much he gave him a job.

Grace remembered her father as a man with a big laugh, who loved to tell jokes, who brought her soaps from the hotels he stayed at whenever he came back from one of his "sales trips"—only years later did Grace realize that he hadn't been in sales. He used to ride her on his bicycle handlebars, before he bought her a bike of her own, which he taught her to ride behind the school. Grace had often wondered where he'd found the money. Even as young as she'd been, she'd known not to ask. That bicycle was one of the possessions she missed most when she and her mother left.

Sam entertained us with tales about his family's estate outside Chicago, the stables, the antique car collection, the plane parked on the back lawn . . . There is much more that Callie would like me to say about this, but it was all so long ago. I feel there is nothing to be gained. What I will tell you is that when Daddy started checking into Sam's background, he discovered that he'd lied to us about his past, his family, and a good deal more.

Daddy began checking because money started disappearing from the company. Joanie was head-over-heels, and none of us believed for a moment it was Sam. But, after some investigation, Daddy discovered that not only was Sam embezzling (which is bad enough) but that he'd been undermining Daddy's leadership, attempting to convince co-workers that Daddy was making bad business decisions and taking the company in the wrong direction. Sam was quite ambitious and felt he deserved a higher-level position. He had big plans for himself and Joanie. And yet, it seems, he didn't want to work for them. By the time Daddy uncovered the truth, Sam and Joanie were engaged and the wedding plans well under way.

*Daddy fired him, canceled the wedding, and forbade
Joanie to see Sam.*

*Callie says that forbidding Joanie was like sending her
an engraved invitation. It's true. She was headstrong, independent, and a totally free spirit.*

Grace pictured her mother: meek, obedient, shackled to her
small, nomadic life.

*She was also bright and talented and could have
had any man she wanted. Any career. Which was saying something in those days, when most avenues were
closed to women. But she wanted Sam Cursio, and so they
eloped.*

Grace thought of Joan's many clerical positions, her days
spent lining up numbers on spreadsheets and cataloging inven-
tory items in databases. What might her mother's life have been
like, she wondered, if she hadn't disobeyed her father and married Sam Cursio?

Her father had never offered any information about his
family, and she'd never asked, because there'd been another
side to him, besides the handsome charmer: a red-faced man
who ordered her to her room—where she was only too happy
to go to escape the shouting, the swearing, the stumbling
about, the occasional falls that resulted in broken tables, lamps,
or chairs. For a time, he stuffed little folded-up bits of paper in
the telephone, so she and her mother couldn't hear it ring. She
thought it odd at the time and only figured out later that it was
to avoid bill collectors. Maybe something worse, she now

thought, than mere bill collectors. Eventually, he stopped paying the phone bill, and the service was cut off.

You may be wondering why she married Sam. We certainly did. What we learned later, of course, was that Joanie was pregnant . . .

Grace hoped desperately that she would next read that there'd been another baby who was the reason for Joan's estrangement from her family and her lonely life.

. . . with you and your twin brother. He died when you were just infants. A fall, Joanie told us, and we chose to believe her. But I must tell you . . . we've always wondered.

Grace looked at the remaining lines of small, tidy handwriting, unsure she wanted to read on.

It took us a while to find Joanie after she eloped; she broke off all communication. Once we did, we wrote back and forth and could tell that she was growing increasingly unhappy, but too proud to come back home with you and Sammy.

Sammy, thought Grace. *I had a twin brother once called Sammy.* Perhaps this explained the hole she'd often felt in her life. The sense that she was being closely followed. Sometimes, when she was young, the feeling was so strong that she would turn quickly, certain she would come face-to-face with someone just a few paces behind her. The feeling had grown dimmer over the years, but every now and then, she still felt Sammy, like a phantom limb. Why hadn't her mother told her about her twin brother? How could she have kept such a thing secret? Grace thought of tiny Abigail and of her mother's attempts to comfort her in the wake of Abigail's death. It must have been terribly painful bringing back memories of her own lost child. While Grace would never know how her brother died, Aunt Corintha's implication was clear enough: Her father had been somehow responsible.

Gar had come in while Grace was reading and begun searching through the drawers in the breakfront. She didn't have the wherewithal to ask him what he was looking for and so simply stared numbly at the letter, trying to assemble the information into some meaningful pattern, in much the same way that the landscapers outside were attempting to fit the small squares of sod into place. She read on.

> *Daddy never knew about you and Sammy. We feel certain that if he had, he would have sent for Joanie. We regret now that we didn't tell him, but Joanie asked us not to. He'd disowned her when she left, and they were both so stubborn and proud.*
>
> *And then—it must have been when she took you and left Sam—we lost her again. Perhaps she was afraid that Sam would contact us, looking for you. Which he did. We were so worried about you both, but also relieved that we could honestly tell him we had no idea where she'd gone.*

So her father *had* tried to find them. Grace had always wondered. Hoped.

Gar had stopped rummaging through drawers, and Grace

glanced up to find him looking at her with concern, holding a ball of twine and a measuring tape. "Everything okay, Short?"

Grace nodded. She was neither ready nor able to share this news, and read on.

We did finally locate Joanie, but respected her wish for privacy, until the last few years. Callie's health is not the greatest, although she insists that she's fine, and we felt it was time. We called her up and asked if we could come visit.

It was a lovely reunion.

I hope this is not too much to tell you all at once. I probably should have sent this letter sooner. (I'm sure you must be busy getting ready for the service and your family's arrival. Joanie told us the names of your children and showed us photos. Twins obviously run in your family.) But it has taken me all this time to decide what to tell and how best to tell it.

Please feel free to call me if you have any question. In any case, we both look forward very much to meeting our beloved Joanie's daughter.

> *With our very warmest regards,*
> *Corintha Weatherby and Callista Clark*

Gar had crept out of the room while Grace finished the letter. Her mother had always told Grace that her grandparents died when she was just a baby. She supposed that in a sense, that was true. So there was no extended family—no grandparents, aunts, uncles, or cousins for Grace to visit. It was one of the reasons she wanted to keep her own family close.

Not once could Grace recall her mother inviting anyone over for dinner, or even coffee. She had lived her adult life in fear of being found. Grace knew this, and now, finally, she fully understood that it was to protect her.

She put the letter in her pocket, stood, and went to the linen closet, where she pulled out five sets of sheets and climbed to the third floor. She opened the door to Sound, knowing that Joy would choose it. She smoothed the freshly ironed sheets on the bed, folding the corners carefully, as her mother had taught her. As she dusted the dresser, Grace caught a glimpse of herself in the mirror. A pale stranger looked back.

Chapter Fourteen ·

JOY

I didn't want to go to breakfast with Tamar and Roger. Honestly, I don't think Roger wanted to go either. It was Tamar who suggested they eat at the Gawker. After I failed to jump and we were getting ready to head back to the inn, Roger said he needed to go into town. My guess was he was going to see Loraine. At Tamar's suggestion, he nodded and asked if I wanted to join them. Not wanting to go back to the inn alone and face my mother's well-meant but unwanted sympathy, I said yes.

Then, after breakfast, the scene repeated itself: Roger said he had an errand, Tamar announced that she was coming with him, and Roger invited me. Which is how we all ended up at George and Kit's.

"What is it in our nature that makes us want to buy stuff?" Tamar was examining a folding plastic water bowl for dogs. "Which came first, the desire to buy or the desire to create? I did not know I needed one of these, but now, I feel I absolutely do." She and I each carried shopping baskets.

"You don't have a dog," Roger said.

"That is precisely my point."

"I'm not sure I'd call this creating, exactly." Roger was holding up a set of four zippered fleece boots. "Not even Sophie would be caught dead in these."

"They're very useful if you live in a city. Keeps the salt off their paws. Besides, they're adorable. How much are they?" Tamar tried to check the tag.

Roger held the booties above his head, out of her reach. "Tamar, step away from the dog accessories and admit you have a problem."

Tamar glared and then tickled his ribs. He surrendered the boots.

Next he held up a pair of moose antlers designed to fit on a dog's head and frowned.

"People who buy those shouldn't be allowed to own dogs," she proffered. He nodded in agreement.

She then turned to me, mouthed, *Love them!* and grinned. I remained silent, still smarting from her comments at the footbridge.

We wandered past a display of Sorel boots and another of Smartwool socks, which I stopped to examine. I had no idea where I'd packed my own socks.

"Joy, please tell me that you do not own any footwear for which these socks would be even remotely appropriate." Tamar tried to tug me away.

"Have you ever tried them? Warm but thin." I dropped two pairs in my basket.

She shrugged and moved on. "I'm just saying, cave people didn't buy stuff and they got along fine. How come we now have this need to buy things?" Tamar was surveying a rack of kitchen gadgets.

"They probably traded," I said. "Think acquire, rather than buy. It's connected to survival. The more meat and saber-toothed tiger skins you had, the more likely you were to make it through the winter."

"Now this . . ." Tamar held up a plastic gadget with a smiling face designed to remove pits from cherries. "Had these been around, no self-respecting cavewoman would have been without one."

"Can't see how that's connected to survival," Roger said.

"I still want one, though," Tamar said.

"Me, too," I agreed, and we each added one to our shopping basket.

"There you have it," Roger said. "Men need *one* thing: women. Women need"—he looked at the items in our baskets—"or, want . . . lots of things, probably to make themselves attractive to men. And men put up with it to get some nookie."

We both looked at our brother.

"That's caveman for sex."

"No, Roger, that's junior high for sex," Tamar said.

"Yup. It's about survival of the species, baby." Roger had moved over to a display of silk scarves beside the walnut-and-brass cash register that had been in the store for probably a hundred years, and now stood proud, if anachronistic, beside an electronic barcode scanner and a credit card processor. It looked like a coastal schooner docked beside two sleek cigarette boats. "It'll go when I go," Kit told anyone who dared ask. Roger selected a scarf in muted purples and pinks, which he bunched awkwardly in his big hands, like a novice magician trying to make it disappear.

"Who's that for?" Tamar asked, clearly suspicious.

"What?" After a brief hesitation, Roger added, "Mom."

"Not her colors." From Tamar's tone, I knew she'd seen through the lie as well as I had. Tamar studied Roger for a moment, then turned and moved down the aisle, stopping in front of an array of watches with bright pink silicone wristbands. "Oh, these are cute. Roger, come here. Should I get them for the twins?"

But Roger didn't move or answer. He'd pulled his wallet from his pocket and was paying for the scarf.

"Can they tell time?" I asked her. "These aren't digital." Very few eight-year-olds can tell time these days, although I doubted my sister knew that.

"Time they learned if they don't," she snapped, and dropped two of them in her basket.

"Ladies, I'm going to leave you and your acquisitive natures to do what you do best," Roger called from the door. He was holding a brown paper bag.

"Where are you going? I'll come." Tamar started down the aisle toward him.

"No. I've got . . ." Roger inched out the door. "You two go on back to the inn. I won't be long."

"Are you going to see Loraine?" Tamar's voice was hard.

Roger hesitated, looked at his twin, and said, "Do me a favor?"

Tamar nodded, eager, vulnerable.

"Buy two different color watches." Then he stepped out of the store, and the door closed behind him.

I recognized her expression. But then, I know well what it's like to be shut out.

Grace didn't have enough rolled oats for the muffin batter, so she borrowed some of Tamar's granola and added a handful of chopped walnuts. She spooned the lumpy batter into muffin tins, inserting chocolate chips into the tops of one-third of them for the twins and Roger. She slid the pan into the oven and wiped her batter-covered hands on her front, only then realizing that she was not wearing an apron. "Damn."

A little later, she heard voices coming up the drive. Then the back door opened and shut, and footsteps—but not enough footsteps, it seemed to Grace—headed into the kitchen. "How was it?" she asked as the twins entered, followed by Gar.

That wasn't what Grace wanted to ask. What she wanted to ask was, *Why the hell didn't you wake me!?* But she couldn't, not in front of the twins. They would be excited from their adventure and want to tell her all about it: who'd gone the farthest, who'd jumped the highest, who'd made the biggest splash, all in an effort to compensate for the fear they'd felt before jumping. She wondered whether Joy had done it this year.

Speaking of which, where was Joy? Where were Tamar and Roger? She looked at her husband. "I was *surprised* to find that you went without me."

"I'm sorry, Short. You were so sound asleep. And last night, when I mentioned it, you groaned like it was the very last thing you wanted to do." He sounded both contrite and defensive. "I know you didn't get much sleep. Waiting up?"

She nodded. "I would have loved to go. I was just . . ." What was the use in protesting now? They could still have breakfast together, and a picnic lunch at Sand Beach. "Where are the kids?"

Grace caught a whiff of something burning. The strata. She searched for her pot holders, which were not in their accustomed drawer, found a dishcloth, and opened the oven. She pulled out the casserole, a little too brown but thankfully not burned, and reset the timer for the muffins.

Gar glanced at the dish now resting on the counter. "They went to the Harbor Gawker for breakfast."

"I made a strata." It was an accusation.

After an awkward pause, Gar said, "It looks delicious. I'd love some."

Grace caught a glimpse of herself in the small mirror hanging beside the phone: her robe batter-smeared, her hair frizzy and unnaturally brown, her eyes underscored by dark circles. "Why didn't you girls go with them?"

"We wanted pancakes," said the twins.

"The Gawker has pancakes." She removed the muffins from the oven.

"Not with chocolate chips," Hal said.

"Made into faces," Nat added.

"How about a nice oatmeal chocolate chip muffin?" Grace asked.

The girls' expressions clouded as they gazed in defiance at the lumpy muffins, bits of granola erupting from their tops. They were close to tears. Only then did Grace notice that the girls' hair was dry. Apparently they hadn't jumped. She remembered many tearful mornings for Joy as her younger siblings crowed about their exciting rides beneath the bridge. "Chocolate chip pancakes, coming right up."

The telephone rang, and Gar answered it. Grace listened as she mixed the batter and poured it onto the griddle, studding the circles with chocolate chip eyes, noses, and mouths. The twins supervised. "I want mine frowning," said Hal.

"Me, too," Nat said. Grace shifted the chips into frowns.

"Uh-huh. Yup. Okay. Sure," Gar was saying. "No, I'm sure they'll be fine. No problem, Frank."

"Who was that?" Grace asked.

"Frank Gilley from the florist. They couldn't get blue hydrangeas, so they're sending something else. What's that on your robe?"

"Did he happen to mention what?"

"Yes, but I didn't catch it." Gar cut himself a piece of strata, poured a cup of coffee, and sat down at the table. The telephone rang again.

Gar listened for a moment. "Oh."

Grace did not like his tone.

"I'm very sorry to hear that. Is there—I see. Same time? And there's no one—" He listened another moment. Grace could hear the voice on the other end, but she couldn't make out the words. "Yes, I guess we'll have to do that." He jotted a name down on a pad of paper. "Thanks, Kathy. Give Bill our best wishes for a speedy recovery."

This did not sound good. Grace lowered herself into a chair and waited.

"That was Kathy Barlow. Bill had a heart attack last night."

Grace gasped.

"He's okay. But she's over at the hospital in Rockland with him and thinks she may not be able to do the service tomorrow. She thinks we maybe should call someone else just to be safe. She thought the Congregational minister might be free, but Jenny Carver's getting married around the same time, and Kathy thinks he's doing that, which leaves the Episcopal priest . . ." Gar trailed off. "Sorry, dear. Want me to make some calls?"

Just then, a knock sounded at the door. Gar grabbed his coffee and headed to the back hall to answer it.

"That'll be the tables and chairs," Grace said. She needed to shower, wash her hair, get dressed; she had so much to do today. The twins looked up from their empty plates as she started out of the room. "Could we have another?" they asked in unison.

Eleanor Findley, her hair freshly curled and lacquered, appeared beside Roger on the sidewalk. The Findleys had lived next door to the Littles for years. "Nice to see you," she said. "When did you get back? You're here for your grandmother's service, of course. I certainly hope the weather cooperates. Grace told me she plans to hold it outside. It's a lovely setting you all have over there, but risky this time of year. Well, any time of year, really. Although I suppose we could just move inside if it looks like rain. She told me she doesn't have a long service planned?" She looked to him for confirmation.

Roger realized that he had no idea what his mother had planned. "No, not too long," he said. "Are you and Jim staying here for the winter?"

"Heavens no. Heading to Vero next month. I used to love winters up here. Not anymore. Please give your mother my regards. Tell her if she needs anything to give me a call. Otherwise we'll see you tomorrow. Best to your sisters." Roger promised he'd deliver the message, although he couldn't imagine his mother needing any help. No one was more capable than she. Eleanor waved as she headed off in the direction of Little Island.

Roger glanced up to the window of A Cut Above. Irrationally, he hadn't figured on there being customers in the salon. What were the chances of running into someone he knew? Pretty good, actually. But he hadn't wanted to call. He was more persuasive in person. Irresistible, some said. Opening the paper bag, he examined the scarf he'd bought at George and Kit's. Would Loraine like it? Maybe he should give it to his mother instead. She did seem a little on edge this weekend. He made a mental note to offer to help with the cooking.

Across the harbor, Walter Fifield's crew was unloading the boat, hosing down the decks, and coiling lines. A pyramid of lobster traps rose from the dock. He had quite an operation over there, Roger observed, and wondered whether he'd like a partner to handle marketing and distribution. Didn't sound like his dad was in any hurry to give up the inn, and it was obvious to Roger, from their short visit the day before in the tool shed, that he still didn't trust Roger enough to turn it over to him anyway. Couldn't really blame him. Even without the crash, Roger had frayed his father's trust to a few thin threads.

If Wally didn't need him, maybe he could open a sporting goods store—he glanced in the window of George and Kit's: they didn't sell bicycles or kayaks . . . The bell at the community church rang ten times. He looked back up at the salon window. Would Loraine be happy to see him? His fantasy of the night before now seemed childish and improbable. But he knew she was "the one," knew it the moment they'd met so many years earlier. He tucked the bag with the scarf under his arm and headed through the doorway and up the stairs.

Loraine was bent over a sink washing someone's hair: Mrs. Albright, the retired postmistress. And there was Mrs. Entweiler, Roger's high school English teacher, sitting under a dryer, paging through a magazine. She looked up, smiled, and returned to her reading. There was no chance she didn't recognize him, and an equally good one that she didn't want to acknowledge him. She was one person who'd remained resistant to Roger's charm and powers of persuasion. So much for not running into anyone he knew.

Loraine was talking in low tones to Mrs. Albright. Roger stood there, undecided and uncomfortable. She looked good. Better even than he remembered. She'd put on weight, but who hadn't since high school, other than Tamar.

"Roger." Loraine had spotted him. She didn't sound completely surprised—his mother would have told her he was in town—but did she sound at least pleased? Not really. He wondered what else his mother might have told her.

He smiled and stood awkwardly by a rack of plastic shampoo bottles, clutching the bag containing the scarf, feeling oversized and undergroomed, still dressed in the clothes he'd worn for the run and dip, unshaved, his hair salt-caked. He should have gone home and cleaned up. Too late now. Should he walk over to her? Talking over Mrs. Albright's reclining body didn't seem appropriate. Besides, Mrs. Entweiler was sitting only a few feet away. True, the whirring of the hair dryer would make it difficult to hear, but Roger remembered well her acute hearing, always calling him out when he whispered to

Walter at the back of the room. And there was that time, when the classroom floor had been recently waxed, when he, Walter, and a few of their buddies inched their desks closer and closer to the door, very subtly, just to see if she'd notice. It took them all period. Just as they reached the door, Mrs. Entweiler, without even turning from the board where she was writing examples of misplaced modifiers, intoned, "Gentlemen, as long as you're that close to the principal's office, you may continue along there." They collected their books and started to stand, when she added. "No, no, at your desks, please. And you will write two hundred words by tomorrow on setting and achieving goals."

Loraine levered Mrs. Albright up to a sitting position and pointed her to a chair in front of the wide mirror. The old postmistress's thin white hair lay wet and close to her head, exposing patches of pink scalp, making her look frail and vulnerable. Roger remembered the fuss she would make over him and his sisters whenever they went into the post office with their mother. One time she gave them each a little book in which to paste exotic stamps. Roger lost his, but Joy dutifully filled hers and won a trip to a convention in Augusta, where she met the governor. Roger was pretty sure Tamar was as jealous as he was of Joy's trip. To this day he didn't know how Joy had gotten all those stamps. She was quite remarkable, his older sister.

Mrs. Albright glanced in Roger's direction but didn't acknowledge him—Roger could see her glasses dangling from a chain around her neck—as she shuffled to the other chair, her neck and shoulders swaddled in towels.

Roger stepped across to the sink, which Loraine was now rinsing. Without looking at him, she stepped into a back room. He followed her into the narrow space, where he watched her select bottles from a row on the shelf and measure their contents into a plastic dish. He caught a whiff of her scent, spicy and sweet, and saw her pulse beat in her neck as she whipped the mixture with a tiny whisk.

"This isn't a good time, Roger," she said.

"Could we talk later?"

She shrugged and looked at him. "Why?" She shifted her glance out to Mrs. Albright, who had put on her glasses and was now openly watching the two of them. "Just a minute, Mrs. A."

"Is that Roger Little?" Mrs. Albright called.

"Yes, it is, Mrs. Albright. How are you?" He stepped back into the salon.

"Getting by."

Roger said nothing, just smiled. *Getting by.* *Is that what everyone works so hard their whole lives for? Jesus.* Loraine was looking at him. *Why* did *he want to talk?* Because he didn't want to sit in a barbershop fifty years from now, a lonely old man, and boast to someone that he was "getting by." Because the news about her divorce was too big to go unacknowledged. Because he'd been waiting twenty years for her to be available. He hoped she'd understand this without him having to spell it out.

"I'll be done at two thirty," she said. "I could meet you at the Flying Bridge."

Not as private as he hoped, but at least she'd agreed to meet him. He wanted to draw her back into that tiny space and press her up against the bottles with their mysterious contents and kiss her, hard.

"I got something for you." He put the brown paper bag on the desk on his way out. "I'll see you later."

JOY

An hour later, Roger was still not back. As I watched my sister power through television channels with the remote control, I started to feel sorry for her. I shared with her how I'd sat at my kitchen table the day before, feeling alone and pointless without my child, how I'd started packing, and then just kept going, needing to claim my life and move away from the sadness. I didn't mention the cutting, of course. That I kept private, like a talisman, to ward off the feelings of inadequacy and isolation I always experienced when with my family. So far, simply pressing a fingernail into the cut was sufficient to keep the wound open and me focused in the present rather than dwelling on the past. Necessary, because there wasn't enough present for me in my family to override our past. I had a pair of fingernail scissors in my room, if something sharper was needed.

Tee continued to gaze at the television as I spoke, punching past golf, football, baseball, hockey, and basketball games, and didn't offer a response.

I should have known better than to expect one from her. "Wait," I said. "Get a score for last night's Red Sox game. Shoot. Okay, move on."

We watched baby otters on Animal Planet, looking like furry corks, learning to swim in wading pools at a California research facility. We watched a dog food ad.

"I'd like to work for dogs," I said.

"I'm sorry, what? Work for dogs? Be easier than working for men, I can tell you."

"No, I mean, on behalf of dogs. Mom said that her aunt Corintha does that. Rescues Great Danes." Tamar only shrugged. She landed on HGTV. "Oh, *Divine Design*," I said. "I love her.

Look, see how she puts everything in that beautiful box? I'd like that in my house. A beautiful box in each room with the fabrics and woods and colors that Candice recommends."

Tamar moved on to a show featuring a group of young people sharing a house. "Reality TV is nothing but sanctioned voyeurism," she said. "I think it should be outlawed." We watched the contestants argue.

"Those people should hire Candice to redecorate their house," I suggested. "They'd probably get along better."

Tamar laughed and flipped through more channels, then returned to HGTV. "I like what she's doing as a light fixture. Brilliant, one could say."

I smiled. "I'd take down that wallpaper and paint. Reupholster in blues and yellows with orange accents—"

"Orange? Be serious. Orange looks like it's made up of bits all the other colors didn't want. It's so neon. Like it's trying too hard to be noticed. No orange."

"Okay, then. What about red?"

"Red is great." Tamar was nodding. She looked at me. "They say that a person's level of happiness is directly proportional to the amount of red in their house."

"Really?" I couldn't think of a single speck of red in mine.

"That's what a friend of mine says, and she's pretty happy."

We chatted some more as the TV demolition crew pulled down a wall, encountered an unanticipated problem, conferred. Candice beamed through it all, unflappable.

I heard the kitchen door open and Roger call out, "Hello?"

Tamar launched herself off the couch, tossing me the remote as she headed toward the kitchen.

* * *

Grace stood at the registration desk planning the menu for Saturday. She felt out of sorts and wished she could go sit in her garden, but Gar had turned on a sprinkler to water the sod. Who needed a church with its endless rummage sales and pot pie suppers to feel close to God? All Grace needed was to study the unfolding pink petals and bright yellow stamen of a rose, or to watch a bumblebee, fat and coated with orange pollen, climb inside the bell of a foxglove and rumble contentedly as it collected nectar. But now, even her garden seemed foreign, no longer a refuge.

Besides, she still had all the food to make for the service. She should probably skip the picnic at Sand Beach and send the others on without her. Let them have the fun. *Why not call a caterer as Gar had suggested?* Because she wanted to cook one final meal for her mother to make up for all the meals she hadn't cooked for her, all the meals she would never be able to cook for her, all the little niceties that she'd skipped because she was too busy.

She sighed and gazed across the entryway, through the dining room, to the window overlooking the harbor. The ferry was making its way out into the reach. Grace longed to be on it, to be heading . . . somewhere. Anywhere. She felt stuck, like when the tide, that tight waistband encircling the island, had ebbed, leaving rocks and piers standing with barnacles exposed, lobster boats on their sides on the rocky, seaweed-covered bottom as though they'd been flung there. Hard aground.

She returned to her ruminations. She could serve the cookies that Joy and the twins had finally made—not exactly what she'd had in mind, but certainly fun. Then she'd serve smoked salmon with capers and chopped egg. As she was writing *boil eggs* and *French bread* on her list, she heard the *clickety-clack* of Sophie's nails. Nearly blind and quite deaf, Sophie had trouble locating people these days. *Click, clickety, clack,* she was heading toward Grace. Grace poked her head out from behind the reception desk. "Sophie," she called. *Clickety, clickety, click.* Grace waved her arms, trying to get Sophie's attention. *Click, click*—Sophie spotted Grace and limped over. "Hi, there. Did you have good snoozers?" Grace asked, scratching Sophie's ears. "Let's go out and do some business."

Sophie followed Grace across the entryway, through the dining room, and out onto the porch. Gar and the sprinkler had disappeared, so Grace carried her down the steps. Once down, Sophie trotted to the center of the decidedly damp sod and squatted. Grace frowned. She hoped the spot wouldn't turn brown before tomorrow.

The day was gorgeous, perfect for a picnic. Clear sky, bright sunshine, a light breeze out of the southwest, although it could change in a minute, Grace knew. *Could tomorrow possibly be as nice?* She would ask Gar for the forecast. Sophie was hunched at the far edge of the lawn now, where it was less soft and marshy. Grace motioned to her. "Come on, sweet pea, let's go check on Roger." She picked Sophie up and carried her into the house, planting a noisy kiss on the top of her head before setting her down. Sophie clickety-clacked across the wood floor as she followed Grace into the kitchen.

Roger greeted Grace with a mini-carrot wearing a turban of hummus. *Delicious.* She'd forgotten to eat breakfast in all the commotion. The uneaten strata sat on the kitchen table. Grace cut herself a slice.

"Want that warmed?" Roger asked.

It wasn't a difficult question, but it stumped her all the same. She stood frozen: *like a deer on the highway*, she thought. He seemed to understand and put the plate in the microwave without waiting for her response. "Sit," he ordered, and went back to pasting together sandwiches. "I've got hummus, turkey, cheese, chips, pickles, napkins, lemonade, and cookies. What else do we need?"

Grace smiled at Roger. He looked so earnest and strangely at home in the kitchen. He looked happy in a way Grace hadn't seen him in years. Hopeful, she might have said. Grace immediately wondered whether Roger's ebullience might not be natural, wondered whether he was high. She hated herself for even thinking such a thing. Roger was heating up another piece of strata and then sat across the table from her. "Can I ask you something?" he said.

JOY

Roger and Mom stopped talking as soon as we entered the kitchen. Tamar looked from one to the other, then sat down beside Roger and ate his last bite of strata. "You two look like the proverbial canary with feathers coming out of its beak." Tamar didn't like others, especially Roger, having secrets from her.

"That would be the proverbial *cat* with the canary feathers," Roger corrected. "The canary wouldn't have its own feathers—"

"Whatever. You know what I meant," she snapped.

"Yes, but only because I lived with you and Mom for so long."

"You didn't answer my question."

"That's because you didn't ask one, counselor." Roger took the two plates to the sink.

"Joy and I are going to pick blueberries. Want to come?" she said in response.

"I'm going to Sand Beach."

"I thought we'd all go," Mom said. "Wouldn't that be fun?"

"I'm still full from breakfast. Besides, you said you needed blueberries." Tamar sounded testy. She looked at Roger. "What are you doing this afternoon? We could go out in the *Kestrel*."

"I could really use some help getting ready for tomorrow, Tee," Mom said, too loudly, too quickly. "Maybe you and Joy could make the cobbler."

I knew she was covering for Roger and, apparently, so did Tamar, who wouldn't look at Roger as she pushed herself up from the table and headed for the door. It was just as well. If she'd glanced in his direction, she would have seen him mouth *Thank you* to our mother.

I shifted a bag of Dansko clogs from the front of the Prius to the back, and Tamar took a seat. "Clogs?"

"They're comfortable," I said. "A lot of shoes hurt my back."

"All I said was *clogs*. The leopard-print ones are actually kind of cute."

The tide was out. Dinghies, overturned on the beach, lay many yards from the water's edge. We crossed the causeway and followed the road leading to Blueberry Hill. It was narrow and winding, and I realized it would take us right past the scene of the crash. I glanced over at Tamar, but she was running her thumb across the face of her phone.

The EMTs had bundled Bonnie onto a stretcher that night, although she was already dead. Tamar, covered in blood, lay in Roger's arms as the EMTs tended to her. They said she needed surgery, loaded her onto a stretcher, and then turned their attention to Roger, who had a dislocated shoulder. The sound he made when Punch Gibbons, also the assistant football coach, popped it back into place haunted my dreams for years. I watched as Roger handed the keys to the patrolman and gave a statement. He'd been drinking, of course, but he had the details of the accident down pat.

I looked at Tamar as we passed the site. But she was still busy with her phone and didn't seem even to notice where we were. Someone had tacked a white cross onto the tree right after the accident, and it was still there. Today, there were fresh flowers beneath it.

Several miles down the road, I pulled into a small lot and parked. Tamar didn't move as I retrieved the empty gallon jugs from the back of the car, their tops severed and strings threaded through holes on each side to form a loop for two-handed picking. I realized I'd forgotten to bring anything to pour the berries into and so dug around until I found a basket filled with pens, pads, and Post-its. These I dumped into the box of clogs. "Are you coming?" I asked as I shut the tailgate.

"I'll meet you up there. Some . . . stuff is happening. At work." She didn't look up as she spoke.

I headed up the trail alone, passing through a fern brake, the bowed fronds slightly yellowed. Sunlight filtered through the branches, giving the woods the feel of a cathedral. I broke off a bit of fern and held it to my nose. It smelled sweetly of hay. Bayberries grew in a stand of dead firs, blown down in some long-ago storm, their trunks and branches grayed and brittle. Aging is a process of desiccation, I thought, as I waded through the ferns and plucked a few bayberry leaves, dropping them into the basket along with the yellowed fronds and a bit of birch bark, papery and white. The trail was padded with fallen needles that filled the air with the scent of balsam as I walked. Bonnie and I used to come here to pick berries every summer. Smiling at the memory, I scooped up some needles, added them to the fern, bark, and bayberry, spied some reindeer moss growing on a large boulder, and put that in as well. A single bright red maple leaf lay on the trail ahead of me. I looked around for the parent tree but saw none and added the leaf to the basket. As I climbed, I gathered a few balsam cones, a russet oak leaf, and, near the top, a stem of goldenrod.

From the top of Blueberry Hill I could see Little Island, the inn looking trim and tiny. The ferry was making its way back to Rockland and, in the distance, the white sails of a coastal schooner slipped silently by. The scattering of little islands in Penobscot Bay looked like the mountaintops they'd once been. If the oceans did rise, as scientists were predicting, which ones would be left? I sat down on a lichen-covered rock and tipped my face to the sun.

Twenty minutes later, Tamar appeared. "No blueberries?" She sat down next to me on the ground.

"No, but this is my living room." I pointed into the basket at a cluster of bay leaf, some burgundy-tipped blueberry leaves, and a few stalks of dried grass. "Here's the bedroom." I indicated the russet oak leaf and bit of reindeer moss. "The kitchen will be birch bark and goldenrod. And the dining room is ferns, cones, and pine needles."

"Where's the maple leaf going?"

"Wherever I want it."

"I like it. I think you have a gift. Too bad you don't have a house."

I felt like I'd been punched.

"I'm kidding. Seriously, Jo-jo, you are not the kind of woman who walks out on her family. You wear clogs and wool socks."

"What does that mean?"

"It means you are practical and prefer comfort to appearance. Redecorating your house is exactly what you need to do. And, your box of items notwithstanding, I'm speaking metaphorically here. You need to find meaningful work. Your kid is gone now. Celebrate! Think of the possibilities!"

"Baseball umpire, explosives expert, hired assassin?" I offered, thinking of my list from the day before.

"Hm." Tamar gave these ideas mock consideration. "Who crossed you?"

I shrugged. "It's not that. They're just so . . . competent. And they seem to be busy all the time."

"Have an affair. That will keep you busy."

"What?"

"Mom had one." Tamar tossed this out casually, as though we were discussing Mom's recent permanent.

"She did not."

"No, actually, she did. After Abigail died. Abby. I think we would have called her Abby, don't you?"

There probably would have been no you to call her anything, I thought. Daddy and Mom would have stopped at two children, I was certain of it. "Why would you even think that?"

"Because I found a card. His name was Glen. Doesn't sound like the name of a lover, does it? More like a car mechanic. Maybe he *was* her car mechanic . . ."

"What did it say?" I asked, in spite of myself. I didn't want to know. It seemed wrong, too private, an invasion, like seeing someone naked without their knowing.

"The card—a postcard, so not terribly private—said 'Thinking, smiling, of you.'"

"Oh, for heaven's sake. That could mean anything. Glen could be anyone. Even a woman. Glenn Close?"

"Not a woman's handwriting. Dated July 1969. Salutation: *Dearest Grace.*"

Around us, insects hummed loudly in the crackling dry grass, and I sat stupefied and furious with my sister for having this information, wondering how long she'd known, whether she'd told Roger or Daniel. *Or Daddy?* I was even angrier with my mother for betraying him.

Tamar finally stood. "What do you love doing and are good at?"

"What?"

"Your career. What do you love doing and are good at?"

I did not have to think about this. "Raising children."

"Then have another one."

I felt a glimmer of hope, then a realization that was as startling and brilliant as that first glimpse of orange in the morning sky. I looked up at my sister and my face must have said it all.

"Again, kidding. You're forty, for God sakes. If you want to be around kids, become a teacher." Tamar added a small stone to the kitchen items in my basket. "Granite countertops. Gotta have them."

I stared down at my assemblage of twigs and bark and moss, and counted my breaths as Dr. Kilsaro had taught me: three counts in, then three counts out, as my sister clambered off the rock and headed down the hill. After twenty slow breaths, I followed.

· Chapter Fifteen ·

Grace, Gar, Roger, and the twins followed the narrow lane to Sand Beach. They could see, just offshore, Spectacle Island, its granite boulders stained white by gulls and topped with bits of grass and a few stunted bayberry bushes. The twins removed their sneakers and trotted in the sand after Roger to peer into a tidal pool stranded by the retreating tide, while Grace spread out an old woolen blanket and Gar set up camp chairs. The sun highlighted the rigid ripples in the wet sand. The twins were poking at something with a stick, while Roger supervised. Grace wished that Joy were with them. She had loved those tiny, bounded worlds of the tide pools.

Grace missed the closeness she'd once shared with her eldest daughter. But, like Roger's car, Joy—and their relationship—had been altered by the crash for some reason Grace could never adequately explain. Despite repairs, the alignment was off, the tires wore unevenly, and what she thought of as Joy's steering wheel always pulled a little to the left.

After a bit, the twins and Roger came up, and the girls

settled themselves into a single chair, while Roger stretched out on the blanket. Gar, who loved to tell stories, now began the one of the long-ago shipwreck just off Spectacle Island. It was a tale he'd told often, and it had grown quite robust over the years. "When my granddad was young, there was a terrible shipwreck right off this beach," he began. "November first, 1906." He gazed out toward the bay.

Roger closed his eyes, and Grace could see a slight smile play across his face. They'd both heard this story many times; with each telling the winds grew stronger, the waves and passenger count higher, the situation more dire.

"Few of the passengers could swim," Gar intoned. "And, of course the water was freezing. One passenger was just a baby. His mother, so desperate to save him, wrapped him in blankets and coats and dropped him over the side.

Grace's thoughts drifted to Sammy and his "fall." She tried to imagine what had befallen him and how her mother had managed to cope with his death with no family nearby to lean on. The one person available to her was perhaps the one who'd caused it.

"My granddad, neighbors, houseguests, and half the men of East Haven came down to the beach with lanterns, trying to help," Gar was saying. "The men had only one boat, which they tried to launch, but every time they set out, a wave sent the boat, and everyone in it, right back onto the beach." Gar was warming to his topic and his voice rose. "They could hear the passengers crying for help, but there was nothing they could do."

"Gar," Grace said, looking at the twins' rapt expressions.

But he evidently didn't hear her. "A few made it up onto Spectacle and clung there, huddled together, until morning, when the tide was low. A miracle, considering the seas were breaking right over its top. Those who tried to swim to shore were carried out by the current."

"Gar," Grace said, louder this time.

But Gar was now quite caught up in his tale and gazing out toward Spectacle, as though searching for survivors. "The ship finally broke up completely. Those who stayed on board were lost. Bodies were still washing up weeks later. They found some, or parts of some, as far away as Matinicus—"

"Gar!"

"Yes, dear?" Gar turned, startled. The twins were staring at him, wide-eyed.

"Did the baby live?" Hal asked.

Gar looked as though he'd completely forgotten who his audience was. "You know, I don't remember," he said. "Probably."

"Yes," Roger said. "Don't you remember, Dad? He was in some sort of a waterproof basket, or, no, it was a little barrel if I remember your story correctly. All tarred and watertight. It floated right up onto the beach. That's what you told me. Not a scratch on him. And, when the baby grew up, he became a lighthouse keeper and rescued many, many other shipwrecked people."

"Is that the boat on Silver Beach?" the twins asked. "The one where everybody died?"

"No, that's a different boat," Roger said.

"Did anyone die in that one?" They sounded eager.

"Not one." Roger propped himself up on an elbow. "They sort of drifted onto the beach and everyone got out and had a nice picnic. Then they just decided to leave the boat there."

Grace dug into the basket. "Are you girls ready for lunch?"

Gar looked out across the mud flats. "Hurry and eat, girls. The tide's low enough for us to walk out to Spectacle."

"I'm going to look for body parts," Nat said.

"Me, too," Hal added, as she bit into her half of the sandwich. "Can we have chips?"

Grace put the picnic basket in the back hall beside the empty blueberry buckets. She surveyed the mess in her kitchen, looked around for berries, found none. It was now nearly four o'clock. What was she making for supper? She checked her list. Nothing, apparently. Sophie was curled up on her bed, in the throes of a dream, legs twitching, the tip of her tongue peeking out. "Just an indication of how soundly she's sleeping," the vet told Grace. "It happens with age." Does anything good happen with age, Grace wondered? Wisdom, she supposed, but to what end? Just as you have a good store of knowledge, you start losing the ability to access it. Too bad you can't transfer memories and knowledge as easily as computer files. Was Gar's forgetfulness the start of something serious or, as he'd assured her, just his wiring starting to wear out?

She shivered, although the kitchen was not cold. In winter out on Little Island, as the lawn went white with frost, and ice turned branches into prisms, cold drafts seeped in through the spaces beneath the windows and doors, seeking refuge. Try as she might, Grace could never quite get warm; days were short as the sun made its shallow arc across the sky. Now, she had a premonition of an ill wind, a sense that things were breaking loose and about to drift away. She filled the dishwasher and the dish drainer, wishing Roger would come in. She needed some company.

The back door banged open. *Speak of the devil.* She could tell it was Roger from the footsteps. "Hello," she sang out, eager to hear how things had gone with Loraine, eager for another mother-son chat. "How did it—?"

He stormed into the kitchen with his leg bleeding and his hands and face smeared with mud and grass. "What the hell is a pipe doing sticking up in the middle of the lawn?" he shouted.

Grace felt herself retreat, fear pulling her away like the tide draining the harbor. *Her father, coming home after work— late—barging into the kitchen, hollering for her mother. Joan telling her to hide.* She wanted to reach out and comfort Roger, but she remained pinned to the sink.

"I mean, why the hell would Dad leave something like that?" Blood ran down his leg. "Christ, he thinks *I'm* the ir-responsible one." The gash, Grace could see, was not serious. No need for a run to the East Haven clinic, or, worse yet, as they'd done the night of the crash, a full-throttled flight across Penobscot Bay to the medical center in Rockland.

Roger tore off a fistful of paper towel and held it to his shin. He looked up at his mother, still clinging to the sink. "How about a fucking Band-Aid?"

Grace grabbed a dish towel from the counter, dampened it, and handed it to Roger.

"Fuck."

She thought about admonishing him, thought better of it, and went instead for the first aid kit. Apparently the conversa-tion with Loraine hadn't gone well.

Tamar rushed into the kitchen. "Oh, my God! What hap-pened?" She knelt beside her brother.

"I tripped over a goddamned pipe sticking up out of the lawn."

"The bird feeder." Gar said, coming in with Joy. "Bear knocked it over."

"Well, why the fuck—"

"Roger, please. Your language," Gar snapped. "The twins."

"Where are the twins?" Tamar asked, but no one seemed to hear her. She'd seen them when she got back from blueberry picking, and they'd twittered on about Gar's famous shipwreck story. They seemed quite captivated, although Tamar was only half listening. She'd heard that story a hundred times and had more important things on her mind.

"—didn't you paint it red, or tie some flagging onto it, or cap it, for chrissake?" Roger finished.

"I planned to. Just . . . hadn't got around to it. Didn't imagine anyone would be . . ." Gar trailed off. *What was there to say, really?* Didn't imagine anyone would be wandering across the yard, drunk, as he assumed Roger was now. They'd been here before. Many times. Roger always coalesced the family around some crisis. This was what they did best, the Littles. They all knew their roles: Grace tended to the physical wound; Tamar supported Roger; Joy drifted to the edges and watched. And Gar? What was his role? To pay for the damages, the hospital bills, the insurance premiums. All he could do for poor Maisie Day was to make sure the family kept her in their thoughts, stopped in often, and offered help. It always seemed like much too little and much, much too late. Perhaps this weekend's crisis was over. If so, Gar concluded, it had been relatively minor. Tomorrow he would buy a can of bright red paint for the end of the pole. He'd meant to do it today and had simply . . . forgotten.

"Well, you imagined wrong." Roger was dabbing at his leg

with the dish towel, his voice calmer. His anger, like a summer storm, was ferocious, unexpected, and brief.

Grace returned with peroxide, antiseptic, and bandages. She still had a good supply on hand.

"You must have taken quite a tumble," Tamar said, bending in to wipe a splotch of mud from Roger's face with her fingers. "Where've you been, anyway?"

"I did, thanks for your concern. Ass over teakettle." He laughed. "Your lawn is really wet. Is that sod?" Grace handed him two Tylenol. He shook his head. "I've got some stuff upstairs, Mom."

"I'll get it for you." Joy started out of the room.

Tamar grabbed her sister's arm. "I'll go. I know right where it is."

SEPTEMBER 9, 1991

It was the day of the annual quarry party. Although Loraine had broken up with Roger two weeks earlier, now she badly wanted to see him. She stopped on the causeway, glanced up toward the inn, turned around, stared down at the water for a bit, then turned and started again for Little Island. Someone was sitting in an Adirondack chair, watching her as she disappeared into the trees, and then reappeared where Roger's dad had carved the inn's lawn out of wild raspberries, jewelweed, and goldenrod.

It couldn't be Roger, she knew. He rarely sat still and certainly would have walked (or run) over to greet her. Besides, he didn't spend much time at his folks' inn. She wiped her eyes with the back of her hand and started across the lawn.

It was probably a guest sitting there. Or maybe Joy. That would be good, Loraine thought, better than seeing Roger right away. But as Loraine drew closer, she recognized the person in the chair. It was Tamar, who stood and waved her over.

· Chapter Sixteen ·

Tamar sat on the edge of Roger's unmade bed. They'd been on the island a full day, and this was the first time she'd been in his room. *What a child he was.* His sneakers, their laces still tied, were tumbled beside the wing chair, his jeans draped over the back. A shirt, still slightly damp and sweaty from the morning's run, lay in a pile on the floor. She pressed her face onto his pillow and breathed in. When they were little, they used to steal into each other's room every night, snuggle into bed together, and tell each other secrets. If they didn't have any, they'd make some up, the more outrageous the better, trying not to giggle so loudly that their mother would come in and separate them. Although her evictions, when they came, never stuck. In high school, they'd sneak out together after their parents had turned off all the lights and go down to Sand Beach, or out to the quarry on East Haven, and sit around with friends. That had all ended when Roger fell in love with Loraine.

Beside Roger's bed was the bottle of Vicodin. She picked it up. He was in pain, sure, but that wasn't why he wanted the painkiller. She didn't know where he'd gone last night, but today clearly he'd been to see Loraine, and obviously it hadn't gone well. Part of her felt sorry for him. She knew, from the way he paused slightly before saying Loraine's name, a little color coming into his face, how deeply he cared for her. And she wanted him to be happy, right? Of course she did. *But, really, was Loraine the only—or even the right—woman for him?* Tamar hadn't thought so twenty years ago, and she didn't think so now. Just as well his old love hadn't greeted him with open arms today. Tamar was sure Roger had said too much, too soon. That was Roger; he wore his feelings like Cub Scout achievement badges stitched onto his shirt. He should have confided in Tamar so she could coach him. But if he had, what would her advice have been? *Don't go.*

She tipped one of the tablets into her palm, studied it, half considered swallowing it herself. The e-mail she'd gotten earlier was not from work. It was from Daniel. He wanted "to talk" when she got back. He'd been trying "to talk" for weeks, maybe months. She always put him off. Too busy, she'd say. True, but really she simply didn't want to hear what she knew he had to say: that he wasn't happy, that their marriage was in trouble. He wanted a trial separation. This weekend had given him time to think, he said. Tamar had hoped, in her absence, that he'd miss all her subtle little touches around the house. Apparently they were so subtle that he'd failed to notice them at all. *Their marriage wasn't really a marriage, so how could it be in trouble?* She supposed he'd been right: She was an absentee wife, and her kids didn't really know her. Was there a pill for that? She glanced at Roger's sneakers and wondered again where Nat and Hal were.

She fingered the white tablet, wondering if she could get away with substituting something else—an aspirin, say—to keep Roger from drifting into a substance-induced fog so she could talk some sense into him about Loraine. She had to act now, she decided, and confront him about his problem with the whole family present. Tomorrow, friends and neighbors and her mother's mysterious aunts would descend on Little Island, and after that they'd all disperse, and who knew when they'd be together again? He'd thank them—her—for this little mini-intervention. Be indebted, even. She was sure of it.

She made the bed, straightened his shoes, picked up his T-shirt and hung it carefully from the upright of the ladder-back chair, and left the room. Down the hall, she opened the door to Puffin Roost and peeked inside; the twins' clothes and shoes were strewn about, the beds rumpled as though the girls had recently been lying on them. Books were piled on the window seat, and pillows stood at either end. Tamar could picture them reading there, feet touching occasionally, confirming the other's presence. Roger used to like the occasional reassuring touch, perhaps a habit developed in the womb as they'd floated for those nine months, blindly aware of the other. His need for her stopped after he found Loraine. The girls must be outside, she thought, as she stood in the hall bathroom and uncapped a bottle of aspirin. She headed downstairs with a single pill resting in her palm.

SEPTEMBER 9, 1991

Roger woke up the morning of the quarry party disappointed in himself. He was hungover and still half-wasted from the night before, when he, Wally, and a few other guys hiked up Blueberry Hill with three joints and a bottle of Wild Turkey he'd pinched from his dad's liquor cabinet. They'd consumed it all. Loraine wasn't with them, of course. Had she been there, Roger wouldn't have gotten so hammered. . . He didn't think so, anyway. He couldn't quite think straight yet. He lay in bed, staring at the ceiling, thinking about her.

She'd told him two weeks earlier that she wanted to break up, wanted them to see other people when they both went off-island for school.

"Other people? What other people? You're going to cosmetology school," Roger had said, too startled by her statement to take it seriously.

"In Portland. Portland's a big city."

"Are you serious?"

Loraine nodded, but wouldn't meet his eye.

"This is coming from your dad, right? Not you." Mr. Fifield had never approved of Roger Little for his daughter. Or as a friend for his son, for that matter. Mr. Fifield didn't know that at least half the trouble he and Walter got into was Walter's idea. Like that party at the inn that Roger knew nothing about until kids started pulling in the driveway.

Loraine shrugged. Roger could now see tears clinging to the lashes of her big, soft brown eyes. He kissed the tears away. "Hey, don't cry, okay? Your dad wants us to prove that we really love each other. So we'll prove it. I don't want to see other girls. I can spend a year not dating, if that's what it takes. Can I at least write to you?"

She was crying now, shredding a tissue, looking miserable. She shrugged again, and then nodded. "I guess that would be okay."

"And maybe we'll run into each other at Christmas. I could drop something off at your house . . . in disguise!" Roger was warming to his plan now, and Loraine giggled and wiped away her tears.

"And you'll stay sober? No drugs?" she asked.

Roger knew this would be harder. Going without both Loraine and booze was a lot to ask. "Can we make the split after the quarry party? Pretend you couldn't get hold of me until then." He wanted a reprieve. Time to talk to his old man about this. See if he'd go talk to Mr. Fifield and convince him that Roger was good for his daughter, although Roger knew this would never happen. First, his father wouldn't give him the time of day, certainly wouldn't sit and listen to him talk about how much he loved Loraine Fifield, how he wanted, someday, to take over the inn. Second, he wouldn't believe that Roger really wanted to turn his life around and would work hard to do so if it meant he could be with Loraine. Third, he'd probably laugh when Roger told him he needed some help doing that. His dad would say something like, *How many times do I have to bail you out before it's enough?* It hadn't been that many, really, but more than most kids' dads. Fourth, his dad could never convince Mr. Fifield that Roger was the right guy for his daughter, because he didn't believe it either. *Shit.*

Loraine looked at him and chewed on her lower lip. Roger wanted, desperately, to nibble on it as well. He couldn't take his eyes off that mouth, her lips so full and soft . . . He leaned over and kissed her, and she kind of melted into him, the way he loved, and his groin stirred the way it always did, but this time their embrace seemed to send shock waves throughout his whole body. From the way she clung to him, as if her knees were giving way, he knew that she felt it as well. God, he wanted her, not just physically—although, Christ, that was true enough—but for always, just like this.

JOY

From where I was sitting—next to Roger at the card table, his leg propped up on a neighboring chair—he looked to be in considerable pain.

"What are we playing?" Tamar asked as she entered and handed him a pill and a glass of water.

"Five-card draw," he said around the pill, which he'd promptly tossed into his mouth.

"Where's Mom?" she asked, taking a seat beside Daddy.

"In the kitchen." I shuffled the cards. "She said to go ahead and she'd step in later." I cut the deck and dealt.

Tamar examined her hand, shifted a few cards, then put them down and took a breath. "You have a disease, Roger," she said, "that tells you that you don't have a disease. The cure is to tell yourself, every single day, that you do."

"Tee," Daddy said sharply.

I mentally buckled my seat belt, preparing for the inevitable turbulence that would follow this statement. (Turbulence, when you think about it, is almost never unexpected.) "It was so beautiful up on Blueberry Hill this morning," I blurted.

"Perfectly clear. You could practically see Spain." My voice sounded unnaturally shrill. "You should take Mom up there. She'd love it." My words came out in a rush. I piled them on, senseless, useless phrases, sandbags against rising floodwaters. "We actually got so caught up in the view we didn't pick any berries! We were collecting—" I was about to move on to the leaves and bark and moss that I had amassed, about redecorating, anything to head us in a direction other than the one in which Tamar was moving, but then I remembered Glen and fell silent.

"They call it recovery," Tamar said, clearly unwilling to give in to my attempted insurrection. "But you're never really cured. It's always there, hanging over you. Like . . . cancer. People who recover from cancer are always thinking, every single day, when will I have a recurrence? And they take whatever steps they can to ensure they don't."

"You certainly are the font of all wisdom today, aren't you? And you are an expert, how?" Roger's words collided with one another in their effort to get out. His leg obviously was hurting like hell. The Vicodin hadn't done a thing. *Because it wasn't a Vicodin.* Suddenly I knew this as clearly as if I'd just read the label on the bottle of aspirin, or antacids, or whatever Tamar had just handed him.

"People with incurable lung cancer don't quit smoking." Roger tossed in one poker chip. "Ante up, sis."

This sounded to me like a challenge. I thought again about us being together here this weekend without the outlaws to referee.

"What?" My mother entered, carrying a big bowl of popcorn. "Who has lung cancer?" She put the bowl on the table beside me and looked around at the serious expressions. "It's like an epidemic. But many recover. Survive. 'Cancer survivors.' That's what they're called." She put an arm across my shoulder.

But I was still angry about the mysterious Glen, who'd apparently insinuated himself into our family earlier, and shrugged her arm off. She looked startled, and then hurt, and I felt so guilty I said, "Except Lee Entweiler. He died last month."

"He did?" My mother sat down heavily in an empty chair. "I hadn't heard. Still, cancer isn't always a death sentence now. Lee Entweiler was just one person. He was much older than Stuart." She checked the expressions around the table, sensed that she had sailed into uncharted waters, and dropped her sails.

"They're the same age, actually," I said, now puzzled. "For what it's worth." My mother seemed to be taking this news of the death of Lee Entweiler, a man she'd barely known, very hard. I wondered whether this weekend—with her unexpected relations turning up, all of us coming home, her mother's death—had been too much for her.

"Really? He looked so much older."

I finally understood. "Stuart doesn't have cancer, Mom." And then, because I could tell from her expression what she was now thinking, I added, "Nor do I. But if I do ever get a fatal illness, I will buy a gun and shoot all the evil, selfish, greedy people on my way out." I glanced at my sister as I said this.

But Tamar was looking at Roger. "I'm talking about Roger's drinking," she said, to no one in particular.

In the silence that followed, I found myself wishing, just for an instant, that we had been talking about cancer. I was sure, from my parents' expressions, that they did, too. We'd been through this with Roger so many times. And the conversations never ended well.

SEPTEMBER 9, 1991
JOY

Bonnie and I came back from Sand Beach that afternoon to find Tamar sitting in one of the Adirondack chairs. She called us over, which was unusual. Tamar didn't much care for Bonnie, who was plump and jolly and kind. Those were traits that Tamar worked hard to combat in herself and avoided when selecting her friends. I assumed she wanted me to get her a glass of iced tea or a book from her room.

I told Bonnie to ignore her and started inside. We planned to execute our new hairstyles this evening before we both left for our senior year of college: highlights for her, layers for me. After we graduated, we didn't know where we'd end up, how often we'd see each other—although we'd talked about getting an apartment together in Boston. But Bonnie was thoughtful and also probably flattered to be singled out for attention from this year's prom queen, school council president, and yearbook editor. (But not, I liked to remind Tamar, valedictorian, which I had been.) And so she ambled across the lawn, her expression curious, open, and trusting, as always. We would make this quick, I thought, as I followed her, and get on with our plans.

"Hi, Bonnie!" My sister smiled up at her as though they were best friends. She definitely wanted something. "How was Sand Beach?"

"Sandy," I said. "What do you want? Where's Roger?"

Tamar gestured toward one of the chairs, and Bonnie sat down. "Is that the new *Vogue*?" she asked my sister.

Tamar nodded and handed it to her. "Take it."

Actually, it was my magazine, but I let it go.

"I was just wondering whether Roger had asked you." She directed her question to Bonnie, but Bonnie was thumbing through the magazine and didn't look up.

"Asked her what?" I said, immediately suspicious. Roger knew and liked Bonnie, but he would have sent any message or question for her through me.

"About tonight."

I froze. "Tonight? What about tonight?"

Bonnie continued to look through the magazine, oblivious.

"He wants you to go with him to the quarry party. He was going to call you this morning. Bonnie?"

Bonnie finally glanced up. "What?"

"Roger wants to take you to the quarry party tonight. He said he was going to call. Maybe you were out?"

"Joy and I were at Sand Beach," Bonnie said, trying to be helpful, although Tamar already knew this. Bonnie, along with every other female under the age of forty, had a crush on my brother. She believed Tamar, of course. She didn't know her like I did. Something didn't ring true. I knew that Roger and Loraine had decided to cool things off. A lot of high school couples do that before leaving the island. I couldn't imagine what Roger had done to cross Tamar, but this smacked of payback.

But my friend looked so happy and so . . . incredulous, that I didn't have the heart to say anything.

"Maybe he left a message with my mom?" Bonnie said.

"I'm sure he did, if she was home. So, we'll pick you up at eight?"

Bonnie looked up at me. She would have said no if I'd shaken my head. Would have said no if I'd given any indication that our plans that evening meant a lot to me. But I didn't. Because I knew what this invitation meant to her.

Roger tossed his cards on the table. "I've got nothing."

After a moment's silence, I said, tentatively, "We haven't drawn yet, Roger. Wouldn't you like some new cards?"

"New cards? Hell, yes, I'd like some new cards." He sounded bitter, which was unlike him. "Be nice if life were that simple, wouldn't it, Tee?" he said. "I'll take five."

"Five?" I said. My job as the emotional fulcrum for this family required vigilance and precision, and I still believed I could manage this one. A slight shift at just the right time could do it. One wrong move, however, would send the whole lot of us tumbling.

"Five. I'll take five new cards," Roger said with the impatience of someone who'd made a reasonable request and couldn't understand why it hadn't yet been granted. "Just like that, a whole new fucking hand."

"Roger." Tee's voice was low, almost cajoling. "I am just—"

"Five it is," I said, keeping my tone light. "Daddy?" He had remained silent during this entire exchange.

"For once, Tee, can we make this not about you?" Roger sounded weary as he spoke.

Damn him, he was going to persist. I could sense the balance tipping beyond my control, a sailboat heeling over dangerously far, cabinet doors banging open, charts, cushions, cups, and anything else not secured crashing to the leeward side.

"About me? I'm concerned about you—about your health." Tamar was leaning toward Roger, as if she were actually on that boat.

"Yeah, right."

"You're my brother, and we love you. We don't want to hear that you're back in jail, or dead in a ditch somewhere. As we all know can happen."

"Do 'we all' know that? I certainly do. I guess I'm glad to know that you do, too, because, from here, this looks a lot like one more of your famous goals: Get Roger sober. A challenge. What difference does it make to you whether I drink or do drugs? Other than the fact that I hold a pretty damned good hand. I chose my life, Tee. Please let me live it."

Roger's five discarded cards lay facedown on the table, and I had not yet dealt him new ones. But I thought hard, right then, about dealing him one. A winning hand. A hand Roger could really play.

"Just one for me." Tamar slid a single card onto the table.

"She's bluffing," Roger said, as I dealt out new cards. "Trust me." He picked up his new hand. "She's got nothing."

His tone was, once again, light, almost joking, and I wondered if this could really be the end of the argument. If so, we'd gotten off easy. "Dealer takes two."

We looked at our new hands, and then Tamar said, "How's Loraine?"

I glared at my sister. Roger shifted his gaze to her as well and left it there a long time, his expression hard to read. Tamar started to look uncomfortable. Finally, he said, "Her son was just killed in a stupid and senseless war. How do you think she is?"

Daddy and I silently studied our cards, shifted them, tossed chips into the center of the table. Mom picked at an imaginary speck of food on the padded tabletop with her fingernail.

"Is that what you went to talk to her about?" Tamar was now staring down at her hand.

I desperately wanted her to stop. Roger clearly didn't want to talk about Loraine. From the looks of him, their meeting hadn't gone well. While I couldn't imagine what they'd have to say to each other after all these years, I supposed he could still have feelings for her. It was obvious that my sister had been jealous of Loraine while she and Roger were dating; Loraine was the first female to supplant her in Roger's life. Tamar seemed off-balance when he hooked up with Loraine; he'd always been the yang to Tamar's yin.

Back then, Loraine hadn't even come to Roger's hearing or visited him in prison. That was what I'd always assumed, at any rate; I didn't really know for sure. We'd all lost track of Loraine. We Littles had let Loraine Fifield drift away, along with so many other people, plans, and priorities.

Tamar took the card I'd dealt her and inserted it into the hand she held. "I'm sorry about Jason." She sounded genuine. I had to give her that. "That was his name, right?"

Roger remained silent for so long that I thought perhaps Tamar had given him a Vicodin after all and he'd dropped into a drug-induced stupor. Finally, he said, "Yes, his name was Jason. My son's name was Jason."

It took me a moment to process what he'd just said. It wasn't that I hadn't heard him. It was that I needed to say the words aloud to make them real.

"Your son?" I said.

My mother now looked as though she wanted to put her head down on the tabletop and sob. I felt the same way and wondered whether the others would mind—or even notice—if we did. Daddy remained silent, his jaw muscles flexed, staring, not at his cards, but through them. Roger, again disappointing him. Jason had been his grandson; a grandson he'd never known.

Tamar looked the most stricken. Her face grew pale and drawn, her hands shook slightly. "What?" It was barely more than a whisper.

He looked at her. "Jason was my son." He paused and chewed on his lower lip, and I thought he might cry. "She found out a couple of weeks after we split up. When I was in prison she came to see me and told me that she'd come by here the day of the quarry party and left a message for me to come see her at the Flying Bridge. She was going to tell me then. I never got the message, never went by, never knew. And then—"

We all waited for him to continue.

"There wasn't much I could do from prison. And, anyway, she said she didn't want anything to do with me, and didn't want her child . . . my child, our child"—I heard the words catch in his throat—"to have anything to do with me, either." Roger folded his cards. "So she married Brian Calderwood and moved off-island."

I put down my cards as well and reached my hand across the table. I knew a thing or two about losing a child. But I'd been able to raise mine, and mine was still very much alive. I wanted to call him, right then, and then call Stuart, tell him how much

I loved him, tell him how stupid and impetuous my leaving had been, how it had meant nothing, that only he meant anything. But that would have to wait.

"Did you know him? I mean, did you ever meet him?" Tamar asked, in a small, soft voice. She was looking down as she spoke.

I don't know what qualifications a person needed to become a partner in Tamar's law firm, but empathy was clearly not one of them.

"Did I ever *meet* him?" The word shimmered in the heat of Roger's disbelief. "You are un-fucking-believably self-absorbed, Miss Little."

"No." Tamar was struggling, clearly desperate to be understood. "I'm just asking. I mean, he was your biological child, but—

"Tamar, stop," I said, with more force than I intended.

"Joy," my mother cautioned.

Tamar glared at me. "Right. This does not concern you, Joy."

"Tee, there's no need to be rude to your sister," Daddy said. It was the first time he'd spoken since we'd all sat down.

"Oh, that's right, protect Joy. Poor Joy. Timid Joy. Daddy's Joy. You have no idea what my life is like, what it takes to do what I do. Every single day." She paused to catch her breath, seemed to want to stop, but the words kept coming. "You live in a fantasy world, Joy. You marry your shrink and he gives you everything. Everything. And you walk out because your child goes off to college. Oh, dear. What a hardship: an empty nest. Do you have any idea how ridiculous that is, Joy? How ridiculous you are?"

I sat with my lips pressed together, staring at my sister. I'd told Tamar all that in confidence. "It *is* hard, Tamar. If you ever spend any real time with your daughters, one day you will know that."

"I spend plenty of time with my daughters. But, if we're dispensing advice here, why don't you try coming up with something a little more . . . normal for your potential future career than hired assassin and explosives expert. If *you* ever work a day in your life, you'll know that."

"I was having some fun. 'Thinking outside the box,' as you might say." My tone was mocking.

"Some fun. Fun? You think working eighty hours a week is 'fun'? Don't you think I wish I could stay home and bake cookies with my daughters, help them with their homework, teach them how to cook and knit and . . ." She trailed off, possibly unable to think of any other activities. Or perhaps, having said this aloud, realizing for the first time that if she applied herself to motherhood the way she'd applied herself to her career, she might well succeed. This only added more fuel to her ire. "You need to stop being so tentative, so timid. Stop waiting for permission to start living, Joy. Do something big and bold and brave for once in your life."

During our exchange, my mother had deflated into her chair, her expression distant, as though wishing herself elsewhere. Daddy's fingers gripped his cards, his gaze now locked on them as though they might provide the key to salvation from this scene, or at least a helpful hint about how to end it.

As I stared across the table at my sister, I realized that if Loraine had come by the day of the quarry party, as Roger had just said, and left a message for him, the only person with whom she could have left it was Tamar. Anyone else would have delivered it.

I thought about that afternoon, coming home from Sand Beach with Bonnie, Tamar waiting in the Adirondack chair, her surprising invitation for Bonnie supposedly delivered on Roger's behalf. But, Roger, I was now sure, had known nothing about it. Loraine must have given Tamar the message. But had Loraine told her everything? Had Tamar known she was pregnant? I thought about sweet Bonnie, her body bloodied, her throat slashed, her life ended at the age of twenty.

"You want big and bold and brave?" I said now. My heart fluttered, as it had the previous night, as I leaned out over the dark water, all alone. And, again, this morning, afraid. Well, this time I would let go and jump. "I'm tired of living my life inside a lie, Tamar, and I imagine you are, too."

My parents shifted uncertain gazes in my direction. I pictured myself approaching a tall building, holding a bag of explosives, hooking up wires and setting detonators, toppling the whole thing from the inside.

"Don't, Joy." Another order. This one delivered by Roger as he stood up, so fast he tipped over his chair. This woke Sophie, who catapulted from her bed, barking.

But I didn't need to take orders. I wasn't part of this team. And I was tired of hunkering belowdecks, trying to keep this family in balance. "Who was really driving the night of the crash, Tamar?"

"Joy, please don't." Roger was now pleading, but the enormity of all that had happened on that long-ago day had already sunk in. Tamar's bogus invitation to Bonnie, my failure to insist that Bonnie stay with me, Tamar's decision not to deliver Loraine's message, my petty jealousy keeping me from going with them to the party, because, if I had gone, I would have driven them all home safely: At different points along the route, if different decisions had been made, the whole horrid outcome could have been avoided.

There are many things in life we cannot control or stop. But I needed to take a stand on something I'd failed to do for decades. I'd gone missing twenty years earlier, because I'd harbored a secret truth that had slowly devoured me from the inside.

My parents were both now staring at Tamar, their earlier expressions of uncertainty slowly giving way to shock. "Tamar?" Mom said, unable, or perhaps unwilling, to formulate the full question.

Tamar's eyes had grown very dark and very serious. "Joy . . ." It was a whimper, really, more than a word, and normally I would have stopped then and there, but then I thought about my too-quiet house, my absent child; about my mother's lifelong admonishment that I must always protect my sister, without knowing just how effectively I had done that; about my mother's presumed infidelity. I pressed on. Tamar had betrayed my confidence. I would do the same. *She's younger*, I could hear my mother saying. True, but no longer young. *We almost lost her*, I could hear her saying. Indeed.

"A person who's just crashed his car wouldn't think to take the keys from the ignition and put them in his pocket. Unless he wanted to *prove* that he was driving, to protect someone. It should have proved—if anyone had been paying close enough attention and been willing to see the truth"—I looked at my mother as I said this—"exactly the opposite." I turned again to Tamar. "Roger's injuries were all wrong for someone in the driver's seat of that car. Yours were just right." I had figured all this out on the night of the accident and had tried, on the boat ride to Rockland, to persuade Roger to speak up, to clear his name. But he'd refused.

Tamar's eyes narrowed. "Why didn't you say anything?" I could hear the hint of a challenge in her voice, her attempt to shift the responsibility and blame to me for having kept this a secret. A bad move. I had a killer's instincts now.

I looked my sister straight in the eye and dug my fingernail into the cut on my thumb. "Because Roger asked me not to," I said. For once, I was squarely on the winning side of two against one.

Tamar fled the room. No one stopped her. And when Roger walked out a moment later, no one stopped him, either.

Gone

. . .

· Chapter Seventeen ·

Grace slowly stood and walked back to the kitchen. The cookie tin, she noticed, was now empty, its lid off to one side, crumbs, sprinkles, and crumpled balls of wax paper trailing across the counter. A scrawled note on the table said, *florist—no delivery*. It looked like Tamar's writing. She would need to ask her what it meant.

So Joy had known the truth all these years, and said nothing. She studied this knowledge as she might an exotically colored beetle in her garden: fascinated and yet wondering if she should be fearful, whether it was one of the bad ones or one of the good. And then there was the news about Jason. Grace certainly knew what it meant to lose a child. But Roger had lost his own child twice. He'd also grown up in the shadow of a lost sibling. *A little time alone is what I need.* She decided to walk up to the cemetery and put flowers on Abigail's grave. It had been weeks since she'd been even that far from the inn. She slipped on her shoes and headed out the door.

The sun was well on its westward trek. A gull, riding the

afternoon breeze, laughed and laughed. Grace smiled. She could hear the waves washing against the rocks, the soft putter of an outboard, the breeze stirring the leaves into a frenzied rustling, a chickadee stating and restating its name. Ordinary, comforting sounds from a time before her world fell into disarray. She so rarely stopped long enough to listen. The bird feeder was down, so she grabbed a handful of sunflower seed from the small metal bin and sprinkled it on the stone walkway beneath the forsythia bush, where the chickadees loved to hide and scold passersby. "For Cynthia," Grace had called the bright yellow bush beside their back door in Bangor, asking her mother who Cynthia was, wondering how she came to have a shrub named for her.

Grace walked down the drive and up the lane, and then followed the path to the cemetery. She hadn't been farther than Sunset Point in, what, two years? Many more than that—six, at least—since she traveled the footpaths that crisscrossed the southern end of the island, looping through the woods and ending at Silver Beach. In all that time, she'd not even gone as far as the fern brake, a lovely open field where she used to bring the children for picnics in the late spring, when it was still too cold for the beach. The hay-scented ferns made for wonderful bedding.

As she followed the path up to the lighthouse, she decided she would make a short loop through the woods to the fern brake and from there take the path to Seal Cove. Then she would follow the Cliff Walk to Little Lane and have an easy stroll back to the inn. She was tired, but surely she could handle this modest walk, which wouldn't take more than thirty-five minutes. And it would be fun, she reassured herself, not quite believing one could have fun with responsibilities hanging about like bored teenagers. She started walking.

Tamar lay facedown on her bed. She recalled Loraine sitting beside her on that long-ago day, pouring out her heart, tearfully telling her how her father had made her break up with Roger. Tamar had listened, all the while wondering how she could drive a permanent wedge, just a small one, between Roger and his girl. She needed him back, fully, in her life. Without him, the world was a troublesome, confusing place: directions no longer clear, jokes no longer funny, days too long, nights too short. Her body had felt as if it were breaking down: her heartbeat irregular, her thinking muddled, her breathing labored without him by her side. She felt that way now.

"Just so you know, Loraine," Tamar had said, her voice oozing with false concern. "I'm sure it's nothing, but Roger is going to the quarry party tonight with Bonnie Day." Tamar had made this up on the spot, knowing that Bonnie was with Joy, would be back soon, and had no real plans for the evening. Bonnie would be thrilled to receive such an invitation. Tamar didn't need to tell Roger anything beyond that they were taking Bonnie with them, which was exactly what she'd told Loraine. It wasn't a lie. She hadn't said that Roger had *invited* Bonnie.

Loraine looked surprised, then hurt, and then angry, and Tamar knew she'd hit her mark. "I just thought you should know." Tamar put her hand on Loraine's, where it rested on the arm of the Adirondack chair.

Loraine withdrew hers and left, saying, "Just please give

him the message to come by the Bridge tonight. My shift starts at five."

Lying now on her bed, Tamar wondered whether she'd intended to deliver Loraine's message that day and it had simply slipped her mind. *Maybe.* No, she had to admit, she'd had no such intention. Would she have delivered it if she had known Loraine was pregnant?

Jason, she thought. *Roger's son was called Jason.* And this made her think about her own daughters, whom she hadn't seen since before the incident in the den. She should go find them, although she doubted they wanted her to. They didn't need her either. They had each other. *God, what a mess I've made of my life.* She could hear Roger's words to her. *You are un-fucking-believably self-absorbed, Miss Little.* She could hear them as clearly as if he were standing next to her. So clearly, in fact, that she turned her head and cracked an eye just to be sure he wasn't. But the room was empty.

Tears trickled down her face. *If I'd just kept my mouth shut, my secret would still be safe.* The worst part was that Tamar didn't think Roger had been drinking today—she hadn't smelled it on his breath when she leaned in close in the kitchen, pretending to wipe a bit of mud from his face—and yet she'd gone ahead with her plan anyway, because . . . Because she needed him to know how much she needed him, how much she cared.

What next? She could enlist her mother's help and together they could talk to her father. Or maybe she could get her mother to talk to her dad for her. She had no idea what he was thinking or feeling right now. She'd never been especially close to him. Unlike Joy. Tamar had always been jealous of their bond, but then, Tamar had Roger and didn't need anyone else.

She thought about Daniel: a nanny more than a husband. Her mother? Tamar had always kept her at arm's length. Joy? Been afraid of her since she was old enough to know fear. Joy was so smart, so competent. She was punctual, polite, placid; everyone liked her better. Except Roger. And now she wasn't even sure about him. And her daughters? She had managed to alienate them as well.

If I weren't a caring person, would I persist in badgering Roger about his drinking? she argued to herself. *Would I want so desperately for him to stop?* In that instant, she came face-to-face with a truth so big and so solid she couldn't imagine how she'd missed it. She wanted him sober because sober, he was easier to control. In the end, it really was all about her.

Where was Roger now? She closed her eyes but felt nothing. She was truly alone. She realized then that not only did she not *need* anyone but Roger, she didn't *want* anyone else. Suddenly, desperately, she didn't want this to be true for her girls. It was unhealthy to depend too deeply on only one other person, because when that person leaves, you become nothing without him, and will stop at nothing to regain yourself.

She stood. *First, find my girls*, she thought, *make sure they're okay, and then go talk with Mom. Apologize. Try to explain—No, just apologize.*

She opened the door to Puffin Roost. No Nat, no Hal. She listened at the doors of the other rooms. Silence. A sense of unease was growing inside her, gnawing at her the way mice used to gnaw the wood inside the inn's walls when she was a child.

The kitchen was empty, too. She saw Roger's truck in the driveway. Okay, so at least he was somewhere nearby. The Adirondack chairs stood in the front yard, their backs turned toward the house, as though shunning her. Something was missing out there, but in her distracted state, she couldn't pinpoint what it was. As the gnawing unease intensified, she picked up her pace and resumed her search.

JOY

I stared at the cards in my hand, the numbers ascending in perfect order from six to ten. I'd drawn to an inside straight. My lucky day.

My mother had left the Games Room shortly after Tamar and Roger, and Daddy excused himself a few minutes later. Before he left, he asked me why I'd never said anything, why I'd kept this huge secret all these years.

"I gave Roger my word," I told him. What I didn't say was that I'd done it because I wanted him to like me, wanted to earn his respect, wanted to have a bond with him like the one he had with Tamar. It all sounded so childish, even for the twenty-year-old I'd been then.

"I so misjudged him," Daddy mumbled, "Can't think how I will ever make it up. What kind of father—" He stopped. "And Tamar . . ." He shook his head as though to clear it and left the room.

My holding Roger's secret had not only *not* brought me closer to him, it had served as a wall between us. A wall between me and my family. A transparent wall, but a wall nonetheless. He must have been afraid every time our family got together, every time I was alone with either of my parents—just as I had been, peering anxiously through that wall—that I would let something slip. Holding the secret had empowered me, but people with power, I now understood, are not loved. They're feared. For twenty years, I'd had the power to shake my family to its foundation, and that knowledge had made me move fearfully through life as though I were carrying a keg of dynamite. Now I'd detonated that keg, and still I stood alone at the threshold, wondering if and when it would be safe to reenter.

It truly was remarkable how much damage even one tiny mouse can do, gnawing through woodwork, Tamar thought, trying to tamp down her rising sense of panic as she raced through the inn, checking for the twins in closets and under tables, calling their names. She had once read that a mouse can get though a hole the size of a thimble, and wondered why they would even need to gnaw if that was true. . . . She ceased her senseless noodling as she burst into the Games Room. "Have you seen the twins?"

Joy, sitting all alone, looked up, startled. "In their room?"

"No," Tamar said, impatiently. "I checked." She fought the instinct to punish her sister, who knew where her own child was, safe in his dorm room; who had known Tamar's terrible secret for years and had kept it hidden.

"Earlier they were building a fort in my old room," Joy said. "Maybe they're still there." Then she added, "Remember the ones we used to—"

Tamar would need to do some serious bridge-building with her sister; later, perhaps they'd be able to reminisce about their childhood. But right now, she needed to find her kids. She bolted from the room and headed upstairs. A fort. Hal and Nat had invited her up to see it this morning, and she'd promised she would—but somehow, she hadn't managed to make it. She'd make a big fuss now, she thought, taking the stairs two at a time and striding down the hall to Joy's old room, grinning in anticipatory relief.

She opened the door to find an elaborate construction of sheets, towels, tables, chairs, and what was probably the old hat rack from the second-floor landing, serving as the center pole. The fort covered nearly the entire room. *Clever, my girls.* Tamar got down on all fours and crawled inside: an ashtray, one of Sophie's dog beds, a magazine rack with her father's old *Field & Streams*, a casserole dish, a few pieces of her mother's costume jewelry, some shells, and a pyramid of smooth, round stones—cannonballs, Tamar guessed—near the perimeter for defense. Beside them—and most surprising of all—were her own running shoes. "Girls?" Tamar called into the labyrinth, although clearly they were not there. Silence. Tamar wished so fervently for them to answer that she called again, not knowing what else to do. More silence.

She rocked back on her heels and listened closely. More closely than she could ever remember having listened before. She listened, until she believed her eardrums might pop under the strain, for the creak of a floorboard, a muted murmur, a soft sigh, a giggle. She heard only the vibration of electricity in the wires, the rumble of the water heater, the clank of the pipes, the distant shuffle of waves trading places on the rocks below the inn. The twins were not here. The twins were not anywhere near here.

Her girls were gone. Truly gone. Not just hiding somewhere. She hardly knew how she knew this, but she did. Her mother had told her once that she'd always known when her children were "around," even when they'd not been immediately visible, maybe not even within calling distance, but somewhere safe. There had been a few times—well, more than a few with Roger, and none with Joy—when a signal would go off in Grace's head, she'd told Tamar, and she'd known, as one does when the alarm on the smoke detector is not simply being triggered by steam from the shower or burned toast, that something bad had happened. Grace had known it the night of the crash, she'd told Tamar. And now Tamar understood what she'd meant.

She ordered herself to remain calm. Panic would not help. Worry would not help. She needed a clear head. Logic. When had she last seen them? Trotting after Roger, Pop, and the others on their way back from Sand Beach. *Had she even remembered to ask if they'd put on sunscreen?* She thought about the girls that morning, standing on the footbridge, afraid to jump. She recalled how impatient she'd been and hated herself for it. When one is having an emotional meltdown, as she had the night of the crash, as she was again now, logic is not always welcome, but it is useful. She longed for Roger's analysis and action orientation, longed for his very presence.

Simply take a step, one step, forward, she told herself. She thought back to that time-management seminar she'd attended. *Do something related to the task.* She remained frozen, however, trembling. Could barely breathe, much less move. Fear. That was what this was. *If you can name the feeling, you can overcome it.* Wisdom from some other seminar. Still she stood. And this time Roger wasn't here for her. She had thought she could safely leave her children on an island with all these adults around: parents, uncles, and aunts. Surely some adult should have kept an eye on the girls. Indeed. Some adult should have. *Me*. She'd abdicated the care of her children to Daniel for their entire lives until this weekend, and now they were gone.

"Not here?" Joy poked her head in the bedroom door. "They're not downstairs either." Tamar stood frozen, her expression blank, and let Joy put her arms around her, although she didn't normally like to be touched, except by Roger. "They're fine. We'll find them. They're just off having a little adventure somewhere." Joy's voice was gentle, and when Tamar choked back a sob, Joy tightened her grip, and Tamar for once, did not rebuff her sister's steady, calm presence. She welcomed it. "Remember how we used to disappear for hours?" Joy asked.

That was the problem. Tamar did remember. She remembered how many foolish risks they'd taken, their parents oblivious: the time she and Roger inadvertently built a campfire over a gas line behind the inn, and the time they broke into the Dietrichs' cabin and nearly burned it down when a hurricane lantern tipped over.

"How about the attic?"

Tamar shook her head. She thought back over the afternoon, willing some helpful memory to appear. Out the window, she could see long afternoon shadows stretching across the lawn to the empty dock. The empty dock. That was what was missing. "The *Kestrel* is gone. Roger must have taken her out. Could he have them?"

Joy bit the side of her cheek. "Maybe. Sure."

Tamar didn't believe the lie any more than Joy did. Roger would not take them without telling her. Then again, he'd been in quite a state. If they'd been down on the dock when he got there . . . He might, just to punish her. . . . That was more Tamar's style than Roger's, but it offered her a thin thread of hope, which she clung to like a lifeline.

Joy kept one arm around her sister as she gently guided her back downstairs. "Come on. We'll try calling him, and then look around outside—"

"What if we don't find them before dark?" Tamar could hear the whine in her own voice. She sounded like a frightened child. Felt like a frightened child.

"Then we'll get flashlights. But we will. Let's not bleed until we're shot. I believe you told me that."

Just down the hill from the lighthouse was the Little cemetery. Grace could see Abigail's stone, there among markers dating back to the early 1800s when the Littles first settled the island. Graves of men and women who'd spent their whole lives there. Just like Abigail: in her case, only three days.

The old stones were slate, now little more than slivers, tilting like buoys in a strong current. They were decorated with trees of life, skulls, and lambs, their epitaphs barely legible—whole lives being slowly erased by time and weather. A fence surrounded the little gathering, and Joy had once asked Grace if it was to keep the dead bodies in so they didn't go around haunting people. Grace had said, yes, that was exactly what it was for, although she herself didn't know. Was it for decoration? Decorum? Keeping animals out? Other than a few coyotes once, long ago when the Findleys had tried to raise chickens, there were only deer, raccoons, and the occasional fox—and now, perhaps, a bear, although Grace didn't fully believe it. So maybe the fence *had* been erected to contain restless spirits. Grace opened the gate and went inside.

Abigail's stone was pink marble, marked with a simple *A.J.L. June 4, 1969 ~ June 7, 1969.* Grace had painted her room pink, but she hadn't spent even one night in it. When Joy was born, Grace painted her room yellow. Pink was Abigail's color.

"She was just too eager to come out and meet her mother," Joan had said, trying to be kind, because Grace was her daughter and Joan loved her, the way Grace loved Abigail. But Grace found no comfort in that intended kindness. She wished, with all her heart, that Abigail had been less eager, that she'd despised her mother, anything that might have kept her on board the full nine months. Grace thought again about the twin brother she'd never known: Sammy.

Grace bought Joan a pink marble stone, too, because Joan had loved pink, although she'd rarely worn it because she claimed that it showed the dirt. The rain had kicked up mud around the new stone, a larger version of Abigail's, and Grace smiled to think that her mother was right: Pink does show dirt.

"We're not having any fun this weekend, Mom. I'm sorry, but I seem to have forgotten how." Grace spoke to the pink marble slab, although Joan's ashes would not be here until after the service. She plucked a few stems of pale blue aster, some goldenrod, and a bit of late-blooming wild phlox and laid the bouquet on Abigail's grave.

Grace had found a poem by John Greenleaf Whittier in Joan's wallet. The paper was creased and as soft as flannel. She'd memorized it and planned to recite it at the service.

No Longer Forward nor Behind

No longer forward nor behind
I look in hope or fear;
But grateful, take the good I find,
The best of now and here.
I break my pilgrim staff,
I lay aside the toiling oar;
The angel sought so far away
I welcome at my door.

For all the jarring notes of life
Seem blending in a psalm,
And all the angles of its strife
slow rounding into calm.
And so the shadows fall apart
And so the westwinds play;
And all the windows of my heart
I open to the day.

The afternoon was warm, so Grace hung her jacket over the gatepost—she would retrieve it on her way back—then carefully closed the gate and walked up the rise to the lighthouse. From here she could see nearly all of Little Island, as well as the harbor and a good bit of East Haven. Out in Penobscot Bay, a few coastal schooners, sails set, slid slowly across the horizon. A few boats were motoring through the channel—one bravely coming in under sail. Bud Carver was rowing out to his yacht. People going about their lives.

She remembered the time, when Roger was in high school, that he and Walter Fifield and a few other boys rotated the

Welcome to East Haven sign 180 degrees and attached to it another sign that read, *At some point in time, the entire world flipped upside down, except for this one sign, on this small island, in Maine. No one knows why.* Grace felt now as though her world had flipped upside down. The recent revelations about the crash, about Roger's son, about her mother, about her lost twin brother. . . . She'd had a simple desire to satisfy her mother's few requests: *Flowers, By the water, Have fun!* And now it had all turned to ash.

Below her, all she could see, stretching from the base of the lighthouse to the edge of Isle au Haut Bay, were the tops of pointed firs. Many more than she remembered. She couldn't even make out the location of the fern brake. After a brief hunt, she located an indistinct depression between two outcroppings of lichen-covered rock; the path was worn nearly smooth, like the inscriptions on the gravestones, and she set off upon it.

JOY

I jogged down the road to the footbridge, following a hunch that the twins might return to the scene of their earlier defeat. I knew something about this. How many nights had I slipped down there, as I'd done the night before, picturing myself jumping into the frigid water and encountering a current as insistent as a guilty conscience?

The tide had only half filled the creek, and although the twins were not on the footbridge, I did spot a piece of wax paper with red sprinkles caught in its creases. Beside it, on the flat rock, lay a chocolate bar wrapper, matching one that had gone missing from last night's cookout. I checked under the bridge. "Hal? Nat?" A dozen gulls and cormorants stood on the rock just offshore. One by one, they would fly off as the tide inched in, until only two or three remained on the single square foot of exposed rock. I used to enjoy sitting on the bank watching them, wondering how they chose who had to leave and who got to stay.

I decided to follow the path to the bathhouses at Sand Beach and then head back along the road to the inn. I didn't think the girls would go as far as the Cliff Walk, and certainly they wouldn't venture into the woods, which had become so overgrown in the past few years as to be almost impenetrable. No one, it seemed, went in there anymore. The last time I tried, I became hopelessly disoriented and turned around. But the bathhouses, now those held real promise. I set off, determined.

Tamar ran up Little Lane to the D'Arcangelos' and Dietrichs' driveways. She'd tried calling Roger's cell phone, but he hadn't answered. Probably out of range. She closed her eyes and tried to summon him, as they'd done when they were kids. She felt nothing.

The two summer cottages stared mutely out toward the reach. She and Roger had loved playing here when they were kids, sneaking in and stealing cigarettes, shifting small items: the teakettle, a side table, sheets in the linen closet. They hardly ever invited Joy. She heard her sister's recent words: *Roger asked me not to.* They stung. How much of an outsider Joy must have felt when they were kids, the same way Tamar felt now.

Both cottages were locked tight. She called out to the twins, tried to summon them as she had Roger, peered in dark windows, made an effort to calm herself. She would find them. Of course she would. And when she did, she would never again let them out of her sight. She would . . . quit her job, become a stay-at-home mom, bake cupcakes for their birthday parties at school. "No need," Joy told her last May when she called for advice on what kind of cake to buy. "Just bring in a can of frosting and ten spoons." Tamar didn't listen, believing she knew more than her sister, who was the mother of a grown child, a substitute teacher, a volunteer in the children's room at the library. She bought an expensive chocolate mocha torte with buttercream frosting. At the end of the party, twelve slices of torte remained, scraped clean of buttercream. She would become the kind of mother who knew these things. A mother like Grace. A mother like Joy.

Running down the rutted lane to Sunset Point, Tamar called and called. She scanned the rocks, exposed now with the low tide and looking like yaks under their heavy mantles of rockweed. There was the Garden Way cart, abandoned the night before when no one had the strength or desire to pull it back. She and Roger had promised to return for it today. She thought back to the cookout. Her mother enthusiastically packing the cart with baskets and coolers. She'd wanted them to walk, but Tamar insisted they drive and had removed all the carefully packed items, giving no thought to her mother's feelings. Just bulldozed her way in, once again, insisting she knew best. *You are un-fucking-believably self-absorbed*, she thought and began to weep.

· Chapter Eighteen ·

Roger needed to get away. Not just from the conversation with his family and the inn, but from the island. He stormed out of the Games Room, looked out the window toward the harbor, saw the *Kestrel*, and thought *why not?* He'd just take her for a quick run out into the sound, maybe up into the basin and drop a line, bring some fish home for supper. A peace offering. He needed some air, some space, some time to think. He'd really believed Loraine was going to be more . . . willing to give him a chance. Drunks often construct fantasy worlds, he knew, furnish them, populate them, even engage in imaginary conversations with the people in them. In Roger's mind it had been a done deal: Loraine confesses that she's never stopped loving him, Roger proposes, they take over the inn, have a pack of kids . . .

No one followed him out, which both relieved and annoyed him. He supposed he'd started it, telling them about Jason. But Tamar had no business bringing up all that shit about his drinking in front of everyone like that. Egging him on about his recovery, imagining that she had all the answers. There wasn't one question about his drinking he hadn't asked himself many, many times in the past twenty-plus years. There wasn't one answer he hadn't examined and dismissed as not good enough to make him give up drinking. Until now.

"Thanks for meeting me," he'd said to Loraine when she arrived at the Flying Bridge that afternoon. "I really wanted to see you, to talk with you . . ." He trailed off, not sure how to continue. He should have rehearsed more. She was wearing the new scarf he'd given her and she looked beautiful.

She nodded. "I'm not sure what there is to talk about. I see your mom pretty regularly. She keeps me informed." She smiled then, and Roger saw the pretty brunette he'd fallen in love with back in high school. She'd worked as a lifeguard at the public beach at the state park and had a great body: tanned, a swimmer's shoulders, big, but not muscular like some women who work out. She was athletic, but still all woman. Her skin smelled of suntan lotion, sun, salt. She didn't have bathing suit lines back then, he discovered the first time they made love. On Sand Beach, late one night, under a full moon. He thought it was just the moonlight that made her whole body seem brown and radiant. He wasn't a complete virgin, but enough of one for lots of fumbling, so excited he didn't know what or where to grab first as she slowly pulled her tank top up over her head, exposing heavy, full breasts, the dark brown nipples flat like silver dollars. And then she unzipped her jeans and slid them down over her hips, wiggling a bit, until Roger thought he was going to pass out. She stood there, all brown and curvy, nipples hardening in the cool night air. He took care of that right away, stripping off his T-shirt, jeans, and skivvies, kicking them away, lunging for her. He craved her body, and satisfied the craving many times that summer.

But it was her smile that he'd really fallen in love with back then. And he was falling in love with it again right now at the Flying Bridge, staring across the table at her.

"Sounds like you're doing well in Burlington," Loraine was saying, bringing Roger back to the cup of coffee slowly cooling on the paper tablecloth in front of him, his cock pressing insistently against his jeans at the memory of her body, her full breasts and ass.

"For now." He nodded. "I have ideas, though." It was too soon to get into how he would eventually take over the inn, offer kayak tours and mountain bike excursions, open the dining room to the public . . . It wouldn't happen right away, but someday. Maybe he could partner with his parents for a while, learn the business, buy it from them over time. Of all his schemes— and Roger knew he'd had more than most people—this one had a solidity and purpose that made him feel grounded. He wanted Loraine with him. Maybe she could move her salon there as a service to their guests . . .

He was getting ahead of himself. "Verbal foreplay," Tamar had instructed him. "Women like to be talked to. Women want intimacy more than sex." They'd been frank and honest with one another through puberty, wondering, each of them, how people without a twin figure it all out. There'd been some touching, him always wondering if it had sometimes gone too far, Tamar telling him she'd let him know.

"How's business?" he asked Loraine.

She smiled at this. "Doing well, thanks. Judy Ladeau, remember her? Closed up her shop last year. A lot of her customers come to me now."

"Mom's hair looked great." Roger sipped his coffee, added some cream. He didn't see how this verbal foreplay would ever lead around to what he really wanted to ask.

"You think? I wasn't sure she liked it."

"No, she did. Very much. We all did."

The waitress came over and asked if they wanted refills. They nodded, and then sat in silence.

"I'm sorry about Jason." Too blunt, and not what he meant. It was hard talking to someone who wasn't Tamar. She always got his meaning, no matter what he actually said. "I mean, I'm sorry I couldn't be there for him, for you, when he was growing up, when he was born. When he died." He spoke haltingly, but it felt good to say it aloud. What he couldn't tell her was the one thing he most wanted to say: *Bonnie's death wasn't my fault. I did the prison time, but I wasn't driving that night.*

Loraine was staring down at the diagram of the island on the paper placemat. He could see that her eyes were red and watery.

"I'm thinking, maybe, of moving back here." *Shit. Too much. Too early.*

She looked up at him, tears again rimming those big brown eyes, as they had the day she and Roger split up, and a few were now making their way down her cheeks. He wondered what she'd do if he leaned over, blotted the tears with his thumb, and then pulled her to him and held her while she cried. They could cry together. He could use a good cry.

"Why?" She wiped away her tears.

It was a simple question, but Roger found himself struggling to find an answer. So he just started talking, right over Tamar's voice in his head, crying, *Stop, stop, stop!* "Because my life ended when you came to the prison that day and told me that you were pregnant and wanted to have the baby. That you were marrying Brian Calderwood, a dumbass jock in our class—who ran three businesses into the ground and did a shit-ass job of raising my son. How could he have let him go to Afghanistan? How could he have let him die there? And because you were moving off-island. I've looked, Loraine, and there's no one else for me. What I want is you. What I want is here. What I want is you here with me." *I can't bring Jason back*, he thought, *but it's not too late for us to have another child. Thirty-eight isn't that old.* But that he kept to himself.

It was as though he had spoken these last two lines aloud, however, because Loraine said, "It's too late, Roger."

She met his gaze. He'd remembered that her eyes were brown, but forgotten about the flecks of yellow, green, and blue in her irises. The longer he stared into them—and he could have stared a good long while—the more colors he saw. She must have seen something in his probing gaze, because her expression softened, and she added, "You look . . . better than you did this morning." She smiled again, and Roger felt his heart expand like a bellows. He watched her shift her glance to one of the waitresses, the one Roger had thought looked familiar the day before. He realized it was probably her daughter. She looked more like Brian than Loraine (poor kid), but could have been a swimmer, judging by the size of her.

Loraine looked at Roger again. Her eyes were filled with regret: regret for the past. *But which past? Being with him or losing him?* No, Roger realized, it was regret for what she was about to say. "We can't—I can't pretend that what happened never happened. I left a message with your sister to come and see me that night. She told me you were taking Bonnie to the party. That hurt, but we had broken up, and, besides, I didn't really think you and Bonnie—" She stopped. "But you never came by. And then you got drunk, Roger, and killed someone. I would never really be able to trust you. I've been there before. My father was—" She stopped herself. "I won't go there again." She stood then, turned, started to walk away, but turned back. "It was really nice to see you," she said.

Roger watched her walk out.

He sat awhile longer at the bar, nursing his coffee, wanting a beer, ordering one but then not drinking it. It was a test. It was one thing to stop drinking by avoiding booze. Quite another to do it, facing it.

The path became less distinct as it dropped in elevation. Grace entered the dense stand of balsam and Douglas fir, ferns and bright red bunchberries growing at her feet. She began to hum as she walked along, her mind first projecting forward to her mother's service, and then dawdling behind, reviewing the events of the past hour. Soon a narrow side trail cut off to her left. Seal Cove, she knew was to the right, so she kept going straight, her thoughts once again drifting ahead to menus and floral arrangements, and then back to Joy's recent revelations. But they were so discomfiting that she could only linger on them for a moment before anticipating the impending arrival of her aunts: equally uncomfortable. Her garden? *Dreadful.* Her mind frantically searched for some safe haven.

The way seemed narrow to Grace, the trees so close that, at times, the path was little more than wishful thinking. After ten more minutes, during which she finalized the next day's menu, she arrived at an intersection: a merging of three paths, one going left and two right. Grace was completely disoriented.

Where was the fern brake? She knew she should have reached it by now. One of the right-hand paths went rather steeply up-hill, the other down. *Would both take her to Seal Cove?* She was hot, and in no mood or shape for scrambling up hillsides, even small ones, so she chose the easier, and more logical, down-hill path.

She walked another twenty minutes, her mind still aimlessly drifting. *This trip is taking too long*, she thought. The ground grew muddy—it had been a wet summer—and Grace began to make detours around muck holes. Mosquitoes hovered, hum-ming in her ears. The dense stand of trees now blocked the sunlight, not only making her surroundings dim and cheerless but further disorienting her, and she wondered if she should turn right around and head back. But she pressed on, enticed by the knowledge that once she reached Seal Cove, she would have a short, easy—and sunny—walk along a well-worn trail to the inn. If she retraced her steps now, she reasoned, she would have to slog her way back through the mud and cheer-less stand of firs. She should have been paying better attention. Now, without the sun to guide her, she didn't even know in what direction she was walking. In fact, she couldn't shake the nagging feeling that she was going in circles.

Gar paced back and forth across the front hall. Every time he glanced out at the empty dock where the *Kestrel* should be, he grew angrier: with Roger, with Tamar, but mostly with him-self. He should never have allowed Tamar to egg her brother on about his drinking. Never have allowed Roger to leave. What was he thinking?

Gar knew he should have done something about Roger's

drinking long ago. He supposed he'd tried, but had he tried hard enough? If he'd only found the right treatment center or counselor, or said the right words at the right time, surely Roger would have stopped. If he'd been more strict, or set better limits, then none of this would have happened, and they would all be sitting around the table enjoying a pleasant game of cards. And Loraine and Jason would be right there with them.

Jason. Gar didn't even know what the boy had looked like. Maybe like Roger: big and burly, with the same affable, easygoing nature. Maybe with his addictions, too. He suppressed a shudder.

Even if he'd been able to intervene with those addictions, though, Bonnie Day would still be dead. His daughter had done that. Gar wondered what the statute of limitations was on such a crime. He would have to call the police, would have to tell Maisie. He dropped heavily into a chair.

He had no idea where Grace was. She'd stepped out to the kitchen after Roger left, presumably to start supper, and disappeared. It wasn't like her not to tell someone where she was going, or at least leave a note. Then again, given half a chance, Gar might have done the same thing. Gone down to Sunset to fish. *Bottledarter.* He tried again to think what he'd done with his pretty new lure, just something to take his mind off the news about his son, about Jason, Tamar, Joy, his missing granddaughters. He was sure they'd turn up. His own kids had been missing more than not, growing up. Always off somewhere. He never gave it a thought back then. He'd abdicated most of the parenting to Grace, who no doubt had worried enough for the both of them. But he'd always believed his own twins would be safe with Joy. What a ridiculous and unfair burden he realized he'd put on her. He stared out the window, and his gaze fell on the empty dock. *Damn Roger! God, I hope he's okay.*

Panic was rising in Grace. *Ridiculous. You're on an island. If you keep going forward, eventually you'll come to an edge.* She knew this wasn't strictly true. The paths wound in figure eights and loops, so she could wander in circles indefinitely—if she was even *on* a path, which she'd begun to doubt. She elbowed her way through the tightly growing trees, her arms scratched and bleeding, and finally came to a wide bog with a profusion of ferns, brown and seed-bearing. Animal prints—she couldn't make out what kind—were stamped into the mud. She laid branches across the wettest part, but they sank as soon as she stepped on them. So she began yet another detour, fighting her way through the ferny undergrowth with her shoes soon caked with mud, until she finally reached firm ground. Mosquitoes feasted freely.

She had completely lost her way during this last detour and now peered back, trying to locate her route. She'd headed left to skirt the muck, so she now bore right, wishing for something on which she could get her bearings: the water, the sun, even a broad patch of daylight would help. But she was engulfed by tall trees and gray gloom. Grace trudged on—aware that the fern-filled mud hole she'd passed several times was probably all that was left of the fern brake—sure she should have come to the Cliff Walk by now. The trail grew steep, and Grace found herself on hands and knees, first scrambling up, and then sliding down on her bum. *Where the hell was she?*

Up ahead, she saw light. She began to jog, tripped over a

root, and went sprawling. She picked herself up and pressed on. The light turned out to be just another clearing, another intersection of three paths. Or, did it look . . . familiar? She called out a few times, "Hello!"—partly to hear her own voice, but partly in the fervent hope that someone might have come out looking for her. Although she hadn't told anyone where she was going, hadn't even told anyone *that* she was going. The woods were dense and silent. Too silent. Grace began to worry that the gray gloom was more than just the tall trees blocking the sun. She began to suspect that it was fog.

Tamar sprinted the whole way to Seal Cove, hollering at top volume. "Nat! Hal?" She'd seen the ferry plowing its way back to Rockland and, for the briefest moment, wondered whether the twins might have, somehow . . . but, no, she realized, they had no money. *What if they sneaked on?* It's not as though she and Roger hadn't done it many times. Security was tighter now. Still, they wouldn't. *Would they?*

She tried Roger's cell phone again. No answer.

"Hello?" she shouted. *There, was that someone calling for help?* She held her breath, willing one of her daughters to call out to her, or to appear magically from behind a tree. *Now*, she thought. *Now.* But there was just the rush of the waves sliding around the rocks, and the wind slipping between the firs. She envied the wind and waves going about their business with no complicated familial issues to resolve, no emotional attachments of any kind.

The sheer rock face fed straight down to the water. Tamar stood at its edge, peering over. What were the girls wearing? Pink, probably. It shamed her that she didn't know for sure.

But she saw nothing pink or blue or yellow or any other bright color disturbing the earthy tones of the surrounding landscape. She thought about heading out along the Cliff Walk, but not even she wanted to tackle that twice in one day, so she couldn't picture her daughters doing it. Then she thought of the lighthouse and the cemetery. Of course! She turned and raced back down the path to the lane.

At the lighthouse, she tried the door and found it locked. She jogged down the hill to the cemetery, spotted something pale blue hanging on the gatepost, and half fell, half scrambled the rest of the way down the hill to find . . . a jacket, much too large to belong to either of her girls. *Whose, then? And why was it hanging here?* Then she saw the flowers on the grave.

Tamar hadn't spent much time in the graveyard when she was little. It had been Joy's domain. Joy had made up stories about all the people buried there, most of them ancestors. One stone marked a mass grave for some Italian immigrants who'd shipwrecked on Spectacle Island, a favorite story of her father's. Tamar made her way between the slanting, lichen-encrusted markers to one that gleamed pink in the sunlight.

JOAN CARLTON
February 12, 1927 ~ June 21, 2011

Her grandmother's gravestone. The woman for whom her mother had made all these weekend arrangements.

Tamar, anxious about traveling alone with the twins, anxious about being back here on the anniversary of the crash, had given very little thought to how her mother might be feeling this weekend. She must have been the one who left the flowers on the grave and the jacket on the fence. The wildflowers weren't by the new stone, but next to Abigail's much smaller, pink stone. The older sister they'd never known. Her memory, a faint shadow always playing across their mother's face. They all knew, without having to be told, not to ask about Abigail. She and Joy sometimes made up stories about her: the forever baby.

She looked again at her grandmother's gravestone. She hadn't been especially close to Grammy, who always seemed rather guarded and watchful when she arrived every September, bringing gifts for the three children. Tamar realized now how carefully those gifts had been selected, often handmade, like the striped stocking caps she'd knitted them, unworn by all three kids. Grace had quietly preserved them in tissue paper and mothballs in a trunk in the attic. Tamar would check when she got back. Perhaps there was something in pink in that trunk that her girls would like. She stifled a sob.

Fog was rolling across the hilltop. She'd seen it—a wall of gray sitting offshore—from Seal Cove. Now she watched in horror as gossamer wisps streamed around the lighthouse and quickly buried surrounding treetops. It looked as though a signal had been given for an army to advance. How was she going to find her children in the fog? What if the girls were on the Cliff Walk? They could so easily tumble off. She started back to the inn, feeling that she had set all this in motion and that trying to stop it would be like trying to hold back the fog. And then her phone rang.

· Chapter Nineteen ·

The fog had indeed come in, thick enough now to form droplets on branches. Grace stood at the intersection of the three
paths, unsure of her direction and having no idea which way to
turn. She went right, hoping it would take her to Seal Cove, but
soon the path dissolved into muck, and she was, once again, at
the boggy area with its makeshift bridge. *Damn!* She wanted
to weep.

Fog both muffles and amplifies sound, and disorients the
listener, making it difficult to know where a noise is coming
from. So, when somewhere nearby a branch snapped, Grace
wasn't sure whether it was to her right or left, close by or some
distance away. "Hello?" Her own voice, so loud in the still,
gray void, startled her. She heard . . . chuffing. "Hello?" she
repeated, softer this time, suddenly unsure about whether
she even wanted to summon whatever was out there. When she
caught a whiff of something intensely animal, and thought of
the prints she'd seen earlier in the mud, she took off straight
across the bog: wallowing, falling, hoping she was heading

away from it rather than toward it. On the other side, she located an opening among the trees and raced through it, her heart pounding and tears stinging her eyes. *Why had she ventured out? Why hadn't she turned around?*

She headed down the path and, a short while later, arrived right back at the same intersection. A loop. She leaned against a spindly pine, her hand growing sticky with pitch. Crying wouldn't help. She could hear her mother telling her so, saying that there would be other boys, or jobs, or parties, or tests to retake, or whatever Grace had shed precious tears over. *Keep moving*, she told herself. This was an island. Her island! She wiped her eyes and took stock, longing for her mother's calm presence. *Think!* She broke a few branches and laid them on the ground, marking the path she'd just taken out of the bog. And there was the path that had just brought her back. That left only one choice.

The fog had settled so thickly now that her clothes were wet, her curly hair limp. As she headed up the path, the ground rose and the trees thinned, and then she was staring into a vast, gray void. The tears she shed now were of relief and happiness. Although she couldn't see the water, she could smell its sweetness, and hear and feel the big swells heaving themselves up onto the rocks below her before sliding back out to sea to gather themselves for the next assault. No sensation had ever been so welcome. The path dipped back into the woods, and Grace followed it reluctantly, wanting to stay where there was space and light, however wet and gray, but needing to move on. She half considered scrambling down the rock face and attempting to make her way back along the water, just to be on the edge of something—happy, for once, for a boundary, longing to stand at the island's rocky perimeter, the middle having been so muddled and ill-defined.

But it would be crazy to attempt such a journey at any time, more especially in the fog. As long as she could hear the hollow, dull thud of water colliding with the rock, followed by the rush and gurgle of waves washing back out to sea, she would be fine. This was the Cliff Walk. This way would eventually lead her home.

JOY

I could see as I approached the bathhouses that one door was ajar. My parents had instructed us kids to keep the doors closed at all times so the chipmunks didn't steal in and eat holes in the towels and store seeds in pockets and plimsolls. *Plimsolls. Why did no one in this country call them that?* A so much more elegant word than *sneaker.* As is *bumbershoot, loo, lift, petrol.* That everything Dr. Kilsaro said sounded refined and erudite had certainly been one of his appeals.

I hurried to the open door and poked my head inside, where I spied two pairs of pink plimsolls. Well, well! I looked out toward Spectacle and noticed two things: the advancing tide had entirely surrounded it, and fog was blowing in. A faint flash of pink out on the rock caught my eye before the mist billowed across the sand, blocking my view. I ran to the water's edge and peered out, but it was as useless as trying to see into the future. I did, however, catch another flash of pink before all went gray. My hands fumbled as I pressed buttons on my phone. I'd call Tamar first, then Daddy. I was certain I'd seen something. Although I hadn't been able to make out before the fog closed in whether I'd seen two spots of pink, or just one.

It was as Roger rounded the northeast point of Pratt's Island that he saw the fog rolling in like a tsunami, overtaking everything in its path. He turned and made a run for the reach, keeping his eye on the rapidly disappearing Pratt's Island, hoping he might make Pratt's Cove before the fog made navigation through the narrow channel impossible. Thankfully the tide was coming in. At low tide, he wouldn't have had a prayer.

He located the entrance and dropped the anchor, occasionally feeding out more rode, just enough to keep the boat from drifting onto the rocks. *So, how was your weekend, Roger?* Ruefully, he imagined a conversation with a friend back home. *Great, thanks. Big family row, everything exposed, lost the one woman I ever loved, learned that my son—yes, my son— was killed in Afghanistan . . . But listen, I've got an idea for a self-feeding anchor rode . . .*

There seemed to be a theme to his inventions: no work. Funny thing was, he didn't mind work. He liked waiting on customers at the store, fixing their bikes, and sizing them for new ones; loved taking groups out on Lake Champlain in kayaks, teaching them to do wet exits (the one thing he'd never been able to get Tamar to do) and Eskimo rolls. The kids were fearless. Jason was fearless. It was what led to his death: He'd been trying to save his buddies, Walter told him. Of course he was. He was Roger's son.

He reached in his pocket and turned on his cell phone, guessing there'd be no signal in this soup. But there were three messages from Tamar. "Roger, I'm sorry, really sorry. Listen, the twins are missing. You didn't take them with you, did you? I mean, it's fine if you did, but could you just call and let me know. Not much of a mother, right? Don't know where my own kids are . . . Okay, so give me a call. Thanks. Sorry. Love you."

He listened to the next message: "Roger, please, please turn on your phone. The twins . . . I think the twins might really be gone. So, if they are with you, which I doubt, but hope they are, please call me. If they aren't, would you please come home and help me find them. I love you."

And the third: "Dammit! Sorry. Just . . ." There was a long silence. "I need you. Again."

Roger tried to make out shapes on the shore as he dialed his sister.

As soon as Joy called, Tamar started running. She soon realized that she couldn't see five feet in front of her and slowed her pace. "Sand Beach. Spectacle Island," Joy had said. *Oh, Christ.* Tamar knew the tide was coming in. How often had she and Roger talked about staying out on Spectacle to watch the water rise and surround the big rock, imagining themselves adrift on a boat, far out at sea. They'd never dared.

Her father was pulling out as she reached the drive, and he ordered her into the truck. "You take the wheel. I'll walk in front with the flashlight." The headlights reflected back as they inched forward into the wall of gray. Once, her father disappeared completely, as though he himself had been turned into mist.

Tamar stopped the truck, panicked, rolled down the window. "Dad!" she shouted. He reappeared, a specter. She rolled the truck forward, opening her eyes wide, trying to find light, shapes, substance. She was afraid he would walk off the road into a ditch, afraid he would trip and she would run him over, afraid her daughters were, at that very moment, trying to make it back to shore and being swept away. Afraid. Afraid. Afraid. She eased the truck forward, inches at a time. It would take an hour to get there at this rate. She stuck her head out the window. "Please give me the flashlight and let me run."

"And do what when you get there?" her father snapped, his nerves clearly as frayed as her own. "They might see the headlights. I've got rope in the back and the two kayaks. If we can find the beach . . ." He trailed off. "Hang on, honey." He turned and dissolved again into the fog, sweeping the light side to side, trying to spot the turn.

Her phone rang. She didn't dare look, didn't dare answer. If it was Joy it was bad news. But what if it wasn't? The girls might have returned to the inn, wondering where everyone was. "Hello?"

"Tee? I'm sorry." It was Roger.

She started to weep. "No! *I'm* sorry. God, I'm such a shit. I'm such a stupid—"

"What's going on?" His voice crackled, the signal was weak.

"The twins are out on Spectacle. They must have sneaked back there while we were all . . . I didn't realize they'd gone. I mean, I wondered where they were, but—" Her words were crushing together, commuters pressing onto an outbound train. She took a breath.

"Tee? Are you there? I'm having trouble—" Crackling and static filled the space between them.

"Roger?"

"Pratt's Island . . . fog . . . wait—"

"Roger?"

"Okay? I really can't—"

"Roger, the twins are out on Spectacle!" She was screaming now, and her father's worried face peered back at her through the gloom. "I need you."

But the line was dead.

"Was that your brother?" Gar asked.

She nodded.

"Where is he?"

"Pratt's Island, I think. The connection was bad."

"He'll be okay. Let's go."

This had to be a nightmare; it couldn't be real. Her entire world had been reduced to the cab of her father's truck and the two feet of road visible in the headlights.

Then she saw her father waving the flashlight. He'd found the turn.

JOY

I waited on the beach as long as I dared, until the fog devoured it completely and I could no longer see the edge of the advancing water. This made me nervous enough to retreat to a bathhouse, where it was dry, safe, and a little warmer. I'd left the inn wearing just a T-shirt, which was now damp. I wrapped myself in a towel and sat on the narrow wooden bench.

When I first spotted that pink smudge on Spectacle, I called out, "Hal? Nat? It's Aunt Joy." I'd listened, straining to hear something over the distant foghorn and the sound of the gong marking the rocks behind Spectacle. Big swells were tossing it to and fro, judging by the near constant clanging.

Once, years ago, caught in a fogbank on the *Kestrel*, Daddy had motored around and around a buoy, always keeping the lonely, hollow tone to our left. He sent Roger, Tamar, and me below, and they played a vicious game of Spit while I sat beside them on the bunk, jaw clenched and knees hugged, believing that only by staying completely still would I keep us all safe.

Now, huddled and shivering in the bathhouse, I realized that I'd been doing just that for the past twenty, or maybe forty, years: clenched and circling around first my family, and then my husband and child, afraid to make a move. Afraid for me, or for them, I now wondered? Today I'd made a move, taken a risk, and my family, so far, remained upright and afloat. I stepped outside and called again, "Nat! Hal! Are you out there?"

Very faintly, I thought I heard a high, thin cry. A gull? The wind?

"Stay there, okay?" I shouted. "Stay up *high*. Are you both there?" The foghorn moaned, the gong swung heavily to its other side, and the water, closer now, whispered to me across the sand.

Grace trudged on. "Just keep moving," she kept telling herself, although she was exhausted and felt like she'd been walking for hours. Then she heard, quite close, the clatter of stones. Seal Cove! She could barely see five feet in front of her, but there was no mistaking the smell of decaying sea life. She plunged forward until the path ran out, and then she stumbled across a stretch of wave-washed stones, caught her foot on something—a tree cast up by a winter storm—and sprawled headlong. She righted herself and crawled back to lean against the trunk, shaking, tears of joy and relief falling freely as though that last tumble had jarred loose emotions bottled up for months. She would sit right here until the fog lifted—she didn't care how long it took—and then have a fairly short, easy walk along the lane back to the inn. The water's edge no longer seemed like a restraint, but a net that had caught her and now gently held her safe.

She sat on the sea-smoothed stones, in the firm embrace of the fallen log, and thought about her mother, and about all that she hadn't known of her mother's life. All those hours that Joan had been at work, while she was off at school. Had Joan been thinking about her son, her sisters and parents? Missing them? Perhaps even missing Grace's father? She must have had regrets. Grace always put on a brave front for her children; had Joan, as well? She thought about all the times she hadn't been there for her mother, the times she had undoubtedly disappointed her. But Joan had never let on. Had she ever asked her mother if she was happy? Would her mother have told her? Was it a daughter's job to make her mother happy? Grace certainly did not expect this from her own children.

She began to make out shapes around her, the first being the hull of an old sardiner. This, then, was not Seal Cove, but Silver Beach. She was on the opposite end of the island. No wonder the trip had taken so long. The easiest way to get home from here was to follow the Cliff Walk up to Land's End, and from there walk up the lane to the inn. It would take her over half an hour, but at least the way was open and clearly marked.

And then the fog vanished, like a dream upon waking, and the sun began to warm the stones around her. She should get started. There was dinner to cook, calls to make, conversations to have, her family and inn to tend to . . . Yet she didn't budge. The setting sun felt so warm and soothing. A bit of blue sea glass, scoured and smooth-edged, glittered beside her, like an offering. She reached for it.

JOY

After what seemed like several lifetimes, Daddy and Tamar arrived at Sand Beach. "Joy?" I heard Daddy call.

"Over here," I said. "In the bathhouse."

"Keep talking, Jo-jo." Daddy's voice was growing closer. I guessed that he would be holding one end of a rope as he attempted to locate my voice. I could hear Tamar calling out to the girls.

"I can see the headlights," I said. "You're not far. I think I heard . . . them calling earlier. I can't be sure. But there was— *is*—almost certainly something pink out there. So, unless seagulls are starting to come in different colors . . ." Daddy suddenly appeared in the murk. "Here. I'm here." He grabbed me around the waist, and we followed the line back to the truck, where Tamar was standing in the bed, shouting. "Hal? Honey? Nat? Can you hear me? It's Mommy." She waited a moment before starting in again. "We're going to come get you, cuties. Just stay where you are, okay?" She was shivering uncontrollably, maybe from cold, maybe from shock, maybe from fear, probably from all three. A high-pitched squeal came through the fog. "Did you hear that?"

Daddy and I looked at one another. "I think it was an osprey, honey," he said.

"No, it's them. I'm sure of it. Nat! Hal! Mommy is coming for you."

As Daddy started to shoulder one of the kayaks from the back of the truck, his knee gave way, and I grabbed him before he fell. "I'll go out," he said to Tamar. "I know the currents better than you. We'll tie the rope to the truck. I'll paddle out, pulling the second boat, get one of the twins, and follow the rope back. Then I'll go back for the other one. It's the only way."

Tamar looked horrified. I didn't blame her. "We can't leave one out there. We have two kayaks. We can both go—" Tamar sounded frantic.

"Only one rope. We have to tie it to the boat. And how would we get the girls back?"

"One pulls the other." Tamar sounded desperate now, trying to picture how her plan might work. She needed Roger. We all needed Roger. "We tie the rope to the first boat, and the person in the second boat holds on to the rope. The girls are small. I think we can hold them in our laps." She waited for Daddy's reaction. "I can't leave one of them out there alone, Dad. I can't."

After a long moment, Daddy said, "Okay. We'll try it. You hold tight to the rope. You drop it, you're lost." He gazed out to where the island lay, invisible. "At least the tide's coming in, so the current will pull us into the creek, not out. Don't. Let. Go." He slid the kayak the rest of the way out of the truck and took a few limping steps toward the water.

"I won't. But, Dad . . ." She hesitated. "I wonder if, maybe, I should go in front and paddle." It was the most diplomatic statement I'd ever heard my sister utter.

Daddy stared at her for a moment and grunted his assent.

"This assumes that, if we make it out there, we can get the kayaks onto the island." He seemed to be speaking more to himself than to anyone else. "I called Hank Leadbetter. He said he'd get the rescue squad here as soon as he can."

I helped my sister pull out the second boat. Tamar and Daddy buckled on life vests and tied the rope to the first kayak, and we walked both boats in the direction of the water, its exact location unknowable. "Okay," I said, as cold water filled my shoes. "Found it." I felt a momentary surge of panic. I waited an instant, and it subsided.

"The current's going to pull us. Let's start farther up the beach." Daddy started dragging his kayak along the sand. Tamar waded beside him, the swells sending water up to her thighs. "Yikes. Cold." She climbed aboard, balancing her paddle across her knees. Daddy waded in, slid into the cockpit, stowed his paddle, and grabbed hold of the rope. "Ready."

Tamar dug in and paddled over a swell as it rolled onto the beach. She had crested it and started down the backside when it hit Daddy's boat. The rope went taut and pulled her right back where she started. Without a paddle to stabilize him, I realized, he was at the mercy of the sea. Tee dug in harder and raced toward the next swell. It looked like she was paddling over a whale. Again the tug as the wave met Daddy's boat. This time the rope jerked her sideways, nearly breaching her. I wondered what she'd do if the kayak tipped over. Would she be able to slip out, or would her legs get trapped? A panic swept over me just thinking about it.

With no forward momentum of his own, Daddy was drifting toward the mouth of the creek and pulling Tee with him. She wasn't strong enough to pull them both. They were losing ground. Her plan was not working.

My mother would have thought to pack blankets so they could have stayed out on Spectacle until the rescue squad arrived. It was the first thought I'd given to Mom, whom I hadn't seen since the incident in the Games Room. Did she even know that the girls were missing?

"The fog's lifting!" I called, although they were still ridiculously close to shore. "I think I can see Spectacle." It was a beautiful sight, but a very long way off. I watched Tamar resolutely dig her paddle into the next wave.

As Grace's clothes dried, the mud on them began to stiffen. She pulled off her shirt—bright red and printed with the logo of Roger's store—and hung it on the log. Then she slipped off her sneakers and propped them up, facing the sun. She glanced around. Why not? Off came her pants. It wasn't as though anyone else would be foolish enough to venture out in this fog. Grace's smile grew a little broader with every layer of clothing she peeled off. Her bra and underpants were soon dangling from branches of the overturned log. She examined her belly. So pale! Paler still, but still visible, were the stretch lines from her three pregnancies. Her thighs were jiggly, but her calves were smooth and tight, and her breasts, though lower than they once were, still had heft.

She and Gar used to skinny-dip here and, afterward, run up the trail to the tiny cottage they called the Rookery and make love on the thin mattress. One time they'd been simply too overcome with themselves and pulled each other down in the tall grass halfway up the hill. Grace smiled at the memory. She searched for more sea glass, even though she no longer had pockets in which to place the green, blue, and amber bits she gathered. She found a piece of driftwood, smooth and pale and round as a finger, imagined it might be all that remained of a once-mighty tree trunk, and wondered what had become of the parts worn away, and then she found a quahog shell in which she could store her treasures.

Down at the water's edge, she placed the shell and its contents on a wide, flat rock and waded into the water. Ankles, calves, knees. Large swells lifted the water up to her thighs. The cold was fierce, and her ankles grew numb. She crouched and let the water wash over her back, removing the sweat, the mud, and the fear of the past hour. She didn't care that she had no towel. She swished her body to and fro, her breasts now light and buoyant, and moved to the shallow water, where she stretched out on the smooth stones, and let the waves wash the length of her. After a time, she stood and began to search the beach for more sea glass, turning at the sound of a distant engine. Without her glasses, she couldn't see who was making their way so quickly through the reach, probably as happy as she was to be out of the fog.

Grace walked back to the log with her bounty and dusted off more of the dried mud from her pants and shirt, turning them so they'd dry evenly. Then she sat with her back against the log, the warm, smooth stones pressing against her bare bottom and thighs. A light breeze stirred, and she spread her arms wide along the log and arched her back, loving the feel of the sun on her breasts and nipples. She was slightly aroused, and she leaned her head against the log and closed her eyes, happy.

As quickly as the fog had come, it was gone. Roger pulled up anchor and headed toward Spectacle Island. He hadn't heard all of what Tamar had said, but he'd caught enough. He pushed the throttle forward and steamed down the reach toward Sand Beach. Sun glinted off the fog-dampened cliffs, turning the whole of Little Island into a glass castle.

As he sped down the southwest shore, past Silver Beach, a spot of red caught his eye. He thrust the throttle forward and grabbed the binoculars. He could have sworn Tamar said Sand Beach, but maybe he'd heard wrong. He trained the binoculars at the shore, scanned, and located the red: a familiar-looking shirt hanging from the branch of a fallen tree trunk. Khakis dangled beside it, along with panties and . . . a bra. Not the twins, obviously. Then he saw a lone figure lounging in the shallows. *Mom?* He lowered the glasses. Why would she be all the way out here, alone, in the middle of a pea-soup fog, swimming, of all things? He put the glasses back to his eyes just as Grace stood up. Roger removed them quickly. "Oh, God!" he said aloud. He eased the throttle back, hoping he could slip past undetected. This . . . sighting would never be mentioned by him, although he had the uneasy feeling that he might never erase the image of his mother's soft, white body from his mind.

JOY

I hoped the girls wouldn't do anything foolish. By the time Roger reached Sand Beach, the two kayaks were still bobbing about in the big swells, only halfway to their destination. Daddy and Tee were both paddling, but neither was making much headway. It didn't look promising. The swells kept lifting them and rolling them back toward shore, the current pulling them a few yards farther into the creek. They should have waited for the rescue squad, who'd be here any time now. They should at least have waited for Roger. Both girls were running along the top of the Spectacle, probably aware that the dry area available to them was shrinking, and the distance to shore increasing.

First Daddy shouted something, then Tamar, then Daddy again, as Roger brought the boat in as close as he could, dropped the anchor, and cut the engine. "You can't hope to land a kayak on Spectacle in these swells," I heard Roger shout. "Not to mention climb up a slippery rock face, wrestle two girls into kayaks, and paddle back." He motioned impatiently for Tamar and Daddy to paddle out to the *Kestrel*, far easier to board than a piece of granite. They both started heading his way. Roger undoubtedly planned to take one of the kayaks out to the island, even with his bad shoulder. Maybe he'd just wait there with the girls.

"Tee! Where the hell are you going?" Roger shouted, pacing along the deck as, without warning, Tamar changed course in her boat and headed straight toward Spectacle. But she ignored him and continued on. She tried once, twice, to get near the island, looking for a place to land, but each time a wave would either send her bobbing away or threaten to toss her up onto it. The girls were on the move, scampering along the small expanse of exposed surface, their eyes on their mother, clearly terrified. They would both try to climb aboard, I was sure of that. Tamar looked frantic as she vainly tried one spot and then another, searching for a place to land. Even I could see that Tamar's plan wouldn't work.

I felt a kinship for my sister at that moment that I had never felt before, an empathy I didn't think possible. When I went to see her just after she'd delivered the twins, I remember her lying in bed with those two darling babies in her arms, looking exhausted and something else. At the time, I didn't recognize the expression on her face, but I did now. She'd been afraid. Terrified, in fact. She used to complain, during those early weeks, about how tired she was, how she couldn't get anything done, how one or both babies were in constant need of something. . . . She never said anything about the giddy happiness of looking into her daughters' faces and seeing herself and Daniel mirrored there, about the joys of motherhood. It was clear now that her daughters' voices coming to her through the fog had stirred something that she'd buried deep eight years earlier.

For the first time, I understood that Tamar's caustic remarks and bravado were merely defenses. She was as clueless and scared as the rest of us. As I watched my sister try first one approach, and then another, to get to her daughters, I knew that, while she'd given up once rather than risk failure, she wouldn't give up now.

But neither did I think she would succeed.

And so it became clear to me what I needed to do. I looked across the nearly fifty yards of dark water that separated me from Spectacle, from my sister and my two nieces. Swells, slightly smaller now, rolled in and heaved themselves onto the beach at my feet. I went into the bathhouse, put on a suit, found a life jacket—so old it looked like it might drag me under rather than keep me afloat—and walked down to the water, rope in hand.

I tied the rope around my waist before wading into the water. It was freezing. With a pounding heart, I silently thanked Stuart both for making me take swimming lessons from the Red Cross at our local pool and for the gift of affirmations, which I now intoned like a mantra. *I have swum before from this very beach. I'm wearing a life vest. I can do this.*

The water was up to my waist now. But going in up to the shoulders was always the worst. Now I was chest deep. Breathless. Christ, I was freezing, despite the Gulf Stream now tugging at my legs, which kept the water on this side of the island relatively temperate. I pushed off and began to paddle forward. My heart was hammering so loudly I was sure the others could hear it, probably mistaking it for distant thunder. I kept my eyes trained on the island. It looked so far away and so small—and when I dipped into a trough, it disappeared completely. But on I went, thinking about my friend Bonnie's sure, even strokes.

I was nearly there when a wave caught me and my head went under. I heard Tamar yell my name, frantic, as the wave sent me sprawling onto the rocks.

Roger threw his father a line and pulled him in the rest of the way to the *Kestrel*. Gar climbed slowly up the swim ladder, and Roger hopped into the kayak with two additional life vests. His shoulder twinged immediately. It was only last week that his surgeon had told him he could stop wearing the sling, and Roger was pretty sure that kayaking wasn't on the list of approved activities. But then, neither was biking, and he'd been doing that for weeks.

Joy had tied the rope around Nat's waist and was now urging her into the water, despite fingers trembling so badly that Roger could see them shaking.

"Jump, Nat," Tamar was calling to her daughter. "Go with Auntie Joy. I'm going to wait here with Hal." Nat was crying, but not as loudly as Hal, who did not like the idea of being left out there one bit.

As he watched Joy begin to make her slow progress back to the beach, her arms around Nat, her hands sliding along the rope, her face wearing a look of complete concentration, Roger tried to think if he'd ever overcome a fear as great as hers. He was so focused on watching her bring Nat back to shore that he didn't notice Hal jump.

Grace began to stack stones, beginning with a wide, flat piece of speckled granite. On that she placed one of gray slate, as warm and smooth as a loaf of fresh bread. Next came a round boulder of pinkish-blue, followed by a hunk of quartz, and then one nearly black, oblong-shaped with a broad white stripe running through its middle. The stack looked unstable, so she took it down and started searching for more stones. Soon her cairn stood a sturdy two feet high. When was the last time she'd done anything so frivolous? Even her gardening had begun to feel perfunctory, more for guests of the inn than for herself. Guests expected not only gardens, but gourmet meals, late-afternoon snacks, and homemade marshmallows to roast over the fire pit in the evening. Each time Grace added something to the list of specialty items she offered, they turned into expectations the following season. She was tired of doing and longed, simply, to be. She added another rock to the pile, and when the pile toppled, she started over.

As Grace held a stone bristling with barnacles, she recalled the pinecone-studded ashtray from so many years ago. She and her mother had assembled that puzzle of state flowers at the Shore View Cabins, and then she'd jumped on the trampoline in the rain, while her mother watched. Afterward, they collected handfuls of tiny cones from the surrounding balsams and went to the office for glue. The manager had none but offered them Scotch tape, which they took back to their cabin and used to stick the brittle, brown cones to the heavy glass ashtray, and then onto the glass in the bathroom. How they had laughed. Later, Grace glued the pinecones on.

It was clear to Grace even then that the getaway was not a prize they'd won—that sad assemblage of damp cabins would not have made even a good second or third prize. Even so, she never asked her mother why they went without Daddy. Not once. Funny, she thought, how children, who question everything, instinctively know when it's time *not* to ask. She'd accepted her mother's story, even after they left the little cabin.

She never saw her father again.

What it must have cost her mother to keep up that lighthearted, vacation attitude for her little girl, especially in such dismal surroundings, knowing what lay behind her, and what probably lay ahead. Grace had memories of her father, vague and blurry, like old home movies: his face contorted in anger, backing her mother up against the washing machine, the stove, the kitchen counter, striking her again and again, with his fists. Never on her face. The day before they left, she heard the crunch of tires on gravel, and her mother said, "Quick, Gracie, let's play hide-and-seek. Hide, and I'll come find you. Hurry now." This was something new, and Grace saw a look on her mother's face that she recognized as fear. So, just as the back door opened, she ran and hid in the linen closet, not from her mother's playful, seeking eyes—she understood this much— but from her father. In all the years afterward, Grace had often wondered whether she was the reason her father was always so angry. She had often wished that she'd come out of hiding that day and protected her mother, wondered whether it would have made any difference.

The very next morning, Joan came into Grace's room to wake her for school, as she did every morning. But, instead of calling out her usual, cheery, "Time to get up!" from the doorway, she came over to Grace's bed and woke her with a light touch on her arm. "I have a surprise for you." She was whispering, but the whisper had an urgent undercurrent. She was holding a new Tourister suitcase, blue with shiny clasps. She looked tired, her eyes red and puffy. "We've won a vacation. Just the two of us."

"What about school?" Grace asked, thinking about her report on Brazil. (Principal exports: iron ore, manganese, and bauxite; language: Portuguese.)

"Never mind that. You can turn your report in later. Now hurry and get dressed. And pack your things in here." She held out the suitcase.

"Where are we going?" Grace asked. "Disneyland?" Newly opened, it was Grace's dream vacation destination.

"No," her mother said, looking like she might cry. "But somewhere almost as nice." Grace did not ask any more questions.

They took a cab to the bus station. "This is part of our prize," Joan told her, as she slid the new blue Tourister case onto the backseat beside Grace, who loved its rough surface, the bright clasps that closed with such precision and conviction. Later Grace would wonder how her mother had managed to save for the trip. It must have taken quite a while to pare enough cash from their meager weekly budget, without sacrificing her milk money, or new school clothes, or presents on Christmas and her birthday. How long had Joan known that she was planning for them to leave?

But the real cost, Grace now understood, had been keeping the whole thing secret, and even making it fun. And here she was, older now than her mother had been then, and feeling like a failure for not being able to make this weekend fun. Then she thought about Joy and what keeping Roger and Tamar's secret might have cost her.

The Shore View Cabins hadn't quite equaled Disneyland. Still, looking back to that jump on the trampoline, to the puzzle of the state flowers, to the pinecones bristling from the ashtray and bathroom cup . . . the weekend did hold a certain magic for Grace.

After three or four days, they left the cabin, took another cab to a train station, and went all the way to Boston, where they rode the trolley ("They have these at Disneyland," a delighted Grace informed her mother) to a hotel. Their room was not quite as nice as the little cabin had been, with its tiny window up high on the wall, looking out to the trampoline. Still, the hotel had an elevator, something Grace had never seen, with a sliding iron gate that crashed closed and levered shut, and black buttons in a brass plate. Even though their room was on the second floor, they rode the elevator all the way to the top several times. The conveyance whined and shuddered as it rose, and you could see the floors as you slid past.

Was it fear or duty that kept Grace from questioning the "vacation" from which they never returned? Was it fear or duty that kept her from questioning the truth of the crash? Another invisible boundary that she had known not to cross, like the electric wire buried an inch beneath the soil that prevented Sophie from wandering too far.

JOY

I wanted to make it those last few yards to the beach unassisted: Alice, emerging, victorious, from her rabbit hole. But the rescue squad arrived, and as the truck doors swung open, four figures hopped out. One of them was now racing toward us, splashing into the water just as my feet touched sand. The current immediately yanked my ankles out from underneath me, sending Nat and me, once again, adrift. But then with another stroke, I found purchase. The young woman wading out to us took a shivering, crying Nat from my arms and helped me the last few yards to shore.

My knees buckled when I reached the beach, and the woman held me up as she threw a blanket around my shoulders. "You okay?"

I nodded, my teeth chattering too hard to speak. Another squad member wrapped Nat in a blanket and started to whisk her toward the truck but then stopped and stared along with the others out at the water. Nat stared, too, swaddled and hiccupping uneven sobs. I turned to see what they were looking at: Tamar paddling frantically, Roger taking halting strokes, Daddy, scanning the water with binoculars from the deck of the *Kestrel*, pointing and shouting. Only then did I realize that Hal had jumped in to follow us. How had I not heard her? I didn't see her anywhere.

Grace dressed and began the trek back to the inn. She had only about another hour of daylight, but she didn't feel like hurrying, wasn't—to be honest—ready to have the conversations that were sure to follow Joy's announcement about the crash. She picked some vetch, aster, and black-eyed Susan as she climbed the steep path to Land's End. The sun, huge, hovered just above the horizon and colored the water orange. Waves exploded onto the rocks below her, and spray shot skyward. Just offshore, a flock of ducks paddled in formation. A gull hung, suspended in the air. She continued along the path, humming softly, occasionally adding to her bouquet.

When she reached the lane leading back to the inn, she spotted the roof of the Rookery. She and Gar had lived there the summer they were married, on a sort of extended honeymoon. And she'd often come by herself the summer after they lost Abigail, needing to get away from the daily grind of the inn—and from Gar. During that time they'd orbited one another, occupied the same space but talked without sharing, listened without hearing. Glen, an artist visiting the island, seemed like a safe harbor, a tranquil cove during that stormy time. She never told him about Abigail or much of anything else about her life.

She'd found him here one afternoon, painting. "The light on the water," he said, "and the wildflowers are perfect." They met only twice. That first time was accidental. The second was not. Grace had come knowing he'd be here. They'd sat on the porch, and he'd sketched her as they talked. How easy, how welcome, it would have been to give her heart, her whole heart, to this stranger, Grace had thought. To leave her life and her grief and the duties of the inn far behind. But soon he would no longer be a stranger. His appeal was precisely that he was unknown, like the many new faces Grace had encountered in each of her new schools in each of the new towns to which she and her mother had moved.

After the second visit, Grace didn't return to the Rookery for several weeks, long past the date she knew Glen was returning to his home in Vermont. When she finally did go back—both hoping and fearing she'd find him there—the porch was empty and, under the mat, was a small sketch of the Rookery. On the back he'd written, "Thinking, smiling, of you." She kept the card in her desk drawer, telling herself that she wasn't hiding it, although she knew that Gar would never look there without asking.

Meanwhile, she and Gar continued to go through the motions of marriage until, one day, she discovered she was pregnant. Their eyes and hearts slowly began to open—like winter giving way to spring. Grace remained guarded, however, knowing how disappointing and damaging late spring snows can be, afraid to grow too close, aware that the frail connection that lay between them might be broken forever if there were another loss. Perhaps it hadn't been fair to name their daughter Joyous. But at the time, there wasn't any other choice for either of them.

The Rookery was surrounded by goldenrod, five feet high, and rugosa roses, pregnant with rose hips. Grace tamped down a path and stepped onto the narrow wooden porch. The two rough-hewn chairs still faced out to sea. She tried the door. Locked. But Grace guessed that the key might still be under the mat.

It was.

Roger turned as he heard his father shout. He saw Hal scrabbling in the waves and dug his paddle hard into the water.

Pain radiated down his arm and up his neck. *Shit*. He could practically feel the stitches popping. The surgeon had said she'd never seen such a mess.

He heard Tamar scream next, as Hal's head went under. Her pink shirt, visible for a moment, disappeared, then reappeared several yards away. Tamar was on the move, and Roger followed, paddling as fast as he could. His father, on the *Kestrel*, had a life preserver and a line at the ready. He'd started the engine but couldn't get in close enough to be of any help.

Roger rolled his kayak and somersaulted out.

It was dark and cold; bits of seaweed sailed past. The cut on his leg stung like a son of a bitch. He came up sputtering, got his bearings, and looked around for his niece. He couldn't see her anywhere, but he could see Tamar paddling up the beach, and he assumed—hoped—she was following a tiny head and a shadow of pink in this sea of green. The current, surprisingly strong, carried him forward at a good clip. But would it shoot him right past her? With his bad shoulder, he wasn't sure if he could fight it.

Each time a wave lifted him, he caught a glimpse of Hal's head, and then he'd drop back into a trough and lose her. *Hang in there*, he told himself. *Think about something else. Gratitudes: That I didn't drink that beer. That Tamar obviously substituted some other pill for a Vicodin*. Another lift. Almost there. He pulled hard into the next wave, felt heat radiate again down his arm and up into his neck. Well, at least there were EMTs here in case he blew all his stitches and couldn't swim to shore. Tamar paddled alongside him. His father shouted out directions each time he picked up the small spot of pink with the binoculars.

Roger could see how badly Tamar wanted to get out of that kayak. Being out of control was intolerable for her. He tore into another wave, felt himself get caught in an eddy. Hal was so close! The eddy spun him past her, but they made eye contact just before she went under again. Tamar brought her boat alongside close enough for Roger to grab her paddle. The force capsized Tamar's kayak, at which point she discovered just how effective fear is as a motivator: She was out of her boat in an instant. The move catapulted Roger closer to Hal, who looked more and more like the flotsam drifting by on the tide.

· Chapter Twenty ·

JOY

I was sitting at the table with Roger when Daddy came into the kitchen. "Where's your sister?" He looked tired and older than I'd ever seen him.

"Upstairs," I said. I'd stood in the shower for a good ten minutes, trying to get the shaking to stop, but every now and then I felt another tremor come on. It radiated down to my ankles and up to my scalp. I felt one now.

Roger was icing his shoulder and must have seen me shaking. "I could go for something hot. Anyone want coffee?"

"You sit. I'll make it." Daddy plugged in the coffeemaker. "You both should be very, very proud of what you did today. Jo-jo, you were incredibly brave." He turned to face me. "I don't know when I've ever felt so proud." There were tears in his eyes.

"And Roger . . ." Daddy's pride and admiration made Roger shift his gaze down to the table. "If you hadn't come along—" Daddy's voice broke, and he turned to spoon coffee into the basket and collect himself. He cleared his throat and turned

back. He stood there, giving Roger the full force of his attention, clearly willing him to meet his eye. But Roger seemed to
shrink under this too-bright light of our father's scrutiny, and
so Daddy addressed his comment to the top of Roger's head.
"I'm sorry, son."

Roger nodded his head.

"Now, if I just knew where your mother was."

"She's on Silver Beach." Roger gave his shoulder a tentative
wiggle. The EMT had done a quick check and pronounced him
good to go but told him to keep ice on it and see his surgeon
when he got back to the mainland.

Daddy looked skeptical. "At this hour?"

Roger shrugged. "I saw her there when I was coming over
from Pratt's Island. Spotted something on the beach, thought
maybe it was the twins, so I grabbed the binoculars and looked.
It was . . . Mom."

"Doing what?" I asked.

"Swimming. Well, wallowing. I saw her shirt. It was bright
red, hanging on a log." Daddy and I were both staring at him
now. "Along with her pants and . . . a few other items."

"She was . . . skinny-dipping?" I asked cautiously.

"I would say . . . yes." He stared down at the table to avoid
our curious looks. "I don't know if she's there now. But she was
there earlier."

A gurgle from Sophie's belly echoed loudly in the suddenly
silent room.

"I'm going over to the Rookery." Daddy checked his watch.
"See if she's there."

"The Rookery?" I asked, as we watched him put two beers
in a bag and add a few food items.

"We used to go there when we were first married. We'd

skinny dip, and then—" He broke off. "I'll be back in a bit. I just want to make sure she's okay."

Roger and I exchanged amused looks across the table after he left. "Nookie at the Rooky," I whispered.

Roger broke out in laughter. "You impressed the hell out of me today, too, Jo-jo." He got up from the table to pour us both a cup of coffee, and stirred two heaping teaspoons of sugar into his. "Not that that's any great testimonial. But you did. It took guts. It's one thing to think up a plan, another to execute it." He gave a self-deprecating laugh. "I should know."

"You're doing just fine, Roger."

He looked startled by my comment.

We'd had few heart-to-hearts in our lives. I'd always blamed Tamar for that, but maybe, the fault was partly mine. *Had I ever initiated one?* This was as good a time as any to find out.

The red-shingled, two-room cottage was much as Grace remembered from her last visit: the curtains slightly more yellowed, the linoleum more worn, but the same light filtering through the filmy windows and settling on the floor, and the same smell of camphor and candle wax. Inside, the Rookery still felt of the unhurried passage of time.

The front room had a deep soapstone double sink in one corner and, beside it, a tiny gas range. Grace thought of her kitchen at the inn with its eight-burner Wolf stove, Sub-Zero refrigerator, two ovens, pantry, pot racks, pans, whisks, and spoons . . . Yet she didn't remember ever feeling wanting the summer she and Gar lived here. They used jelly jars for glasses and ate off chipped, mismatched plates. Grace smiled; she still favored mismatched china and picked up old sets at yard sales to use at the inn.

Back then she and Gar made wood fires in the small stove on bright, chilly mornings and damp afternoons, the heavy air infused with the scent of roses and pine. Each morning, she would fill the battered aluminum percolator and set it on the range, and they would stand together with their arms entwined, watching the coffee grow darker and darker as it bubbled up in the glass knob. They would take their mugs out onto the porch and sit in the chairs, draped with towels to avoid splinters, and dream about their future.

She stepped farther into the room and ran her hand across the table Gar had made from driftwood they'd found on Silver Beach. It still stood against the window, across from the sagging sofa, now covered with an old bedspread that Grace did not recognize. She laid her bouquet on the table and found two jelly jars in the single cupboard. She tried the tap, and after a few coughs and sputters, the water streamed out—rust-colored at first, but soon running clear. She made two bouquets, one for the dining table, the other for the bedroom.

A curtain that Grace had sewn from blue-checkered tablecloths and hung on a slender cord still separated the two rooms. As if they'd needed privacy, with just the two of them. She was impressed that it had held up all these years. The pale blue metal bed, its coverlet still tucked neatly around the mattress, stood in front of the single window, yellow with film and coated with cobwebs. Even so, Grace could see that daylight was rapidly fading. She pulled back the coverlet to see if there were sheets. No such luck.

She stepped out onto the porch and stood, stock-still, breath held. Everything—sky, water, rocks, trees—glowed violet rose.

She leaned against the porch rail and watched the colors deepen and shift. Just offshore, on the real rookery, gulls and cormorants rose like clouds of smoke to sail off and feed. It seemed as if she could see forever.

A truck door slammed behind the cottage, and Grace heard footsteps. She knew it was Gar before his head appeared around the side of the cottage. "How's my best girl?" he asked.

"*Best* girl?"

He smiled. "I heard you went skinny-dipping without me."

How on earth did he know that? "From who?"

Gar looked abashed. "Our son."

"The boat." She remembered now that she'd seen one motor by, too far out to identify. "Oh, dear."

"I think he'll get over it in ten or fifteen years. With lots of therapy."

Grace chuckled. "And you knew I'd be here?"

He nodded. "Pretty sure."

"I think I might stay."

"Forever?" He'd taken a position at the rail next to her, the picnic basket between them.

She shrugged. "Probably be a bit chilly this winter."

"I could come and keep you warm."

Grace looked out to the horizon, now a deep red with smudges of purple. "I got lost."

"Oh?"

When had it started? Several months ago, after her mother died. Or maybe much earlier. "This afternoon. I tried to find the fern brake where I used to bring the kids and . . . got lost." She stopped, once again unsure which trail to take.

Gar sensed that Grace needed silence, so they sat companionably for a little while, watching the sky grow dark. Finally Grace said, "Did you bring any wine?"

"Two beers. I was in a hurry."

"Even better."

Gar popped off the caps, and they clinked the necks of the bottles together.

"It's so mild," Grace observed. "Strange for this time of year." She knew they needed to talk about the crash, about Roger, Tamar, Joy, but she couldn't just yet.

"Tropical air from that hurricane down south."

"Oh, no. Rain tomorrow?" Grace hadn't checked the forecast.

Gar shrugged. "Maybe a shower or two in the afternoon. Some wind. Late. We'll be okay." He didn't sound convinced, and neither was Grace. He was keeping something from her. "What is it?" she prodded.

Gar recounted the events of the afternoon: Tamar discovering that the twins were missing, the fog, the search, the rescue. "You were in the fog, Short. No wonder you got lost."

Grace listened wide-eyed and silent. "How are they? How's Tamar? Oh, I should have been there. Let's go back right now—"

He put a hand on her arm. "Everybody's okay. We managed without you."

Grace took a long swallow of beer. Was she relieved or disappointed to hear that they hadn't needed her? "Do you think you could . . . manage without me a bit longer? I want a little more time."

Gar looked pensive. "I could, but I'd rather not."

"Just for tonight."

"You really want to stay here by yourself?"

She did.

"All right, then." Gar kissed her lightly on the cheek, told her he'd send Joy and Roger back with some additional supplies, and walked to his truck.

After he left, Grace sat for a while, staring out into the dark. She was exhausted after her trek through the woods. Still, she was being given an opportunity to witness something important about life: her mother's, her family's, *her own*. When she realized that she was holding her breath, she let it out very softly, as one might during a game of hide-and-seek. Who, or what, was she hiding from? Her grief about her mother's painful marriage? Her remorse over all the kind things she hadn't thought to do for her mother as an adult and now never could? Her guilt about the long-ago car crash?

Or was it merely frustration at not being able to make this weekend fun?

At the time of the crash, she had to admit, she'd wondered. . . . Something about the event hadn't rung true. Roger's injuries had seemed out of line with what would have occurred to the driver—everyone said so: EMTs, doctors, police. But Roger was insistent. Joy was right: It had been easier for them all to believe it was Roger's fault than to look for, and see, the truth.

In the picnic basket, she found Tamar's jar of organic peanut butter, half a box of crackers, a few individually wrapped cheese singles, an apple, and a chocolate bar. Not bad, she thought. Suddenly she was very hungry. She remembered the note on the kitchen table. Would the flowers be delivered? She had no idea. At least they had the garden—although she cringed at the memory of the kale in those awful urns and the billowing ornamental grass. She could, at least, honor her mother's request with a beautiful view of the water. But fun? Grace simply did not see how that was possible. Because tomorrow, after the service, they would need to sit down, as a family, and sort through what happened today, and what had happened twenty years ago.

Grace folded the square of cheese into quarters and popped it into her mouth. When was the last time she'd laughed with abandon? As a child she had loved jumping on a trampoline, playing jacks, jumping rope, playing dodgeball. As an adult, she'd also once found pleasure in the simple tasks of cooking, sewing, gardening. Now everything seemed like a chore. Had she grown too tired and worn out to have fun or simply forgotten how? Was it too late to learn again?

JOY

I watched Roger knead a round of pizza dough.

"I was thinking of an aerosol," he said. "Tamar suggested pillows, like the balsam-scented ones . . ."

"Sachets?" I offered.

"Right. What do you think?" Roger pressed his fingers into the dough, flattening it.

"Creosote-scented sachets? I'm going to need to think about that."

Roger laughed.

When Daddy returned from the Rookery, he told us that Mom was going to spend the night there.

"Why?" Roger asked.

"She needs . . . a little time alone, I guess, to sort things out," he said, and asked us to take her some sheets and towels. Then he went upstairs to check on Tee and the girls.

"Virginia Woolf," I said, after he left. *A Room of One's Own*. It's every woman's dream."

Roger waited. When I didn't say anything more, he said, "You know what would be excellent on pizza?" He had created a perfect round.

"Winter squash," I said. "With capers and white sauce."

"Hm. Interesting. I was thinking lobster, sweet red pepper, and vodka cream sauce."

"Oh, that would be good. I love lobster in ravioli. Ever tried wild mushrooms?"

"Morels, chanterelles, ramps, and fiddleheads. Awesome."

"Black trumpets and smoked salmon," I countered.

"No, stop!" Roger said, in mock distress, as if this last description were too much without a sample to try.

I smiled, but I was thinking about Mom, alone in the Rookery, taking some time away from the rest of us.

Roger glanced over, noting my silence. "Fairy-ring mushrooms with prosciutto?" he said, with a twinkle in his eye.

"We'd have to have leeks with that," I said, smiling back. "You seem to know a lot about cooking, or at least about wild mushrooms."

"I like to cook. Have a buddy with a restaurant." Roger was now stretching another mound of dough with his fingers. "I work there on weekends."

My brother: full of surprises. "Let's take those sheets and towels to Mom," I said. "You mind driving? My car's . . . kind of full."

Roger's expression was somber. "Yeah, what's up with that?"

"Guess I overpacked for the weekend."

Roger's gaze grew even more serious. "I saw your thumb, Jo-jo. The cut."

Roger and I had never talked about my cutting. I would have said that he knew nothing about it, but actually, he looked quite concerned. "I missed Rex," I said. And . . ." I looked at my brother, uncertain how he'd react to my next statement. "I was worried about this weekend." He and I had not yet spoken about my blurting out the truth in front of everyone earlier today.

Roger laughed. "I know that feeling."

"I hated having that secret, Roger."

He grew serious again and fiddled with the round of dough. "I know. I'm sorry. I didn't intend to put you in that spot. It was just . . . Tamar thinks she's tough, wants people to think that, but she isn't. I don't know, though. Sometimes I'm not sure I did her much of a favor."

He was pressing the dough into a larger and larger circle. "Maybe," he said to me now, "you just need a room of your own."

I stared at him for a moment before standing and heading to the linen closet. My brother: full of surprises.

Although it seemed that they'd all been submerged quite enough for one day, Tamar ushered her girls upstairs as soon as they reached the inn and into a tub laced with lilac-scented bubble bath. She sat on the floor beside them, her hands resting on the rim. The nightmare was over. *That* nightmare.

She finally left them, but only to sit in the hallway with her back against the bathroom door, well within earshot should the room grow too quiet or a small voice call out for help, and used her phone to call Daniel. As she waited for the connection to go through, she thought about Roger, his son dead at nineteen. Had he been right the day he teased her about not having a heart? How many such comments had *she* made to him, to Joy, to Daniel, to countless others?

Startled by the sound of her own voice on her home voice mail, she hung up and sat for a moment, listening to the twins chanting and splashing, before dialing Daniel's cell phone. She thought about what she would say to him. "Hi, it's me. I'm just checking in." *Too impersonal.* "Just wanted to say hi." Except that *Hi* wasn't at all what she wanted to say. "The girls wanted to say good night." She didn't want to tell him about the afternoon's events but knew she had to. She pressed the phone to her forehead. She was done with secrets, done with lies. She would take the phone into the bathroom and let them tell him about their adventure, and then explain, as truthfully as she could, the events of the afternoon. But how on earth would she tell him about the crash? About how she'd let her brother take the blame for her all these years, let him go to prison, lose Loraine, lose his son. . . .

When Daniel didn't pick up, Tamar didn't leave a message. She'd been angry when they talked that morning. "A separation?" She'd actually laughed. "Don't be absurd, Daniel." Now she was frightened. Why wasn't he answering? Where was he? Earlier today she'd watched Hal be nearly swept away. Now she was watching her marriage go, too. Wouldn't that be a kicker: Just as she recognized what was most important—family—she lost it all. Her life felt like one of those annoying puzzles with the little silver balls that roll around, resisting one's attempts to settle them each in its own pocket. What was it Joy had said to her earlier? *Don't bleed until you're shot.* Was that really one of Tamar's workshop aphorisms? She could hear the bullets whizzing by.

She toweled off the twins, trying not to think about how foreign their little bodies looked to her. At home she often checked her e-mail as they changed into their pajamas and hopped into bed. Multitasking, she thought, is possibly the worst affliction of the twenty-first century.

Tonight she tucked the girls into her own bed—she would shift them later—and climbed in between them. Although it was much earlier than their normal bedtime, neither complained. Each twin had stacked a pile of books beside her, which delighted Tamar. Her usual one-story-each rule seemed like something she'd instituted a lifetime ago. She would lie there all night with her girls, if they'd let her.

"Where shall we start?" Tamar asked.

Hal handed her *The Counterpane Fairy* and proceeded to unwrap a candy bar. Another rule broken! Tamar smiled and stretched out her palm for a piece. Hal broke it in three not quite equal pieces. Each girl hugged a stuffed animal to her chest and wriggled down beneath the covers. Tamar had turned off the fan because a warm breeze was wafting in through the open window. "Are you cold?" The girls shook their heads. She wiggled down as well, savoring the feel of her daughters' two warm bodies pressing against hers. The smell of chocolate hung thick in the air, mingling with the lingering scent of lilac. "The Princess of the Golden Castle," she began. "Chapter First . . ."

· Chapter Twenty-one ·

JOY

"I am sorry I told," I said in the dark cab, as Roger and I bumped along the lane to the Rookery. "I mean, I'm glad for you: You deserve for people to know the truth. But I'm sorry I didn't keep your secret."

Roger said nothing for a long moment. "When you build a house, one wrong measurement can send the whole thing slightly off. It will stand okay, but doorjambs and walls aren't even, so doors don't stay shut, and pictures never hang straight. Some contractors shrug it off; 'Can't see it from my house,' they'll say. I never liked to do that. Guess it's why I never made any money at it. But someone's going to live in that house, and they'll know something's not right. Maybe now . . ." He trailed off.

We drove on in silence, and I wondered whether the doors and windows in our family would now shut properly. "How did things go with Loraine?" I asked, as Roger pulled up in front of the Rookery.

Roger reached for the door handle. "Not well. She can't get past the drinking. Or the crash."

"But—"

He held up a hand. "I know. It wasn't my fault. I wasn't driving. But I had been drinking. Was drunk, in fact. I've stopped now—again—but who knows if it'll stick this time. If I hadn't been drunk that night . . . Well, things would have turned out differently for all of us, wouldn't they?"

"You are an amazing man, Roger," I said, because I believed it and because I wasn't sure he'd ever heard that from anyone before. "Generous, kind, fun, caring, sensitive. Loraine deserves to know the truth. You deserve for her to know the truth."

Roger shook his head and opened the door. "Maybe so, but I can't be the one to tell her. If it's meant to be, it will be."

Grace was sitting on the front porch holding a beer when Joy and Roger arrived with a kerosene lamp and an armload of sheets and towels. On the table beside her were the uneaten apple, several empty cheese wrappers, and the open jar of peanut butter. Grace was not displeased to see them, but hoped they wouldn't stay long. She was enjoying her solitude.

Roger dropped into the other chair. "Man, this is amazing." The moon's fat, white face gazed down at its wobbly mirror image in the shifting surface below. Crickets sawed enthusiastically in the tall weeds. "You guys should fix this place up. We could charge a bundle. Rent it as, like, a private getaway. Maybe put in a hot tub out here . . ."

"Roger," Joy said quietly, "let's go make up Mom's bed for her."

Roger picked up the apple and took a large bite. "Oh, sure," he said, and they disappeared into the cottage. Grace resumed her meditation of the night, letting the silence steal back, like a small animal scared from the room, and slowly settle around her. The moon had moved a few inches in the sky, and more stars had come out, and Grace was imagining them as peepholes in a giant curtain, through which the dead could peer down at those below. Everyone waiting for the show to begin. She gazed up, wondering if her mother was peering down, and, if so, what she saw.

For years she and her mother had come to the Rookery after picnics at Sand Beach. They climbed the bluff, just the two of them, and sat right here. Just like this. Once, Gar took their picture, and Grace put it in the album. Grace had been thirty-five, her mother fifty-five. Nearly ten years younger than Grace was now. One day, Grace realized, she would be eighty-four, and then just a pinprick of light in someone's night sky.

Joy returned a few minutes later, alone.

"Where's your brother?"

"Mentally renovating. Which is an appealing concept, when you think about it."

Behind them, Roger's heavy footsteps paced out the dimensions of the cottage. Grace could feel Joy's smile match her own in the dark. Her son, irrepressible and resilient. Grace envied him those qualities.

"Was this your dream?" Joy asked. "A room of your own, no family around . . ."

"Some might object to your use of the past tense there."

"Sorry. Is this your dream?"

"No." Grace had spent too much time alone as a child to have such a dream. She thought for a moment. "For a while, when I was young, I dreamed of becoming a stewardess."

Joy raised her eyebrows at this and smiled.

"I wanted to wear a crisp, blue suit and a snappy hat set at a jaunty angle, my hair and makeup perfect. To fly to exotic-sounding cities with names I couldn't pronounce." Grace glanced at Joy, certain she would be judged for having such an uninspired dream. But she saw her daughter gazing at her with rapt attention, as though picturing herself in just such an outfit, deplaning in Caen, Nizhny Novgorod, or Kyaukpyu. She'd missed this daughter, who'd grown so distant since the crash. Grace now understood why.

"I was 'too short,' they said. And then I met your father, and you kids were born, and we took over the inn. And after that . . ." Grace thought, but didn't say, she'd been too busy for dreams. Then she realized that she did have one other dream. "I dreamed of having a home I'd never have to leave." A rustling in the grass nearby signaled some small, nocturnal animal out hunting. "What about you?"

Joy picked up the peanut butter jar, stared into it. "Tamar said that to stop procrastinating, you should do anything related to the task."

"What have you been procrastinating about?"

"My life. Rex is gone, and I have no idea what to do with myself." Joy dug her finger into the jar, stared at the wad of peanut butter, and sucked it off her finger.

Grace nodded and reached for the jar. "I don't remember how to have fun."

The two women sat in silence, handing the jar of peanut butter back and forth.

"You need to 'get off dead center,'" Grace said.

"Tamar?"

Grace nodded, and they both smiled. Grace wanted to pull her daughter onto her lap and rock her, tell her that every mother goes through this when her children leave. Inside, Roger was dragging furniture across the floor. Grace thought about her own mother, living alone all those years, while Grace was busy with the kids, the inn, her life. The excuses she made were real enough, but they were just that, excuses. The truth was, she felt she'd needed to establish her independence. It pained her now to think how much her absence might have hurt her mother. And yet, wasn't it a mother's job to raise her children to become independent? "We want and don't want our children to grow up and leave us," she said as much to herself as to Joy. "We're both proud and resentful when they do."

"The emptiness was too much. I was afraid, am afraid, that without Rex there'll be nothing holding Stuart and me together." Joy's voice grew soft and broke slightly as she said this.

"I thought I could run away from sadness and uncertainty once." Grace was thinking of Glen. "From loneliness and pain."

"What happened?"

"I decided to face them instead. It seemed like such a long way around." Grace put the lid back on the peanut butter jar and stared at it. "I was thinking, earlier, about the time—I doubt you even remember—when you were about three, and I found you in the kitchen, all alone, smashing a package of peanut butter crackers with the end of a kitchen knife because you couldn't get it open and didn't want to bother me."

"Of course I remember! I still have a hard time opening those things." Joy reached for one of the empty cheese wrappers and began folding it.

"I felt so negligent: my child, foraging for a simple snack. What if you'd cut yourself?"

Joy glanced at her thumb and noticed that the salt water had gone a long way toward healing it. "Remember what we did after?"

Grace did not remember. She peered back in her mind's eye, but saw only light glinting off the sharp blade, her daughter's noiseless tears. Her beloved little Joy, all her silent rage channeled into the unyielding wrapper.

"We went for a picnic on the rocks. Just you, me, and my dolls."

Grace had no recollection of that whatsoever and doubted it could be true. Who would have looked after the twins? "Did we? I'd forgotten that."

"One of my favorite memories. We had ladyfingers and butterscotch pudding."

Now Grace was sure Joy had made this up. When had she last bought ladyfingers? When had she ever? "Sounds quite elegant."

They listened to Roger dragging more furniture. "Do you have any regrets, Mom?"

Regrets. "I regret that I didn't ask my mother more about her life while I still could." As soon as she said this, Grace remembered that her aunts were arriving the next morning. Only yesterday it had seemed a somewhat unwelcome intrusion. Now it felt like a gift from her mother. She glanced up at the starry sky. Then she thought of Gar, back at the inn, bearing the burden of this afternoon's revelations without her. And about Tamar, alone with her twins, her secret exposed. And dear, resilient Roger, whose footsteps had recently disappeared into the back bedroom—she wondered, briefly, whether he'd curled up on the bed and fallen asleep. Funny that Roger was the one she and Gar spent all their time worrying about, and he was the one who probably needed it least. *She had a home she never had to leave. Why was she sitting here?*

She pushed herself up out of her chair. "I'm going home."

Just then, Roger clomped out onto the porch and heaved the apple core into the night. "We could easily turn this into a really nice suite: bedroom, sitting room, kitchenette. Kind of what you've got now, but really swanky. . . ."

Grace bent down and kissed her daughter, who remained seated. "I think I'll catch a ride back with you and Roger."

Joy stared out at the expanse of dark water. "Do you mind if I stay?"

At some point we all need to stop running, Grace thought, hoping her daughter would one day realize this as well. She whispered to Joy, "A child's needs change, and the truth of that change cuts deep and takes a long time to heal. But it does heal. I've missed you, Joy. I'm so glad you're back."

Joy smiled. "Good night, Mom. I love you."

It had been many years since Grace had heard those words from her daughter, and they brought tears to her eyes.

Roger looked from his mother to Joy and shrugged. "Whatever."

And as she made her way to the truck with Roger, he detailed his plans for the cottage renovation. Grace smiled. *Some things never change*, she thought.

· Chapter Twenty-two ·

JOY

The sun, still low on the horizon, momentarily blinded me as I followed the lazy circles of the osprey. I tried to imagine what it would be like to soar silently, effortlessly, above the woods, the rocky shoreline, the water—completely free, to peer down and see fish swimming, unsuspecting, beneath the surface.

I'd sat on the Rookery's porch nearly half the previous night, staring out into the dark, thinking. As the hours slipped by, I watched the moon travel the width of the sky, and then, knowing I needed sleep, forced myself inside, where I found the new toothbrush I'd brought for my mother, resting in a glass in the tiny bathroom, which smelled now of pine disinfectant and sandalwood soap. I found my mother's nightgown on the neatly made bed, the piece of chocolate that Roger had placed on the pillow. I could get used to this kind of service. But when I climbed in between the sheets, the mattress was lumpy and smelled of mildew, and I lay awake, listening to the scuttle of tiny paws beneath the floorboards, wondering whether Stuart was home, whether he'd noticed that I'd packed far more than I'd need for a weekend on Little Island, and had called the inn.

When I woke from my few hours of fitful sleep, dark had given way to gray, and I longed for my own bed, for Stuart's even breathing and familiar shape beside me, for a hot shower and a steaming cup of strong coffee in my own kitchen. I wrapped myself in the bedspread and went back out onto the porch. The moon had long since vanished, along with most of the stars. Those remaining had slowly slipped away in the dim light of dawn, replaced by a pinkish prelude, and then the sun's slow ascension.

The osprey pulled up suddenly, hesitated, and then rocketed toward the water. As it neared the surface, it swiveled, its feet like clawed landing gear. There was just the slightest splash as it grabbed its quarry and began to rise. Or tried to. The osprey flailed, as though something had grabbed it from below. *Fish catches bird. Now there's a headline*, I thought.

The osprey flapped furiously, but the fish, impaled in its talons, was enormous. The bird could not get airborne. Nor would it let go. It now looked less like an efficient, aerial killing machine and more like a lumbering transport. I imagined the bird's eye, no longer glinting with confidence and bravado, but glassy and fixed. *Let go, you fool*. If the fish were somehow able to draw the osprey under, the bird would drown, because ospreys, unlike ducks and gulls, cannot fly when their wings are wet. A different sort of fish tale, one the fish could tell. Daddy would enjoy that.

The osprey's wings hammered the surface of the water, and the fish thrashed. I wasn't sure which I was rooting for. The fish was certainly the more defenseless, but the osprey might have young to feed. I watched, spellbound, as the bird finally got a little air under its wings and rose a few feet. I could see the effort and strength this small action required. Bird and fish flew low for the opposite shore, toward a nest on one of the platforms, provided by the local Audubon chapter. I wondered what the fish made of this new, superoxygenated mode of travel. The pair didn't have enough altitude; it looked like both bird and fish were going to slam into the trees. But then, two huge pumps of the osprey's wings, and they rose onto the platform. *Damn.* I guess I'd been rooting for the fish.

I leaned back in the chair, turned my face to the sun, and listened to the waves wash against the rocks. Nearby, a seagull enjoyed a good laugh. I had no idea what time it was, since I'd left my watch at the inn.

"Ah, ram, sam, sam! Ah, ram, sam! GOOLIE GOOLIE GOOLIE GOOLIE ram, sam, sam!" Three voices were approaching: the twins and Tamar. The singing grew louder. There was the sound of running feet. "Aunt Joy!" Then Hal and Nat were beside me, one climbing into my lap, the other taking the empty chair; now both in the chair, arguing about who would sit there; now one—Hal?— climbing back into my lap; now both nesting there. They wiggled and twitched, and the utter stillness and calm I had been enjoying just moments before vanished without a backward glance, the way Pinklepurr sometimes did when too many people suddenly filled a room.

"Girls, girls," Tamar said. "Go inside." They both hopped down and scampered into the cottage. "Don't touch anything!" she commanded. "There isn't a back door, is there?" she asked me, nervous.

I shook my head.

Tamar looked as if she hadn't slept. Her eyes were puffy

and she wore no makeup and had a bad case of bedhead. "I owe you an apology," she finally said. "More than one. Lots." She set a picnic basket on the table between us. "A peace offering." She pulled out a thermos of coffee, some yogurt, and two muffins.

"Did you make these?" I asked, eyeing the perfectly browned and rounded tops.

"Roger made them, actually." Tamar poured coffee. "I am a terrible cook. One more thing I've never spent any time on."

"Tee—"

She waved me off. "Excuse me." She popped into the too-silent cottage. "Girls? Okay. Nothing. You're fine." She resumed her seat. "On the couch playing with a bit of twine. Very *Little House on the Prairie*. I should have brought some books or something. I have a lot to learn. You were so right."

I took the coffee she passed me, and we stared out at Isle au Haut Bay. The sun lifted itself higher on the horizon. Below us waves worried along the shore. Another gull had a good laugh as it hung on the morning breeze.

"Remember how we used to come here as kids and play house?" I asked to fill the silence. "Funny sort of game, when you think about it. If we'd had any idea how long we'd be *doing* house, as opposed to playing it . . ."

As soon as I trailed off, Tamar started talking, almost more to herself than to me. "Roger was in the backseat that night and was thrown out of the car. One of those freak times when not wearing a seat belt paid off. He dragged me out with his good arm, and then . . . we decided to say he was driving. I was so scared."

I knew most of this from Roger and didn't feel the need to go over it again. But then I realized that Tamar probably did.

She, too, had been alone all these years with the truth swirling around inside her.

"I was hysterical. In terrible pain, only slightly less drunk than Roger, but I was sure I was okay to drive. He knew he wasn't. That's the difference between us, Joy. Roger knows his limits. It hasn't always served him well, but it would have that night.

"The whole thing was like a nightmare, surreal. Impossible. Like yesterday, with the girls missing. I just kept thinking, *How could this be happening to me?* Not, *How could I have let this happen*, mind you. God, I really am self-absorbed." Tamar settled into a moment's silence. "If only I hadn't asked Bonnie to come along. If only I'd given Roger Loraine's message. If only I'd told the truth that night."

I waited a moment to see if she'd say more. "There's no 'if only' in life, Tee," I said, not willing to let her off quite so easily. "There's only 'because.'"

Tamar nodded and continued, her voice low. "We didn't know how badly Bonnie was hurt when we decided on our plan, didn't know that she would . . . die. And by the time we did, it was too late." Tamar paused briefly and added, in a whisper, "I'm so sorry, Joy." She looked at me, and then looked away. "It *seemed* too late, anyway. Now, though, I think that I was just being selfish and afraid. It was so easy to let him take the blame." I handed her a napkin to wipe her tears.

"Here's the thing—ironic, really—Roger has served his time. But I never have. And I've never quite forgiven him for that. Which sounds, I know, really bad. But, if I'd known then what I know now, I would have confessed."

I divided a muffin and offered her half. "The question is, what can you do about it now?"

Tamar tore her half muffin in half—and then again, and then once more. "Regret is its own punishment. Really, a worse punishment than one might think. You were right about that, too. And I do have terrible remorse. It's like dry rot."

I could see that my sister was truly suffering. Had been suffering for years. I wanted to ease her pain but knew I couldn't. Only she could do that for herself. But I had an idea.

"What Roger did was unselfish and generous," I said. "And there is something equally unselfish and generous that you could do for him."

Tamar looked up at me.

"Tell Loraine."

She looked utterly miserable and started pushing the muffin crumbles around her napkin. "I need him, Joy. I know it's not right, but I really . . . love him." Her voice was very soft.

"And he loves you. He will always love you, Tamar. He's your brother. But you need to let him go. He deserves happiness, right? You want him to be happy? Because if you don't, then you're not really loving him." And as I said this, I thought about Rex. Inside the Rookery, I could hear the twins softly singing.

I'd asked my mother about regrets, and as I got ready to leave the Rookery I wondered if I had any of my own. My conscience was clear for the first time in twenty years, but I realized I did still have one regret. And so, after Tamar left, when I started back to the inn, I took the longer route, across Sand Beach and around the point to the footbridge. The sea was choppy, a strong wind blowing. But that wasn't going to stop me.

At the footbridge, I took a seat on the smooth, flat rock. From there, I could see the roof of the Findleys' house, its small dock jutting out from the rocky shore. Beyond it was the causeway, and what looked like Roger's truck crossing it, quite quickly. Tamar, I hoped, heading over to see Loraine.

I dropped the terry-cloth robe I'd put on at the bathhouse, stepped out onto the narrow wooden bridge, and for a long time I watched the water eddy and swirl below me. So long, in fact, that I was still standing there when Roger's truck came back across the causeway. Down the channel, in the other direction, Spectacle Island was a small hump in a vast expanse of dark green. I eased myself over the railing, held on tight with my hands, leaned outward, and closed my eyes.

I stayed that way for a long while, too, trying to slow my racing heart, knowing that I should wait until someone could be here with me. But what if I chickened out? No, I needed to do this alone. I had no idea what time it was, or how long I had until the service, but I sensed that it was getting late. The aunts would be arriving soon, and my mother needed my help. As far as I knew there was no food, no flowers, and no minister. *Jump, Joy. Just jump.*

Still I clung there, a voice deep in my unconscious warning me that this was not a good idea. I kept telling myself that it was nothing more than the voice of fear, the voice that had held me apart from others, including members of my family, all my life. I was tired of that voice running things. I bent my knees and jumped.

It wasn't far down, but time seemed to slow as I fell. I could feel the air, slightly cool against my skin, and see the sun shimmer on the water's surface. The boats moored across the creek all had their bows pointing toward East Haven. The Harbor

Gawker prints a "Sheet of Useless Information" for tourists. One of the items reads, "Yes, the boats in the harbor are all required to park facing the same direction. The wind and tide decide which way." Daddy talked endlessly of wind and tide when we were growing up. I either hadn't been listening or had forgotten how this worked. What I did know, as I sailed through the air—like the osprey!—was that the boats, unlike me, were securely moored.

No regrets. I saw droplets of water clinging to the underside of the splintery railing and, below, bits of seaweed being borne along with the current: Commuters, old hands at this ride. But wait, I thought just before I landed. Shouldn't the seaweed be going the other way?

Grace and Gar had fallen into bed, exhausted, sometime after one A.M. after a long conversation with Roger and Tamar about . . . everything. Grace had cried, as had Tamar, and even Gar. Only Roger remained dry-eyed and looked slightly bemused through it all. Gar said he would make calls to their lawyer, and then the police, on Monday. He was sure the statute of limitations had expired, but wondered whether anything could be done to clear Roger's name and record. Grace and Gar had not awakened until after nine, to the smell of coffee and bacon.

Grace arrived in the kitchen to find Roger, wearing a baseball cap with long blond braids, leaning against the counter. He was grinning as he listened to an elderly woman who stood beside him, chopping onions as she spoke. On her head she wore a bright red beaded cocktail hat, with a billow of black lace pluming up from its back. Another elderly woman sat at the table, rolling silverware in paper napkins and tying the napkins with bits of pink ribbon. She wore a mound of pale yellow feathers that reminded Grace of Big Bird.

They all turned when Grace entered the room. "You must be Grace," said the woman at the counter. "I'm Callista Clark, and this is my sister"—she gestured to the woman in the feathers—"Corintha Weatherby."

"Hats," said Corintha, in response to Grace's startled expression. "Our family always wears hats to funerals."

"I'm so terribly sorry," Grace said. "What time did you arrive?" she asked. "I'm so, so sorry I wasn't there to meet you."

"Your very handsome son picked us up," Corintha said, tying off another napkin. "He looks, by the way, very much like our father."

Grace studied Roger as she accepted the coffee he offered her and sat down across from her aunt. "For the service." Corintha indicated the rolled-up flatware.

"I'm not sure there's going to be a service," Grace ventured. "As such."

"Nonsense. We came to celebrate Joan's life, Carlton style." Corintha gestured toward her hat.

By now Gar had entered the kitchen and he stood staring silently at the two women in their feathers and beads and Roger with his long blond braids. Grace introduced them.

"We don't think Joan had much fun in her life," Callista said. "And that was her goal, after all. So it's imperative that we give her a fun send-off. Hats at funerals are a Carlton family tradition. Your mother must certainly have followed it, and so should you. We insist. I assume you can each come up with something?" She looked at Grace and Gar.

"I've got just the thing!" Gar sailed out the back door.

Grace watched him leave. "But, you see, we have no minister, no flowers, no food—"

Corintha cut her off with an upraised hand and looked toward Roger. "We're all set on that score." Roger smiled. She handed Grace half the stack of napkins and a spool of ribbon. "Start rolling."

Grace began bundling forks, knives, and spoons into napkins. After a moment she asked, "What did you mean, fun was her goal?"

Corintha tied off a ribbon and said, "Oh, when we were little—Joanie was maybe ten, I was twelve, and Callie nine—we sat on the beach one day, asking each other silly questions. Mine was, 'What will you name your first child?' And Joanie picked Grace."

"That's you," Callista added, in case Grace hadn't understood. "Joanie asked us, 'Where do you want to live?' We all said, 'By the water.' We know Joan didn't live most of her life there, but she did, finally, get that little bungalow on the pond."

Grace nodded, trying to ignore the sharp tapping at the edge of her unconscious.

"And then, this was Callie's question and very silly, I thought—"

"Pooh to you," Callista said, smiling.

"What will you wear in your hair at your wedding?"

"We both said veils and long trains. But Joan said—"

"Flowers?" Grace said weakly.

"Yes!" the two sisters said, looking at Grace in delight. "How did you know?"

Grace stood and walked over to the table that served as desk and catch-all. There, on top, was her to-do list and, paper-clipped to it, her mother's note to her. Or what she had taken as Joan's note to her. In the drawer was the photo of the three girls on a beach. She brought both back to the table and showed her aunts.

"Oh, my." Corintha put a hand to her mouth.

Callista sat down heavily in the chair. "Our father destroyed every photo of Joanie when she left. And look, Cornie, here's Joanie's list."

Grace sat silently and watched tears fill her aunts' eyes. "Have fun! That was her answer to Cornie's question, 'What are your goals in life?' We both said, get married, travel to Europe. Cornie wanted to raise dogs, which she did. I wanted to be a professional chef. Well, that didn't happen, exactly, but I do own a restaurant. Joanie just said, 'Have fun!' How clever she was. We always thought she was so clever."

The three women sat for a long, silent moment, gazing at the faded photo.

After their conversation, Grace went up to the closet in the attic, where she'd hung the items of her mother's that she'd removed from her bungalow after her death. Among them were the dress and the hat that Joan had worn to every family occasion. She carried them back to her room. The dress, brown with white polka dots and a white plastic belt, was a little snug, but fit. Tears welled when she looked in the mirror. She put on a pair of brown pumps, and a pair of her mother's earrings, and then lowered the pink Plaza Suite simone—with a rosette on one side—over her brown curls. The one pink item Joan had owned. Grace did not recognize herself. She didn't think it was just the borrowed clothes.

Grace knew that she no longer needed a service. She had

already come to terms with her mother's life and death, reached an understanding, said her good-byes, and let her go—but she realized that others might. Her aunts had come all this way. Yesterday she had grieved her mother's death. Today they would celebrate her life.

She would tear out every ridiculous plant she put in this year and start over with her wildflowers and her no-fuss perennials. What fun! Yes, Grace realized, fun is all a matter of perspective.

JOY

I hit the water and felt a tug as fierce as labor bear me down and away from the bridge and out into the bay. Daddy once told me that it is a different force that drags the water out of the harbor than the one that drives it in: gravity versus inertia. The outbound tide did seem determined, even greedy in its efforts to drain the harbor and take me out with it.

The act I'd just committed was foolish, that much was clear, as I hurtled along in the viselike grip of that current. If only I'd told someone. If only I'd worn a life preserver. But what had I just told Tamar? Life has no *if only*, it only has *because*. I'd done this so I'd have no regrets. Well, I had one now.

My head throbbed, from cold, from fear, from holding my breath. . . . The current held me with what seemed like a vindictive intensity. I tried to calm myself. What would Stuart have me say? *I am strong. I can swim. I will survive.* Gravity was out of my control, just like my fate. *Les jeux sont faits.* Roger's voice. *Always pray* before *you roll the dice.* Was it too late for me to pray? My lungs felt ready to burst. Another eddy caught me and spun me around. I was sure I must be halfway to Owl's Head by now.

I thought of that fish, caught earlier in the osprey's talons. Nature has her own agenda, to be sure. I wondered what my family was doing now. Perhaps sitting in the Adirondack chairs, enjoying a second cup of coffee, wondering when I would return. Or, perhaps they'd all gone out on the *Kestrel*. I pictured them peering over the side, watching jellyfish and seaweed float past and then seeing, suddenly . . . me, zipping along with the current! I would have laughed at this but for the water buffeting me. Despite this, I felt . . . alive. How ironic if the only way to feel fully alive was to look death squarely in the face. I thought now that I understood something of Roger's need to drink, to drive cars too fast, to test the limits of the law.

On and on I went, just another bit of flotsam being borne out on the tide. I wondered how far the current intended to drag me. Its unrelenting clasp was beginning to infuriate me. I flailed about, unwilling to let it win, desperate to regain some control of my movement and direction, aware that I must look like a parody of a drowning person, and then I realized that I might actually *be* a drowning person and grew light-headed. This was why and how people drowned: They passed out from fear. But I kept fighting. I would not go down, literally, without a fight. I thought again about the fish and the osprey.

My need for air was profound. I kicked some more, not even sure which way was up, not knowing if I could free myself from the current. Then I felt myself spinning upward, still being borne along by the surging water, and then darkness gave way to light, and my head broke the surface. I sputtered, coughed, gulped in air, kicked hard, and felt the dizzying motion of the current lessen. Disoriented and salt blind, I gulped in more air, sure I would, any second, be pulled under again. But although the current still carried me along, I remained afloat. I had jumped into the outgoing tide, all alone, and survived. No one else in my family had ever done that. I rubbed my eyes and opened them and, before me, saw a dazzling, endless expanse of wide-open sea.

But just how far past Little Island had I been catapulted? Would I have the strength to make it back? I swiveled, craning to see above the chop. Spectacle Island lay just a few dozen yards beyond me. It felt like I'd been underwater for fifteen minutes or more, but my entire voyage had extended for only about twenty yards. Not chump change, but not exactly a transatlantic crossing. I giggled and set out for shore. As soon as I was free of the water, I collapsed, laughing, onto the sand.

Back on the rock, my terry-cloth robe looked like the discarded skin of my former self. Why was Daddy so afraid of the outbound journey? How many of us live lives driven by rules and assumptions that we never test? I stood a moment, watching the tide slip out through the channel, feeling a new sense of freedom and an understanding that we are only as stuck as we allow ourselves to be. With that, I headed back to the inn.

I hoped I could slip in unnoticed, but as I entered the back hall, I heard voices in the kitchen.

"How about stars?"

"Stars would be good."

The twins were talking to someone. I didn't recognize the voice and assumed it must belong to one of my mother's aunts.

"Hearts?"

"Hearts would be very good, too."

"Dog biscuits?"

A slight pause. "Unusual, but I like unusual and so did my sister. I say yes to dog biscuits."

"I think trees would be good."

"Then make trees. Why not?"

"Why not," agreed the twins.

I stepped into the kitchen. My two nieces were kneeling on stools, pressing cookie cutters into biscuit dough. Each wore an apron over shorts and a T-shirt, and a green-and-red-striped stocking cap, which I recognized as the ones that Grammy had knitted for me and Tamar when we were little. My recently deceased grandmother was, in fact, standing at the sink, doing dishes. She turned to face me.

It was not my grandmother, of course, but my mother, wearing Grammy's hat and dress. "Hi!" she said. "You're home! And you've been for a swim. You've turned into a regular little fish."

A woman wearing an apron and a red beaded cocktail hat stood beside the twins. "We didn't have any French bread," she said, as though I'd asked for an explanation about the biscuits. "So we're making these to serve with the smoked salmon. You're low on flour, by the way." This she directed at Mom, who nodded. The twins exchanged uneasy looks across the table.

"Joy, this is my aunt, Callista Clark. Aunt Callista, my daughter Joy Kilsaro."

Aunt Callista beamed at me. "How was your swim?"

I simply did not know how to respond that question, so I just smiled.

"What do you think of witch's hats, Aunt Joy?" Nat asked.

No one had commented on the odd headgear nor offered me an explanation, so I said, "Hats seem to be a theme today. Why not?"

"Hats," Callista said. "We always wear them at funerals."

"Why don't you go shower," Mom said. "Daddy and Roger are outside setting up the tables and chairs. Tamar went to get flowers and run some other errands. I think she's outside now, too."

My mother seemed . . . lighter than she had in the past few days, but I felt lighter, too, and wasn't sure which one of us had done the changing. I decided it didn't matter and started for the door. "Did Stuart call?" I asked.

My mother shook her head.

"Let's see, chèvre-and-smoked-trout scones, spinach-and-leek panini bites, and . . . what else are we serving?" Grace asked Callista.

"Mozzarella, basil, and grape tomatoes on skewers." Callista pressed a cookie cutter into the biscuit dough. "And I told Tamar to get a tenderloin, pastries, and a cake."

I wandered out of the kitchen and into the dining room, where I could see a pale yellow feather-duster passing beneath the window. Aunt Corintha, or so I assumed, materialized beneath the feathers and strode across the lawn to Daddy and Roger, who were setting up several dozen chairs in a semicircle on the still-startling emerald lawn. Several buffet tables stood off to one side. Roger was wearing the baseball cap with long blond braids attached that I had given Daddy as a joke gift on his sixty-fifth birthday. Daddy had on an old hat that he'd decorated for last year's New Year's Eve party with assorted fishing lures and political slogan buttons: *McCarthy for president*, *Vote Yes on #1* . . .

I went upstairs and took a long, hot shower. After I changed, I went to my car to look for a hat.

Wearing a pith helmet with bug netting furled around its brim, I joined my mother on the porch. "Bought it for gardening," I explained when she turned and saw me. Tamar, in a red-and-black-checked hunter's hat with the earflaps down, was arranging stems of pink gladiola, freesias, and carnations on the makeshift altar. Sophie wiggled her way out from beneath the potentilla, a challenging task, what with the moose antlers on her head. We laughed loudly, and Tamar turned, saw us, and waved.

"Poor Sophie!" Mom called, pointing.

"I almost got her a set of boots, too, but Roger would have had a fit," Tamar shouted back. Roger grinned at her, and Sophie disappeared around the side of the porch, almost certainly embarrassed. I felt light enough to lift right off the porch and float out over Penobscot Bay, where I could see a line of dark clouds forming.

At half past one, we greeted the Findleys and Bonaventures, Judy Ladeau, and a dozen others, who cast odd looks at our assorted headpieces but politely said nothing. When all were seated, Roger stood at the front of the semicircle by the makeshift altar, where my grandmother's ashes rested in their butternut box. The dark clouds had advanced, and a southwest wind was kicking up, roiling the surface of the harbor and fluttering the cloths on the buffet tables. I could see my mother eyeing them nervously from her seat.

Roger's voice carried above the sound of the waves rolling around the rocks as he read the Whittier poem that Mom had found in Grammy's wallet and taped to the refrigerator door after she died. "No longer forward nor behind I look in hope or fear; But grateful, take the good I find, the best of now and here." I could feel wet soaking through the soles of my shoes, and noticed that others had hooked their heels around the crossbars of their seats, seeking escape from the damp sod. I could also feel the legs of my chair sinking slightly, and so shifted, trying to find firm ground. As Roger was calling on me to say a few words in memory of our grandmother, Sophie, in her moose antlers, wandered across the front of the circle, squatted, and relieved herself, before trotting over to her den beneath the potentilla. Guests and family members tried, mostly unsuccessfully, to stifle smiles.

"Thank you for sharing, Sophie," my brother said, never losing his respectful demeanor. The twins giggled uncontrollably, trilling like two lovebirds.

I made a wide circle around the newly dampened area and approached the lectern. Just as I took my place and started to speak, the wind strengthened and slipped beneath a tablecloth on the buffet. Daddy leaped up and grabbed it just before lift-off. The decorative grasses in the garden waved wildly. I felt a drop of rain splatter on my arm, and then another. My mother had just suggested that we move inside, when Sophie bolted from beneath the potentilla and shot across the yard, barking ferociously. People turned in their seats to see what had caught her attention.

A young black bear, who, having lapped up all the sunflower seeds that my mother had thoughtfully sprinkled on the front walk for the chickadees the day before, was now approaching the buffet table. The guests who were watching it had thrown just enough weight on the backs of their chairs to send them deep into the soggy sod and, one by one—like dominoes, Roger would describe it later—they tipped over backward, feet shooting skyward.

"A bear!" Tamar screamed, grabbing her twins and hauling them toward the inn. Everyone scattered. They needn't have worried; the bear had eyes only for the smoked salmon.

My mother grabbed Grammy's ashes, while Daddy and I rushed over to help the overturned guests. Roger charged the bear. "Perhaps not my smartest move," he conceded later, but it turned out to be a successful one. The bear took one look at Roger, with his arms windmilling, and his hat's blond braids bouncing, and cantered off around the side of the inn, squealing. The guests made it safely onto the porch, the aunts insisted that they were fine, and we all stood and watched as the wind finally found its way under the now-unsupervised tablecloth and sheared it off, sending platters of salmon, baklava, panini bites, smoked salmon scones, skewered tomatoes, and the cake tumbling onto the bright green sod. Then the heavens opened, and the rains came, slicing in sideways, soaking the carnage.

A small set of wilting moose antlers appeared in the garden near an urn of ornamental kale.

"Oh, my God, Sophie!" My mother bolted into the kitchen, grabbed dog treats from the counter, and dashed back out into the rain before anyone could think to stop her.

"Sophie! Sophie, come!" she commanded. To no avail. Sophie, even if she weren't deaf, had her nose down and was tracking the bear. Mom ran across the rain-drenched lawn, holding treats in her outstretched hand.

"Grace, come here!" Daddy shouted. But she paid no more attention to his command than Sophie did to hers.

The bear now reappeared around the side of the inn and

made straight for the buffet on the lawn. It scooped up a paw-ful of baklava, sat back on its haunches, and started eating, completely ignoring my mother, who stood, unaware, just a few yards away, entreating Sophie, now wisely hiding in the garden.

Roger examined the bag Mom had left by the door. "So Mom is out there with the bear, baiting Sophie with salmon jerky?"

It was a small bear, we could now see, little more than a cub, and quite content with the feast before it, but when Mom finally turned and saw it sitting just a few yards away, she dived into the garden, overturning one of the ridiculous urns, scooped up Sophie, with her antlers drooping, and held her protectively in her arms. The bear couldn't have looked less interested. Mom sidled back across the lawn. The bear helped itself to a smoked trout scone.

"Hello?" A voice called from the kitchen. Loraine, in a black dress and bare feet, her shoes dangling from her hand, poked her head into the living room. "I'm sorry I'm a few minutes . . ." Her voice faded as she took in the limp feath-ers, the wilting moose antlers, the mud-spattered dresses. ". . . late," she finished.

Mom started to laugh, and then everyone joined in—Callista, Corintha, Daddy, Tamar, the twins, and me. We col-lapsed into chairs and leaned against doorjambs. Only Roger wasn't laughing. He was staring at Loraine. "Nice braids," she said to him.

"Honey?" Mom said, when the laughter died, pointing to Daddy's hat. "I found your bottledarter."

· · ·

Out in the harbor, boats reared and bucked at their moorings. The bear eventually ate its fill and ambled off in the direction of the lighthouse. Daddy called Comry Leadbetter, the chief of police, to report the bear, and learned that it belonged to an artist who was visiting East Haven. He'd been using the bear as a model, and she'd wandered out of the yard three days earlier. Hadn't Gar seen the notice in the *Island News*?

"Haven't seen a paper," Daddy admitted. "Had a houseful." He had removed the long-sought bottledarter from his hat and was admiring it as they talked. "Anything else of importance I should know about? Any escaped leopards or alien sightings?"

Comry just laughed and told him that the dump fee was going up, the school board was still trying to balance the budget, and Maisie Day's dahlias had taken first place at the Blue Hill Fair. He then promised to have the artist come retrieve the bear as soon as the rain let up. "Maybe you could put out a little food?" he suggested.

"Yup," Daddy said. "We'll do that." And then the power went out.

Our guests departed, having refused apologies, insisting that it was, by far, the most entertaining memorial service they'd ever attended. We all removed our hats, changed into dry clothes, and gathered in the living room, where Roger built a fire before disappearing with Loraine. I caught Tamar's eye as the two left the room; she smiled and gave a shrug of feigned indifference, but I knew what it must have cost her.

Mom produced a bag of her marshmallows for toasting. "Let's put some out for the bear," Hal suggested.

"When it stops raining," Tamar said.

I went into the Games Room, wondering why Stuart hadn't

yet called, too worried and embarrassed to call him. Tamar told me that she'd finally reached Daniel and let the twins tell him about their adventure. He listened quietly, she told me, not interrupting once. When the girls finished, Tamar had sent them off and told him about the crash.

"He didn't level any *what-if*s at me about any of it," she said to me. "Didn't play the guilt card. We'd have had a chance, if he'd done that. But all he said was, 'Something needs to change.'"

I nodded, not knowing what to say, knowing that saying nothing might not be acceptable either.

Tamar glanced at me, seemed about to take my head off, but then her expression softened and she said simply. "I'm afraid it's too late to save my marriage."

I was wondering the same thing about my own, which I seem to have cavalierly tossed aside two days before. "Remember Hagbard Celine's second rule?" I asked her.

She shook her head.

"'Communication is only possible between equals.'"

"Did I tell you that?"

I shook my head.

She thought about it for a moment, then raised her eyebrows and gave me a sardonic look. "You might consider mediation, or even diplomacy, Joy, for your future career."

I only smiled, having already decided which career path I would follow.

Grace found Gar in the dining room, slipped her hand in his, and they stood, staring out the window to the sodden lawn, the rain pelting the flowers and drenching the harbor. "What would you think about Roger coming on board and helping out with the inn?" Gar asked. "I think he has some good ideas."

"I'd like that," Grace said. Then she smiled. "But he can't have the Rookery."

"I've never stopped loving you, Roger. Maybe because Jason looked, and acted, so much like you. It was as if I had you with me all those years. Losing him was like losing you again, too."

They were huddled in the business center. Roger couldn't take his eyes off Loraine's hair, where little droplets of rain had caught and sparkled like some sort of exotic jewels. She was tan, and he was pretty sure the tan sailed, uninterrupted, the length of her. He figured he must be dreaming and kept his eyes on the sparkling drops, winking in her curls.

"Brian did run three businesses into the ground," she continued. "It's true. But he actually did a pretty good job of raising our son. He tried to stop him from going to Afghanistan, but Jason . . . Jason had his own ideas, always chasing after some dream or other."

She was so close that it seemed the most natural thing in the world for Roger to put his arms around her, almost rude not to. But he didn't want to wake from this amazing dream. She'd just said she'd never stopped loving him.

Then Roger realized it couldn't be one of his dreams, because his dreams never came true, never even had endings, let alone happy ones. As he stood there, uncertain about what to do or say in this dream that wasn't a dream, Loraine stepped even closer and put her arms around him. Then she untucked his shirt and slid her arms up his back. "I've missed you so," she whispered.

He buried his face in her hair and wept.

JOY

After Tamar left, I continued to sit in the Games Room, still hoping Stuart might call, wondering what I would say if he did, worried about what I would do if he didn't. I put the last pieces of the jigsaw puzzle into place, started memorizing the state flowers. It was my mother who answered the knock at the kitchen door and found Stuart standing on the granite step.

"The place looked so dark, I thought you might all be out," Stuart said. Mom invited him in and gave him a hug.

"Oh, Nan's marshmallows. How splendid," I heard him say as he came into the living room, where the twins were toasting them on the fire.

"Stuart!" I heard my sister say. "I'm putting together a brownie, peanut butter, marshmallow sandwich. Would you like one?" Tamar had found a plate of brownies in the kitchen that had somehow been overlooked.

"Perhaps in a bit. Joy?"

Tamar must have nodded toward the Games Room, because he soon appeared in the doorway. He looked wrinkled and exhausted and even more handsome than I remembered.

"Did you know that the state flower of Maine is the white pinecone and tassel?" I asked as he entered.

"I did not. Nor am I quite sure what a pine tassel is," he said, sitting down beside me.

"It's the thing that turns into the pine cone. Not a true flower, according to this, but the cone has a fragrant, gummy resin," I read, frowning over this last part.

"Ah." He didn't sound impressed. "What about Massachusetts?"

"Trailing arbutus," I reported, trying not to smile. "Otherwise known as mayflower, shadflower, ground laurel, mountain pink, or . . . gravel plant."

"I'd say any of those, except, perhaps gravel plant, would be preferable to trailing arbutus." Stuart took my hand.

"Habitat and range," I read. "Newfoundland to Michigan and Saskatchewan, and south to Kentucky and Florida."

"Doesn't seem quite fair that Massachusetts got saddled with it. Perhaps we could convince one of those other states to take it over." Stuart studied the puzzle.

"This plant," I read, "generally referred to in the drug trade—oh, dear—as gravel plant, has rust-colored, hairy twigs bearing leathery, evergreen leaves from one to three inches long and about half as wide."

We sat in silence.

"I think we should lobby for something a little more . . ." Stuart paused. "Exotic? What's Hawaii's?"

"Pua aloala," I read.

"In English. Not cabbage wort or some such, I hope?"

"Hibiscus."

"Sounds nice. I think we should check it out. In person. A little in vivo exploration. What do you say? We'll have time now with Rex gone."

I looked at him and asked, "Why did you come?"

Stuart took both my hands in his and looked into my eyes. The love I saw there spoke volumes. "Because I don't know where you keep Pinklepurr's medical charts, and I think he's due for his rabies shot."

I nodded.

"Also, I haven't any idea how to cook your grandmother's lasagna and I couldn't bear the thought of going through the rest of my life without it."

I nodded again, grinning now. "Top drawer of the file cabinet under Pinklepurr," I said. "Google 'Grandma's Best Ever Lasagna.'"

Stuart looked stricken. "Not your grandmother's?"

I shook my head. "Hawaii, you say?"

"Just for research purposes."

"Of course."

He smiled and kissed me, and we sat together, reading the names of the state flowers, and listening to the chatter from the other room and an occasional verse of "The Cow Kicked Nelly in the Belly in the Barn."

"By the way," Stuart finally asked, "How was your grandmother's service?"

Out in the dining room, Grace took a seat at a table with her aunts. A bottle of wine and Joan's hat rested on the table between them. The rain had stopped, and a few dark clouds shot across the moonlit sky, as though late for their next appointment. A tablecloth that had fetched up on one of the decorative urns gleamed brightly, and chairs, upended and scattered across the lawn, looked like sculptures. She could see the occasional glow of a serving platter on the pillaged remains of the buffet. Grace wondered whether they'd apprehended the bear, poor thing. "Someone should clean that up, I suppose." Grace didn't move.

Corintha shrugged. "Wait until morning."

"Maybe the bear will come back and do it for you," Callista added.

Grace opened the bottle of wine and poured for the three of them. They clinked glasses and toasted Joan.

"So, how would you rate this service?" Grace asked.

"A ten," Corintha said at once.

"Definitely," her sister agreed. "At Daddy's, the minister said the wrong name: 'Arthur Castleton,' he kept saying, instead of Carlton. We could hardly contain ourselves. And we had some dignitaries come for Mother's—she had all the money, you know."

Grace hadn't known.

"They all stayed at the Black Point Inn, Secret Service and all," Callista continued.

"Not Secret Service, bodyguards," Corintha corrected.

"No, we had a former attorney general, who traveled with Secret Service," Callista insisted. "Anyway, they all stayed at the Black Point Inn and caused quite an uproar. One of them managed to get himself locked out on a porch roof. He had to hail Woody Comstock, who was just coming back from a round of golf, to let him in!"

"And one of the waitresses claimed that her boyfriend was after her with a chainsaw!" Corintha took a sip of wine.

"But I don't believe we've ever had a bear."

"Positively not. And a hurricane!"

They clinked glasses again. "Joanie would have been delighted."

·   ·   ·

"We're going to ride the rip!" Hal exclaimed as the rest of us burst into the dining room.

Mom checked her watch. "It's nearly ten o'clock. Why are you still up?"

"Too many marshmallows," Tamar confessed. "And chocolate brownies."

"Come on, Short," Daddy said. "You missed it yesterday morning. The tide is just right. We'll skip the run around the island, of course. It's balmy outside, full moon. It will be gorgeous!"

"What is it they want to do?" Callista asked. Mom explained.

"Oh, this I've got to see," Corintha stated, standing. "Ladies?"

Callista stood, followed by my mother, who linked her arms through theirs.

"We've got to hurry, the tide turns in about thirty minutes," Daddy said.

"Is that terribly important?" Corintha asked.

"The outgoing tide could shoot you clear over to Owl's Head. Very dangerous crosscurrents all through there."

I just smiled at this and slipped my arm around Stuart.

"I've never even jumped at night, but Grace has," Daddy said. "All by herself. Quite the free spirit, that one."

"Takes after her mother," Callista said.

I looked at my family: Tamar, with her arms around her twins; Roger and Loraine, looking disheveled, his shirt untucked, her hair mussed; Daddy, still wearing his silly hat, minus the long-sought bottledarter, so eager. "You know," I said, "I think we'll stay here."

The others said nothing, they simply filed out, singing, "Boom, chicka chicka, boom," at top volume. After they'd gone, Stuart and I sat down at the table. Grammy's water-logged hat, with its rose sagging, rested between us. I put it on and poured wine into two glasses.

"I want to go back to school, Stuart. Get a degree."

"Sounds wonderful. What will you study?"

I smiled shyly, this being the first time I'd said it aloud. "Architecture. I want to design houses that are sound, with doors and windows that shut tight, and pictures that hang straight."

If he wondered about any of that, he didn't say. He clinked my glass, and I closed my eyes and pictured the osprey suspended on a current of air, and before me, the dazzling, endless expanse, without visible boundaries or limits, of the wide-open sea.

Little Island

· · ·

1. In the beginning of the story, Joy has just seen her only child off to college. In this moment, how does Joy identify herself? What qualities does she use to describe herself, and how does this change after her weekend at the inn? As you get to know her family members, how do you think they see her?

2. Why is Joy the only character who narrates her parts of the story in first person?

3. Joy feels like Alice in Wonderland, falling down the rabbit hole out of control. Do you think she intends to leave her husband forever when she packs up all of her clothes and belongings into her car to take to the inn?

4. Describe Tamar. Is she a likeable character? Does she have any redeeming qualities? How do you feel about her by the end of the book as compared to the beginning?

5. There are three sets of twins in the Little family stemming from the maternal side. What is the significance of twins and pairs in the story? Do you believe there is a special bond between twins that other siblings don't share?

6. Edgar says, "An island, especially a small one, isn't right for everyone. It required planning and time to get to and from Little Island. This was as it should be. But some people didn't like boundaries, felt hemmed in by them." How does the setting of a small island help shape this family's story? How would this story be different if it were set somewhere else?

7. Motherhood is a central theme in this story. Describe Joan, Grace, Joy, and Tamar as mothers. How are they similar and how are they different? What do you think the author is trying to say about motherhood by weaving their stories together?

8. Why doesn't the Little family ever talk about the crash?

9. What was your reaction to learning Tamar was the driver in the crash? Why do you think Roger took the blame and, if you were Roger, would you be able to forgive Tamar?

10. Does Joy feel guilty for keeping the secret about Tamar driving in the accident? If she hadn't, how do you think everything would have turned out differently for the family?

11. After Joy jumps into the tide, she muses, "How many of us live lives driven by rules and assumptions that we never

test?" and realizes "we are only as stuck as we allow ourselves to be." Do you believe in this statement? In what other ways is Joy held back by her rules and assumptions (besides her water phobia)? In what ways are her siblings and parents also "stuck"?

12. Grace believes her mother wanted her memorial service to be fun, and worries she won't be able to honor her mother's wish with her family that weekend: "*fun* was not a word she associated with their gatherings." Near the end of the book, after meeting her estranged aunts, Grace realizes having fun is a matter of perspective. What is fun to Grace? To her aunts, husband, and children? Does the memorial service turn out to be fun?

13. The note Grace finds left by her mother that says "Flowers, By the water, Have fun!" turns out to be a to-do list for Joan's life, not her death. What list would you make for your own life right now? What would the list have been like when you were a teenager?

14. Roger uses the metaphor of building a house to describe his family's dynamic after the crash, suggesting that after Joy reveals the secret of Tamar's fault, their house will stand a little straighter. How does this metaphor resonate with Joy? Do you like this metaphor for the Little family? Does it hold true in the end?

15. What do you think future reunions hold for the Little family at the inn?